SISTERS FOREVER

Sharon D. Martin

AmErica House
Baltimore

First printing

ISBN: 1-58851-589-3

PUBLISHED BY AMERICA HOUSE BOOK PUBLISHERS

www.publishamerica.com

Baltimore

Printed in the United States of America

Dedication

To the Slaves whose blood, sweat and tears soak the southern soil. Your spirit and strength has been inspirational in writing this novel. I salute your courage and would be honored to find one drop of your blood running through my veins.

This novel began as a dream and was supported by the keeper of my dreams, my husband Steven Martin. Without his love, support and encouragement it would never have been completed.

To the nuns at Spring Break who gave me the freedom of their plantation house and grounds, and the special room they fixed for my solitude in the completion of this novel.

For my mother who taught me Christian values and supports me with her love. To my children who have always stimulated my imagination and have listen to my stories all their lives.

For my sisters who love me and have shared with me laughter and tears.

To Lena and Andy who created my beloved husband and lifted me up with their prayers.

To my brothers that think they can out fish me let them forever dream.

For my Circle of Friends who lifted me up and kept me going till I reached the finish line.

Chapter 1

The Births

Screams sliced the darkness like a knife through flesh. All of the slaves on the Cothran Plantation hurried to dress by the firelight in their small cabins, their hearts filled with fear.

Lately they had grown used to being afraid. Just two months earlier, in the city of Charleston, a planned slave revolt had been put down. Denmark Vasey, a respected freed slave, enlisted an army of nine hundred freed and bondage slaves from the surrounding area, and designed an attack to kill the whites and take control of the city and its ports. Weapons had been gathered for some time and a large armory had been established.

The date set for the revolution was June 16, 1822, a time when most Charleston residents would be vacationing on nearby Sullivan's Island. In May, a slave named Pete informed Colonel John Prioleau of the planned revolt. The slaves incriminated by Pete were captured and tried by the magistrates. Of the thirty-five who went to the gallows, five were from the slave cabins on Cothran plantation. Forty-two were exiled, and sold to planters in other states, forever separated from their families. One old man, loved by many, was spared his life after being whipped for his involvement.

The screams that terrified the people of the cabins came from the second floor of the big house, where Miss Betty was in labor. She had been seen in the garden that very day by all whom now rushed towards the house. Apparently something had gone wrong, terribly wrong. All who huddled outside in the cold could see the candlelight's inside moving frantically. Those who peeked inside the parlor window saw, for the first time, their master taking orders from someone else. Doctor Albright, who was obviously in control of the situation, was making him to sit in a chair near a fireplace.

Some young men climbed the large oak outside Miss Betty's window. They saw their mistress lying in a pool of blood, screaming so loud they felt she would spit out her soul.

"It be Miss Betty," one yelled down. "She ain't long to dis world. Lordy, she lying in a river of blood. Oh Lordy.... help us all!"

Miss Betty was loved and respected. She treated them with kindness, and was understanding of their suffering.

"It's a baby, she done had her baby. Lordy, it's a girl. Miss Betty done had a girl," cried out Paul to the others.

The screams of Miss Betty now were replaced by the loud crying of a newborn baby. Those below began to whoop and holler at the joyful announcement. Then they remained shivering in the yard, waiting to hear the news of Miss Betty's fate.

"I think she be dead. Yep, don't look like she breathing. We done lost Miss Betty, she gone to meet her maker," cried out young Augustus.

Women began to weep as they walked back to the cabins a few hundred yards from the big house. The cabins, made of brick fired on the plantation, did little to keep the January wind from chilling the bones of those inside. One cabin housed up to ten people.

With the breaking of dawn, word spread that Miss Betty was alive. Her labor had ended with a breech birth. The doctor had to turn the child while it was still in Miss Betty's womb.

Miss Betty's personal maid, Suzy, had a young daughter named Cecil who was sent to the master's house to help her mother with Miss Betty. Cecil was dying to see the master's new child. Four days after the birthing, Suzy sent Cecil to the bedroom with clean sheets for Miss Betty.

Cecil was six years old and small for her age. She had dark skin, unlike her mother. Until that day Cecil had stayed at the children's cabin during the day with the others under the age of twelve. Now she was proud to be chosen to help her mama care for the master's wife.

Cecil opened the door an inch at a time, and entered Miss Betty's bedroom. She gasped when she saw Miss Betty, who looked more like a ghost than a living being. Miss Betty heard her and opened her eyes.

"Cecil… you seen my baby girl?"

"No, Miss Betty, I ain't never seen no white baby 'fore."

Miss Betty leaned over to look into the basket holding her daughter.

"Come look, but be quiet. I don't have the strength to get her back to sleep," she said softly.

"Isn't she the prettiest baby you ever laid eyes on? She reminds me so much of springtime that I've named her April. April Marie Cothran. Don't you think she looks just like a little flower?"

Cecil's eyebrows rose up in disbelief as she thought, 'Dat sure be a funny looking baby. She ain't got a hair on her head. Looks like she ain't got teethes either. She be so wrinkled and squished up looking. Dese white babies, dey ain't much to 'em. I ain't never seen a flower dat looks like dat.'

She looked up at Miss Betty and smiled, showing her missing front teeth "Ooh wee, Miss Betty… dat be a fine looking baby."

Miss Betty reached out and pulled the blanket down so that April's little body was exposed. April wiggled about in her basket and moved her head.

Cecil gasped and her eyes widened in disbelief when she saw the baby's sleeper. April had on a pink cotton sleeper tied at the bottom, that had embroidered little bunnies around the neck and a large bunny on the front. She was amazed to see a baby with such fancy bedclothes. Little slave babies wore clothes made from scraps of cloth that were sewn together.

"Goodness gracious, I ain't never seen a baby as fancy as dis one."

Miss Betty laughed at this comment, then gently covered April. She lay back on her pillow and motioned for Cecil to leave.

Cecil looked down at the sleeping baby and waved her hand in a gesture of good-bye. She walked to the dresser and laid down the clean sheets. As she closed the door, she peeked in once more to wave to Miss Betty.

When April was only a few weeks old, Miss Betty was told she could never have another child. The doctor told her she was lucky to have given birth to April. The news hurt Miss Betty deeply. She didn't want her child to be raised alone. She'd wanted to fill her house with the laughter of many children.

In February, the slaves prepared for a birth at the cabins. Slaves weren't allowed to take time of for birthing. Those having babies during planting or harvesting seasons were expected to work until labor began, then go back to work the day after giving birth if possible. Some even gave birth in the fields.

Eleven years after the ratifying of the Constitution, slave trade with areas outside the union had been deemed illegal, except by the state of Georgia. In the year of 1803, however, South Carolina once again opened its harbors to slave vessels because of a need for labor to work the growing rice and cotton fields.

Slave traders during this three-year open window brought over thirty-nine thousand humans into Charleston harbor. The slaves were brought into the city shackled and chained, at the rate of one thousand a month. Many were branded with the passage ships' initials or with formal seals. The marks stood as white scars against their dark skin while they stood in the Slave Market, the brands flesh on their breast and shoulders.

Before the sale, slaves were rubbed with oil and shaved so white hair, exposing age, could not be seen. The price of an adult slave ran from two hundred to five hundred dollars. Children sold for much less, with bids beginning at fifty dollars.

A young girl, named Lilly, was due to have a baby at any time. Her baby had been sired by a "Mandingo warrior" owned by a neighboring plantation, the Jackson's.

Cecil felt sorry for the young girl who was only thirteen. She had played at the children's cabin with her just the past year. Now she was old enough to work the fields and make the master new slaves. It sure was a strange sound that Lilly was making, like the cry of a wounded animal. Cecil made a promise to herself right then. "No slave babies will ever come from me!"

Early the next morning word was spread that Lilly had a baby girl. The master was hoping for a boy from the African yet he was pleased, knowing girls would grow up and have more slaves. Miss Betty came down to Lilly's cabin that very day, even though she herself was weak. Being happy Lilly's baby was a little girl she began clapping her hands and holding them in the air.

"Thank you Lord.... Thank you Lord!" she cried then gently picked up Lilly's baby.

Never before had Miss Betty fussed over a slave baby. She looked her over, then decided on a perfect name for her.

"This new baby's name will be May, because she was born one month after my April. I think that's a fine name for such a beautiful baby!"

She gave the baby one last hug, then handed her back to Lilly. Miss Betty watched them together for a few minutes more, then left the cabin smiling.

"I'll send down some more coal for you, so the baby will stay warm. You stay in and rest a few days. I'll make sure you have all you need," she called out over her shoulder.

Lilly was confused by the fuss Miss Betty made over her baby, but grateful.

Cecil finally got to see Lilly's baby when May was three days old. She couldn't get over how cute she was. There was enough hair on May's head to share it with Old Bald William and she were prettier than Miss April. She became concerned when she saw the baby didn't have teeth.

"Let me see dat baby. Why ain't she got no teeth? How come babies don't come with teeth?"

Those in the cabin laughed at Cecil and led her to the door.

"How come I's gotta leave? I's ain't gonna hurt dat baby. I's just wanna see her some more. She be prettier dan Miss April, don't y'all think?"

This remark made them all laugh harder as they gently pushed her out the door.

Cecil was the 'little rascal' of the plantation. She always said what was on her mind, and she kept the others in stitches. She'd stand up to the biggest man if he made her mad. The others used to say she had bobcat blood in her. She never considered herself to be a child. She use to say she was born a grownup and was getting younger by the day.

It was an easier life on most plantations for small children. They were given time to grow up before being sent to the fields or into the city to work for their masters.

That week word came for Lilly to pack her things. The master was calling her and her baby. Lilly was frightened, thinking she'd been sold for not having a boy. She cried as she packed her gunnysack with the few things she owned, then hugged everyone good-bye and headed towards the big house.

On the way up to the big house, Lilly passed Wilma, April's wet nurse. Wilma was crying uncontrollably, as if something terrible had happened. Lilly became more fearful. The master wasn't mean, but she was afraid he could turn mean. She was teary eyed when she knocked on the kitchen door.

"Child, why are you crying? Don't you know why you is here? Miss Betty done want you to be her baby's wet nurse. She wants your baby to be raised with little Miss April. You holdin' one lucky baby," said Alice, the cook.

Lilly couldn't believe it, never having heard of such a thing. She reached down and kissed her baby's head, grateful to know she wouldn't be separated from her.

It was known that Miss Betty had a hard time feeding little April. Her milk had begun to dry up, and April wouldn't accept a bottle. As soon as Lilly arrived, she was expected to nurse both girls, which she easily did. Later, other women of the house liked to tell how Lilly beat out all the cows in making milk. They claimed she produced so much milk that it could be stored in jars. Within a week of Lilly's arrival, April's constant crying ceased.

One day Cecil asked her mama if she could go see the babies. Suzy once again sent her upstairs with clean sheets, this time to Miss April's room. Cecil was impressed with what she saw. This was a room for just the girls and Lilly. Lilly had a nice bed with a feather mattress. April had a fancy basket made of white bamboo with a veil that hung down from the high ceiling. May had a box at the foot of Lilly's bed made from cedar, which filled the room with a fragrant smell. What Cecil loved most was the chair that rocked. Lilly let her sit in it and rock baby May.

"Dis here chair be fine. I's sho do wish I's had me one jes like it. One day I'm gonna git me one. Yessiree, I's need one of these bad. You ever don't need dis one; you just let me know. I's be glad to take care of it for you."

Lilly laughed at Cecil's fascination with the rocking chair. It had been the first rocking chair that Lilly had used too.

"Now you know dat chair ain't mine. It belongs to da master. I's just git to use it for his baby girl. It is a fine rocker though. You can sit dere a while longer. I's don't mind."

So Cecil sat there and rocked for at least an hour. Rocking back and forth. Singing softly to herself and the baby.

Before Cecil left, she noticed Lilly's hands were no longer chapped and dry from hard work. They were now soft and pretty. Miss Betty had given Lilly new dresses that looked like Sunday's best, and she wore them every day. It was hard for Cecil to imagine wearing good clothes every day. She now understood why Wilma was upset when she came back to the cabins.

Later that day Cecil walked up to some older slaves and heard them saying May might start thinking she was white when she grew older. Cecil found this thought funny, a slave girl thinking she was white.

"How's she gonna figure she's white with dat darky skin. Y'all jealous jes like my mama says," stated Cecil.

"If I git to be white, I'd be a good white. I'd git everyone's together and says, y'all not slaves no more! From now on, you jes like me. It don't matter no more bout your color! Nosiree, it don't matter at all. Now let's go grow us some food!" declared Cecil in a loud voice, her hands on her hips.

The older slaves laughed at Cecil's bold statement. Cecil then skipped away from them in pursuit of someone to play with.

Because of April's difficult birth, Miss Betty spent most of each day resting. April and May were both demanding babies, Lilly was only thirteen and it was hard for her to keep them content. Sometimes Lilly felt she'd get more rest working in the fields. When Miss Betty became well enough to help, Lilly was extremely grateful.

While the girls were toddlers, the whole house stayed on alert. April quickly learned to open the bedroom door, so the two were always escaping. Lilly would turn her back for a moment, and out they'd run, straight for the staircase. Sitting on the top stair, they'd try to scoot all the way to the bottom. Squeals of delight could be heard as Miss Betty and Lilly scooped them up. The vision of stairs brought terror to the hearts of their mothers, but pure joy to the girls.

"Lilly, we must do something to alert us when the girls get out. They're becoming such good little runners; one day they'll get hurt. Why don't we tie a bell to the door knob so we'll always hear them open it?"

"Yes ma'am, Miss Betty, I's git one of dem cow bells. Dat oughta do da trick."

A cowbell was attached to the girls' doorknob. As they grew older, they'd grab the bell when running out the door. Yet the crude alarm helped Lilly carry them through their toddler years. Nothing, however, could prepare her for the mischief that would come as they grew older.

Soon the girls turned five years old. For the first time they began to notice that they weren't the same color, and sought ways to remedy this problem.

One day April found a way to become dark like May. She decided that soot could do the trick, and found a mound of soot outside a shed that she proceeded to roll in. Soon every hair on her head and all her clothing were black. The sisters were joyful that finally they matched, at least a little. Miss Betty and Lilly chased after April for a good fifteen minutes after they were told of the blackened child.

"No mama, no! I don't wanna be white; I wanna look just like May! Please let me stay this color. Please!" April screamed as her mother caught her arm.

Lilly helped grab April, and together they carried her to the washtub. May followed behind, pleading for April to stay black.

"Don't change back colors, April! Stay my color; you said you'd stay my color!" cried May.

The soot was washed off April, although she fought with all her might to stay black. The ones who gathered to watch this noisy event thought it was the funniest sight they'd ever seen. They all thought April was growing up to be one crazy master.

"Dat April be a mess. She gonna be one heck of a master one day. She be plum crazy! It won't surprise me none if she don't try to whitewash May next," laughed Big Joe, the field hand.

In fact April did try to paint May, but the color washed off when it began raining.

One time Cecil found them outside playing house in an old shed. April was carrying around an old sock full of flour. She would take the sock and beat May over the head with it, until every part of May was white. They played for hours as Cecil, now eleven, sat under a large oak and watched them. Every time May's dark skin would appear, out would come April's sock. Cecil laughed so hard she cried.

Once the girls got Marlou, the children's cabin nanny, to fix their hair. April had little corn rolls all over her head. When April's hair was finished, the girls decided it was time for a party. They gathered all the cats and dogs into the barn as party guests, and closed the large doors. Each girl chose a partner and started dancing around the barn as they hummed the music they knew so well. The animals didn't take kindly to close contact with each other. An old tomcat got upset about the barking and howling of the dogs, and scratched April's face.

"April, you're bleeding, " cried May.

April reached up to her face and wiped off some blood.

"I am bleeding," April said looking at the blood in disbelief. She ran for the big house crying, with May in hot pursuit.

The party had ended.

Most of the time the girls played outside. April's papa felt that sun and fresh air would keep them healthy, although mischief was never more than a thought or two away.

One of the scariest times in the girls' lives happened when they went into the dogs' pen. Masters kept dogs that were trained to hunt and catch runaways.

These dogs were mean, especially to black people. They were trained to hunt and trap runaways in buildings or trees, and given the chance, they'd kill. Slaves had a true terror of these dogs.

Many dogs lived on the plantation, some of them strays and others the pets of the workers. April and May played with them, and didn't understand that the dogs in the large pen were different.

The girls, now six years old, were playing in back of the big house when the slave dogs began to howl. The girls believed they wanted to play, so they ran down to the large dog pen. April opened the gate, and they both went inside.

Lilly was helping Miss Betty do needle work when they heard the screams. Field hands came running to the dog pen. Miss Betty and Lilly dropped their work and followed them.

April was standing in front of May with her arms spread open. The screams had been April's.

May's mouth was open wide in silence, as she stood frozen in fear behind April. The dogs were trying to get May, biting at her as they growled. April tried her best to protect May. She kicked at the dogs, and screamed for help. Master Cothran ran to the dog pen with his gun. He opened the gate and fired into the air, but the gun blast only excited the dogs more. They began to attack him as he reached down and grabbed both girls. As he threw the girls out of the pen, a large gray dog bit deep into his left leg. Cursing in pain, Master Cothran turned and shot the gray dog in the head. He limped out the gate, fell to the ground and grabbed his leg and screamed in pain.

April and May, covered in scratches, with clothing in tatters, held each other's hand, and cried as their mothers carried them to the big house. Though their wounds were found to be minor, the girls were terrified that the dogs would come after May.

"April, do you think they want to kill me still? Why were those dogs so mean? We never hurt 'em. I don't understand."

"Aw, now I know why papa keeps them in a pen. Them dogs are crazy mad. That's why they went for us. They just plain mad," April said.

"Let's just play in the house for a while till they forget we exist. If they be mad, they won't remember us."

"Let's do that."

They wouldn't leave the house for three weeks.

The girls often went to the children's cabin and played in the yard with them Marlou, who cared for the children, prepared beans and cornbread for their supper, using a large feeding trough into which the food was poured. Marlou cooked the beans in big black kettles, ringing the supper bell when everything was ready. Children with dirty hands would run from play to the feeding trough, leaving it muddy when they'd finished.

The girls found this way of eating fun. They'd all play games and pretend to be different kinds of animals. April was best at acting like a hog, making the best hog noises. Everyone laughed at her grunts and snorts. May preferred to act like a cat and slowly lick her food. May could meow so well that kittens sometimes came running to her.

Occasionally Master Cothran came to the children's cabin. He'd line the children up in neat rows, check their teeth, and register their heights and weights in a logbook. April liked to get in line, pretending she was a slave child. Her papa acted like he didn't know her and checked her too.

"Marlou, this one isn't getting enough sun. I do believe her color has fallen off. Make sure she gets enough sunlight from now on," Master Cothran playfully said.

The children all laughed when the master made this comment. They wondered if he was telling the truth. For weeks thereafter the children were seen jumping from shade tree to shade tree, trying to make their color fall off. It was a known fact the color of one's skin affected what work was given. Those who were darkest-skinned were used as field slaves; those with lighter complexions received duties in the big house or jobs in Charleston. Masters seemed to treat lights with more respect, causing many arguments among the slaves. When Cecil overheard a group of slaves talk of this matter; she couldn't help putting in her two cents worth.

"My mama told me my grand pappy done come here from a place called Africa. Says he got here on a big ship. Lots of others were with him, but none of them wanna be coming here neither. She says they was chained up together and took to market when they gits here, just like animals. My grand pappy gits lots of money to buy him. He was big and black. He made a good field hand for his master."

The others standing around the oak listened carefully to Cecil as she continued to weave her tale. She was still a young child, age of twelve, but a gifted storyteller.

"Y'all know dat May's daddy be a African too. He done come on a big ship just like my grand pappy, but not the same one. I hear tell he be a warrior over there; he got papers to prove it. Y'all know he lives at the Jackson Plantation down da road. Dey says he done got forty-eight chillins. His master gits money for him to make babies. His chillins git papers too, cause he be da daddy. I's never seen him. I wonder iffin he be pretty like May. Everyone keeps telling me dat he does all his working at night."

They all burst out laughing at this last comment. They were aware of the mighty African. Many had seen him walking about in his feathered hat, following behind his master. Some of them envied his work, but most didn't want to be forced to father children they would never know.

When the girls were eight years old, Master Cothran decided they'd become too attached, and were acting like real sisters. He determined that it was time for them to separate, so he sent Lilly and May back to the cabins. His face was stern as he told April what he had done.

"April, you're big enough to be without a wet nurse. I've tried to make your mother happy by letting May be raised with you, but things have gotten out of control. You act like she's your sister, and this must stop. I care about May too, April, but she is our slave. People are beginning to talk of this strange relationship you have. April, you are an only child. I'm sorry, but you'll never have a real sister or brother, and you must deal with that fact starting today," lectured her father.

When April understood what he said, she lost control and attacked him.

"You bring her back. She is my sister. She's always been with me, always. Don't take her away. You take her from me and I'll just die. Bring her back home to me!" cried April, her fists flying.

She continued to hit her father until he grabbed both her arms. Even though he could stop her attack, he couldn't stop her crying and she wouldn't allow him to comfort her.

"You hate me! That's why you're doing this! I won't eat until May is home eating with me!" wailed April.

April ran to her room and refused everyone who came to her. For days she cried, the house growing quiet only when she slept. At first she would stand on her balcony and scream for May to come home until her parents pulled her in. Finally she wouldn't even leave her bed. No one could make her eat, not even a bite. When food was forced, she would throw up. It was as if she was willing herself to die. After many days of this behavior, the doctor was called.

"David Cothran, I know this is not what you want to hear, but you're going to have to give in. Your child's body cannot take much more. She is dehydrating at a rapid rate. Her internal organs will soon start to dry up. This seems to be her only problem but it is a problem that will take her life. That little slave may be just a slave to you, but to April she is her sister and she is in deep mourning for her. My advice is give her back May."

David couldn't believe the effect this was having on April. He realized the girls' relationship had endured for too long. There wasn't any way to break the bond. His only child had chosen a sister, one that didn't agree with the natural law. He'd have to accept it.

Betty came to his side and took his hand in hers. She spoke softly.

"Look upon the face of our beautiful daughter. She doesn't ask for much. I understand her need for a sibling, for I have felt it all my life. We have a large home, and there's plenty of room for May. April has spent her whole life forming a bond with May. Is it really that important their race may differ? Is separating them so important that our daughter should die? I took responsibility in the beginning for this bond to be formed, and I think it's healthy for our daughter. Please reconsider, and let May come back home to April." Betty pleaded with David.

He looked at April lying asleep in the bed, and then at Betty. He pulled Betty close and kissed her cheek. "All right, I give up. This is the craziest relationship that's ever been. That slave may be considered April's sister, but she's not our daughter. It's wrong to treat them as equals; it could cause them to turn against us. Send someone to get May, but don't bring Lilly. It's time for her to go back to the fields."

David walked out of the room, as Betty bent over the bed to awaken April.

"April, I'm sending for May, it's over. From this day forward you'll never have to worry about her leaving again. Papa is giving her back to you. Now it's time for you to begin eating and getting well. May will be wanting to play."

April smiled when she heard the news. Then, weakly, she sat up in bed and began waiting for May.

"Mother, as soon as May arrives we'll both eat. I couldn't stand eating without her. She's been missing me just like I've been missing her. We have to be together."

May heard of April's private battle to bring her back to the big house, and believed she would be returned. During the day she had waited patiently at the children's cabin and at night she had cried herself to sleep.

Within a matter of days, April had regained her health and her sister. Joy once again came alive at the Cothran Plantation.

Once when the girls were 10, they invited Cecil to come play in the corncrib with them. April had found some cottonseeds left over from the previous year. She and May had invented a game with them. It involved eight metal buckets lined up in a row. The girls would push a cottonseed up one nostril and hold the other closed with a finger as they blew the cottonseed out. They would thrust their heads forward to get an advantage in distance. Cecil always won, making the distance of five buckets.

Once the game ended when May had her nose plugged with a cottonseed, then needed to sneeze. She almost sucked the seed up to her brain. It took May ten minutes to get it back out using all her might to blow. After the scare was over, the girls laughed themselves silly thinking of May with a crop of cotton growing in her nose.

Chapter 2

The Incident In Charleston

April's room was on the front side of the house. Two large glass doors opened onto a long porch filled with white wicker furniture. During the spring and summer the girls spent many nights out on the porch. They'd carry out pillows and make pallets on the floor with quilts. Both girls loved the night songs the animals and insects made. Sometimes they'd hear the screams of owls as they grabbed prey and carried it away. Once a woodpecker worked all night on a small tree near their porch. The girls giggled at the thought of the tree falling because of a woodpecker's effort.

April's room was lovely. She had a large mahogany bed with carvings on the headboard and four posts that connected to a canopy top. Soft blue silk formed the canopy. Her dresser was heavily carved, with a large golden-framed mirror behind it. At the foot of April's bed stood a cot for May to sleep on, although she never spent a night there. April and May slept in the same bed, sharing their thoughts and dreams each night.

As the girls grew older, they began to take trips away from the plantation. They were allowed to go alone to the small nearby town of Cainnoy, but others supervised trips to Charleston because David Cothran felt the city wasn't safe.

In the city many Negroes were to be seen. Some were free men; others were slaves working at trades needed to keep Charleston growing. Negroes worked as butchers, blacksmiths, wheelwrights, pump or block makers, cabinet makers, painters, glaziers, gold and silversmiths, tailors, tin men, tanners, coopers, shoemakers, barbers, hatters, rope makers, handicraftsmen and mariners. The business of hiring out slaves was widespread and profitable.

Charleston fishermen were usually Negroes. They registered their boats and tackle, with the number of hands on board, along with their names and whom they belonged to. Punishment for failing to do so was thirty-nine lashes and withdrawal of the fisherman's license. Fishermen were the only class of slaves who could lawfully own their vessels.

The city of Charleston had three markets. Two were for vegetables, meats, and other provisions such as clothes, handmade items and the third was for fish. The market opened each morning with the ringing of the bells. Those caught selling before the bells rang were subject to penalty. If the shop owners were free Negroes, the penalty was a fine. If they were slaves, it would be thirty-nine lashes and confinement to the stocks for six hours.

Masters gave slaves tickets, which set forth what they could sell. Negroes were only supposed to sell what the master gave them permission to, but this law was hard to enforce. A few of the Charleston craftsmen were free, but most were slaves. The masters purchased licenses or tags for each year the slaves were employed. The tags, made of brass or copper, gave the slave's name, his trade and his master's name. Free slaves also needed to purchase tags proving their freedom. Freed slaves were the upper class of Black society, and were seen in the city dressed in fine clothes. Some of them served as custodians of the slave system. There were some freed men who owned their own slaves, which they treated as the white masters did.

Once, while in Charleston, the girls caused quite a stir. They were 13 years old and thinking themselves to be grown. April overheard a group of men on the street talking about "the Cothran slave" who dressed as a lady in fashionable clothes. She blazed with anger.

"What is this you say? One cannot be a lady if her skin is black? Do you realize how foolish you sound? You are jealous of the beauty of this so-called slave! She is my sister, and has the right to dress as a lady. Why don't you speak of something you truly understand, like for instance, the price of cotton!"

After her comment to the group, April grabbed May's arm and stormed away.

May was surprised by April's outburst. When they walked around the corner, away from the men, May begin to laugh.

"Those men thought you were a wildcat! You came at them scratching with both paws. They didn't even see you coming. Did you see the look on their faces? 'The price of cotton'; why the tall man almost choked on his cigar when you said that."

"Well it served them right. They don't know anything about us. You know they were speaking of us. I ought to have slapped them all!"

April's father was furious when he heard what happened in Charleston. Although May was dark skinned and clearly wasn't of mixed blood, rumors spread about David Cothran's slave daughter. Master Dayton told David of the rumors.

"April, if you speak to anyone in that way again, I swear I'll sell May. Everyone now thinks I fathered this slave. I've papers to prove her lineage, yet people believe what you said. She is not my daughter nor your sister!" David said sternly.

April was shocked to see her papa in such a rage. He picked up a stack of books and slung them across the floor, cursing the day May was born. As he lost control of his emotions, April realized she was seeing a side of her father she'd never seen before. Her heart pounded in fear of the man before her, not knowing what he might be capable of. David's embarrassment over the event was far more than he could bear, and worst of all, it was being inflicted upon him by the person he loved most.

"Papa," April cried out, "I'm sorry that I've upset you, but those men made me mad. They had no right to speak of May like they did. I didn't mean to suggest you were her father; I just meant she was my sister."

"You are never to speak of her in those terms again. May carries our family name only because we own her. She is neither my daughter nor your sister! Now leave before I do something I will regret!"

April fled the room, and went to find May. Eventually she found her under a pecan tree near the slave cabins. May sit with her knees drawn up to her chest.

"May, are you all right? I know you must have heard Papa, but he didn't mean it. He's upset over the rumors people are spreading about him. Don't cry May, Papa really loves you. Remember when he saved you from the dogs? It almost cost him a leg. He knows we are sisters; he used to call us his white and black angels--don't you remember?"

"Sometimes April, you make me feel like we're sisters. Then someone comes around to make sure we realize that we're not. You're all I have. Sometimes I think we're only fooling ourselves."

"Now listen May, as long as you and I know, that's all that matters. No one else can go inside us, and see how we feel. You will forever be my sister." April placed her arm on May's shoulder as they both sat in silence with tears forming in their eyes.

Cecil came up and asked," Lordy, what y'all crying bout. Someum done happen?"

"We're crying' cause we're sisters. It doesn't matter anymore what people think. No one can stop how we feel," April said.

"I's ain't never seen no one cry cause dey be sisters. Dat shore be a funny thing to cry over. Y'all should be happy, not sad." Cecil said.

"May, I just got an idea. You stay here with Cecil, I'll be right back."

April returned with paper and a quill with ink. April sat down under the tree and drew a large heart on a sheet of paper. In large letters she wrote -SISTERS FOREVER-inside the heart. Then she wrote her name on top, and let May write her name on the bottom.

"This is our pledge of sisterhood. As long as this paper stays hidden, we'll always be sisters. We will put it in a special place so no one can touch it. We can never remove it from its hiding place, unless one of us dies. Then it will go to the grave."

April folded it once and handed it to May for a second fold. They walked side by side to the big house as though they were on a great mission. They found a loose brick in their bedroom fireplace and slipped the paper behind it. When they replaced the brick they hugged, and once again felt like true sisters.

With the passing of time, May become more beautiful. The young men of the cabins argued about who would marry her. She had dark complexion with perfect skin. Because April helped May do her hair, she never wore rags on her head, as was custom with the workers. Soon her beauty surpassed all the local women, white or black.

May's mother, who was thirteen when May was born, never married. Lilly was treated differently by the slaves because of her contact with the Mandingo warrior. Males considered her used and not acceptable for marriage. If she'd been raped, she would have been accepted. The males believed she had chosen to take part in the contract with the African, though such was not the case.

David Cothran had said, "Lilly, tomorrow night you will receive a visit. You must obey the man sent to your cabin. You will be made with child. Don't be afraid of him; his coming is for the good of the plantation. You will wait for him alone."

Lilly cried that night and the next during the painful visit with the African.

Master Jackson, who owned the stud African, came to the Cothran plantation frequently. All were concerned that he was trying to buy some of the Cothran slaves. The thought of belonging to Jackson brought fear. It was known that Jackson beat his slaves, and worked them beyond reason. Sometimes, late at night, strange sounds could be heard coming from the direction of the Jackson plantation, and the people of the cabins believed the sounds were the screams of Jackson slaves carried in the wind. Many of the Jackson slave children were light skinned and resembled their master.

Master Jackson dealt mostly in the slave trade. Although he made money from cotton, indigo and rice, most of his wealth came from the interstate slave trade. Some believed he was also smuggling slaves on the coast. This crime could lead to two to four year's imprisonment and fines up to $10,000. When naval vessels captured smuggling ships, the ownership of the ships passed to the Navy.

Once David Cothran was overheard saying to Master Jackson," I'd rather not fool with the market. I'm satisfied with my plantation, and I don't think I'd be good at trading. It pains me to see what those people have to endure. They come in scared to death and have obviously been treated like animals before they get here. My father traded for a while in Savannah, but decided to stick with raising crops. I don't see anything wrong with working a slave, because work is good for them. Nobody needs to be lazy, nothing ever comes from laziness."

Cecil was twenty-one years old when the girls turned fifteen and considered an old maid. Cecil desired to be free one day, and kept all the money she'd saved selling handwork to pay for her freedom. Cecil made baskets from sweetgrass and Master Cothran allowed his workers to keep thirty per cent of the money they earned selling their crafts. Cecil kept the jar full of coins she had earned in a secret place.

"One day dis money gonna get me freedom shoes. Den my feet will start walking away from here."

Cecil learned from the house workers that Master Jackson was trying to buy May. She rushed to warn May, but wasn't taken seriously.

"Thank you for telling me what you have heard, but April told me I'd never leave again and I believe her. Don't worry; I'm not going to be sold for any amount of money," May said playfully, pushing Cecil.

"You best listen to me May. Dis here ain't no game. You better pray dat Master Jackson don't git you. You look like a grown woman, but you act jes like a child. Master Jackson wants you cause you pretty. Heck, he ain't da only man dat wants you. I don't know iffin you be lucky or cursed with dat beauty."

"Don't worry Cecil, I'll be fine."

"Let me tell you a story I heard. It happen down on da Jackson plantation. Dis slave woman had a boy four years old. Dey told her one day he was to be sold da next day, so she decided it was time to run. Late dat night they ran.

Early next morning master found out she is gone. He went and got the dogs and overseer to hunt dem down. Da woman was caught trying to climb a tree when dey found dem. Da child was torn right from his mother's arms as da dogs attacked his body. When da master reached the site, dem dogs don torn off the child's arm. Da mother was high in da tree, screaming da child's name. She got beat when returned to the plantation, and her child died from its wounds. Da master was shore mad at her cause no one gonna buy a dead boy." Cecil finished the story and looked at the fear on May's face.

"Dat ain't all I hear. Some nights when da moon is jes right, dey says you can hears dat boy crying for his mother. He wants her to be free like him, and wants his arm back too. You know he died cause his soul done slipped out through the hole in his body. Dats what I's hear anyway. I hope to never hear him cry for her, but I listen. You want a master like dat to own you? You better watch out, cause he shore enough got his eyes on you!"

May couldn't wait to find April to tell her the story. Maybe they could hear the child crying from their porch, when the moon was just right.

Four months later April was baptized in church. She decided since she was an experienced baptized Christian that she could prepare others for heaven. She began with May and Cecil and took them down to the lake.

"I baptize you in the name of the father, son, and their ghost."

She dipped them in the lake as they held their nose. Pulling them up she said, "Are you saved yet?"

"Not yet," called out Cecil. She was a very good swimmer, and it took awhile to get her saved. After six dunks, she was saved.

May didn't like water on her face, so she was saved right away.

That summer nearly all the workers were baptized by April.

Chapter 3

The Jubilee

Excitement filled the air at the plantation as everyone prepared for a party at the big house. People from as far away as Savannah were invited. Once a year the masters from different plantations threw large parties inviting others to see how they'd prospered.

For the first time in years, slaves from the Jackson Plantation were invited to the Cothrans' for a special party to celebrate those 'jumping the broom'. Master Cothran owned one hundred and thirty slaves, with forty of them working in Charleston. Master Jackson owned one hundred and fifty. Those who worked in Charleston were coming home for this special celebration, which they chose to call 'Jubilee Day'.

'Jumping the Broom' was a symbol among the Negroes of sweeping out the old life, and bringing in the new. Once two people standing, side by side, jumped over a broom they were married. This tradition had been passed down from Africa; one of the many handed down from generation to generation, only the masters accepted this one.

The masters had given them six hogs to roast over open pits, and the smell filled the air for miles. Meats and vegetables simmered in large kettles, and outside ovens blazed with the smell of baking breads and pies. Tables were brought outside from the cabins, and lined up in rows, each of them bearing blue mason jars filled with fresh flowers. The masters had also given the slaves two barrels of corn whiskey.

"Dey's here y'all!" screamed Cecil at about 11:00 o'clock as she saw the Jackson slaves approaching.

Holding onto her hat, she ran towards the approaching wagons as if in a race. You would have thought the Jackson slaves were kin, the way Cothran people ran to greet them. Everyone was dressed in Sunday's best, the women wearing fancy straw hats made just for the occasion.

They hugged each other as they jumped down from the wagons. Some brought instruments, and began to fill the air with music. Little children played 'Da Bones'; made of hog and cow ribs banged together to make a beat. Banjos, fiddles, guitars and jugs were also played. Banjos were African instruments brought over with the first arrival of slaves many years before.

"I be so happy to see all y'all, I'm feeling like I might bust wide open with all the joy inside me. Let's git to partying fore dis fine day ends," Cecil exclaimed.

The big house also filled with people and music on Jubilee day. Slave musicians from a plantation in Charleston entertained them, a big moneymaker for their master. Black people working in the big house were allowed to take turns coming to the Jubilee.

"I's don't know bout y'all, but I's just got to dance. Can't stand still no more," said Cecil as she began to dance.

April and May managed to slip away from the stuffy event at the plantation and ran to join the fun at the Jubilee.

The whiskey and food were being served. Some danced as others began to eat and talk. It felt so good to be together.

"You like your master?" one of the Jackson slaves asked. "Ain't never heard such a tale before. Masters is a child of the evil one. Dey like to see blood and hear men scream out in pain. Dat pleasures dem in ways we can't understand. Dey all evil."

"Dey is not. Master Cothran ain't one of da evil ones. He be good. He only whips a slave who don't know nothing 'bout hard work, and one who talks back. You work well for da master here, den he treats you good. Simple as dat," replied the man known as Monroe.

"Well, I shore ain't never heard no other slaves talk good of the master like y'all. You all just plain lucky. Simple as dat," said the Jackson slave.

"Why over on our plantation, you look master in da eyes he's gonna knock dem out. You gotta keep your head down when he speaks at ya. Iffin he wants to see your face, he says, 'Show me your ugly face, slave'. Iffin he is mad, you better stay out of his way. He treats his hound dog's better dan us. You know he's got lots of light colored young'uns running all over our place. Some of da women folks must not be too ugly for him," the Jackson slave named Leroy said with a chuckle.

"We watch two whippings every week. Iffin no one be bad, he just picks someone to whip. Says it keeps us in place. Dat place be called hell, if you ask me," Cece said.

April and May fixed their plates over flowing with food.

"May, I see your pappy. There he is sitting under that willow. It looks like he's shackled to that tree. Someone should take him a plate so that he could eat too. Maybe one of the men would be brave enough. Let's ask them," April said.

"I'll take him a plate. He is my pappy. I ain't afraid of him. I always wondered what it would be like to meet him. I betcha he don't even know he's my pappy. Fix me a plate. I'm going."

Cecil and April began to pile a plate high with goodies for the African.

"You sure you wanna do dis, May? I's go take it to em. You ain't gotta go. Heck, I always did want to see em. Heard so much about him, you know. He sure looks tall. Betcha he's mean too. I heard he eats chickens live," Cecil teased.

"Nope, he's my pappy, and I'm going. Give me that plate and get out of my way. I'm going to see him if it's the last thing I do. Might not ever git this chance again."

Cecil and April stood side by side and watched May march off to meet her pappy.

"Here is your supper. I hope you like what I fixed for you. Don't really know what you like to eat. Heard you eat lots of chickens though," May said, as she handed him a heaping mound of food.

"Get out of here girl, fore I hurt you. Didn't they tell you to watch out for me? Why you think they got me shackled to this here tree?"

"I think it's because you important and they don't want you running off. You don't scare me none. I ain't afraid of you now or never," said May, folding her arms and glaring at him.

She noticed he had her skin, and when she handed him his plate, she saw her own hands reaching out to take it. Now she looked into his eyes, and saw her eyes looking back. He had gray hair, and looked tired and worn out. His ankles showed scars of many shackles. But still, he was a beauty of a man. His chest muscles were large and his face was perfect. She wondered if he shaved, for there were no signs of facial hair.

"You really a warrior?" she asked.

"You really a slave?" he replied.

"I ain't or never have I been a slave. I'm the sister of the master's daughter. I live in the big house with them. She's standing right over there. You see her?"

"What's the matter girl, you crazy or someum? First you come over here; then you tell me a wild tale like that. Get on out of here. I ain't got time for you."

"What you gonna do? Sit over here all by yourself all day? Why they got you chained up? You have been trying to run, haven't you? I bet that's why you out here all by yourself."

"Woman, you don't know nothing about nothing. He got me out here to show me off. Just like his prize horses, he wants me to stand out from all of you. He wants to find me more work. You know what kind of work I do child? You'd faint straight away iffin you knew. Now get on out of here before I commence to telling you."

"You ain't scaring me none."

The warrior then let out a roar like a mighty lion, jerking at his shackles as though to free himself.

May took off like a scared cat. She fell trying to reach the others, and heard the African laughing his head off.

"Oh May, are you all right? Did he try to hurt you? What was that dreadful noise he made? What did he say to you? Did he know you was his child? May, tell me everything!" April said as she grabbed May's arm and helped her up.

Cecil and April were both jumping up and down with excitement.

May stood and brushed the dirt off her shirt and skirt. She took her time answering the questions they were both shooting at her. Her time with her pappy was private, and even April would never know what was really said.

"He just told me it was nice to meet me and thanked me for the food. That's all he said."

"May Cothran, you're lying to me. I saw you talking to him. Now what on earth did he say?" April said, pulling on May's shirt.

"That's all he said."

May never told April anything more. In her heart she knew she'd never see her father again, and she was right. Three months after their meeting, he was shot in the back while trying to run for freedom.

Single girls made new brooms for Jubilee in hopes of being chosen for a bride. The straw brooms were decorated with flowers, and kept near at hand. Cecil had made a broom, with the help of May and April, but left it inside her cabin because she felt too old to wed.

Brooms were made by sitting on a bench with a broom vise on one end. Straddling the bench with a pole sticking out the vise, straw was bunched to the pole and string was wrapped tightly around and around. The girls laughed at their first attempts then finally made one suitable for a wedding. Cecil beamed with pride.

April and May also helped Cecil make a special bonnet with a large red bow tied in the back. They swore to Cecil that it would catch her a man.

"Now you just wear this hat, and you'll see a man come running into your life. This red bow will draw them like flies to sweet butter. You better be ready, cause you'll catch a man for sure," May said as Cecil tried on the hat.

"It's gonna take more dan a hat to catch me a man. It will take a beauty stick beating me over da head for at least two days," replied Cecil, studying her reflection in the mirror.

April and May fell to their knees in laughter as Cecil pranced around them in her fancy new hat, with its bright red bow. Cecil wore the hat with pride, but didn't have much faith that it would help her.

Early in the evening, the big dance started. Everyone was dancing and Cecil was busy dancing a fast jig that she'd made up. Then someone tapped her on the shoulder.

"My name is Henry, and I come from the Jackson's," said a tall dark man who stood at Cecil's shoulder.

Cecil stopped dancing and turned to face the intruder.

"You want me to stop dancing so I can hears your name? You crazy or someum?" replied Cecil.

Henry looked down shyly and took off his straw hat. "I's been watching you all day, and I think you purdy. My wife died last year, and I ain't got no woman. I'd be happy and proud iffin you would jump da broom with me. You don't know me yet but I'm a good man, and I'd make you a good husband."

Cecil almost passed over right there. She didn't expect anyone to really ask her to jump the broom. She circled him and looked Henry over real good. He had a kind smile and all his teeth. He looked to be ten years older than her, yet it could just be the fields that had made him look that way. She found him handsome in a plain sort of way. He still had a head of hair, with some on his face. He stood there smelling strongly of whiskey, swaying a little as he waited for his answer. The ones who knew Cecil shouted words of encouragement.

"Cecil, don't let dat man gits away. Say yes! It's 'bout time you married."

Cecil stopped walking around him and placed her hands on her hips.

"You wait right here, and I be back with your answer."

Cecil ran to find April and May.

"Y'all ain't gonna believe it. Dis here hat works. Dat man over there wants me for a wife. I don't know what to do. Should I say yes, he's waiting for an answer."

"What man, Cecil? Show us!"

"Dat tall black man with dat silly grin on his face. He got on da green shirt. Y'all see him? He ain't ugly you know. Tell me what to do."

"Cecil, you got to decide. He looks like a good man and you want a good man. You right, he ain't ugly. I think he'd make a fine husband. He probably could help you make some pretty babies. You know how to make babies? You'll learn if you marry him," teased April.

"Now hush your mouth. I ask you for help, and you just wanna tease. I guess I done made up my mind without y'all. Move out of my way."

Cecil marched off towards her cabin. She returned carrying her newly made broom. When Henry clearly saw what she carried he let out a loud cry.

"Whoopee!" he yelled, reaching for Cecil and twirling her around.

"You ain't never gonna regret dis day, I promise you right now. Dis day is gonna be a good one." he said with a big smile.

Later that evening both masters came down to watch the slaves jump the brooms. Twenty had decided to join together. The masters had them line up holding hands in pairs; then told them all to jump.

"Jump over and be married!" they yelled.

After they'd jumped over, everyone came to shake the newlyweds' hands and bid them well. Cecil was happy to be married. As she and Henry danced, she thought to herself, "I hope da master let me keep any babies dat come from Henry and me. I wonder iffin it be da whiskey or dis big bow dat made Henry want me. I guess it won't be bad to be married. Heck, I only has to see him on Sundays. I feel like we gonna be real happy together." Cecil smiled at her man as they started towards her cabin.

Chapter 4

Lye Soap

Time has a way of changing all that lies before it. Two years had passed since the day of the great Jubilee. The crops that once had been plentiful refused to grow in the great drought that affected the southern states. The situation on the Cothran plantation echoed throughout the south.

April was in the parlor drinking hot tea when she heard someone knocking at the front door. The butler soon ushered Master Jackson into the hall. Master Jackson said he urgently needed to speak to David Cothran. April was curious and went to the parlor door.

"Why good morning, April. You're looking mighty pretty today. How are you doing?" Master Jackson said as he handed the butler his hat.

"Fine, thank you," replied April. "Mr. Jackson, I hope there is nothing wrong on your plantation. Is everything all right?"

"Everything is fine, April. I just need to settle some business with your papa."

April didn't like the thought of her papa doing business with the Jackson's. Master Jackson's main business was buying and selling slaves. She knew he had several men he hired out just to sire children. Her own papa had paid a large sum for the Mandingo warrior to sire May. She knew this, for she'd found the papers. She had even let May read them to prove how special she was. Her papa had paid one hundred dollars for the warrior to visit Lilly.

Her papa greeted Master Jackson when he came down the stairs. He then said they'd go into the library to discuss their business. When she saw the library door didn't shut all the way, she tiptoed to the door hoping to hear the conversation that was beginning.

"Now David, you know this is the best deal you're ever going to receive on the sale of one slave. I'm offering you ten times the amount she's worth. You know I did own her father, until he tried to escape, so I want her in my breeding stock. That's the only reason I'm offering you this amount," said Master Jackson.

"Yes, I realize the deal you're offering is great. But you don't understand the relationship between that slave and my daughter. I swear those two acts like they're real sisters. Once before I tried to separate them and April wouldn't eat for a solid two weeks. She almost died! Doctor Albright said she was grieving herself to death for May. When May came back into this house, April's health return. They've been together ever since that happened eight years ago. I've never tried to separate them again. April just can't handle it," David finished in a concerned voice.

"David, I'm only going to offer this once. If I leave here today without papers on that slave, you'll never hear this offer again. And let's face it, your crops didn't do well these past two years. You, my friend, really need this money. You own many slaves, and they must be fed and cared for. Winter is coming fast; you'd better give this offer some serious thought."

David turned his back to Master Jackson and began rubbing his forehead, trying to decide what to do. One thing was certain, he needed the money. He stood there wondering if April could let go of the relationship that she'd formed with May? Was she old enough to understand the value of a slave? After all, May was just a slave. A good slave, but just a piece of property, nothing more. These thoughts filled David's head.

"Jackson, I will sell you May on one condition. You allow her to stay here a few more days, and let me have time to work it out with April. I will sign the papers today, and give you full ownership of May if we can work together on the time of delivery. You just don't have any idea what this might do to April. The only reason I even consider your offer is the fact that winter is coming, and I must care for all my people. God knows I would never do anything to hurt my child again and I too have become accustomed to May," David spoke with tension rising in his voice.

David turned again to face the now smiling Master Jackson.

"Well David Cothran, you got yourself a deal. Let's sign those papers now and seal the deal with some whiskey. This is a good day for us both. You have made me a happy man. I've wanted that girl since she was ten years old. She will be my prized possession. No harm will ever be placed on her. I give you my promise." Master Jackson reached out with both hands to shake the hand of David Cothran.

April's heart was beating so fast, she was afraid they might hear it. Her legs had turned to rubber, and the room was beginning to spin. She had to lean against the wall to keep from falling flat on her face. It was hard to breathe.

"Oh my God, what has he done. No Papa, No! What am I going to do? May sold to Master Jackson! Oh sweet Jesus, this can't really be happening. Papa promised us both never again. Never again," April thought to herself.

April thought of how much May meant to her. She was her only friend. She always encouraged her and supported everything she did. She was the one who comforted her when she got the bleeding disease that now affected her monthly May eventually caught it too. No one in her life meant as much to her as May Suddenly she realized there was only one thing she could do. She would find May, and they would run far away from Master Jackson. April was young, bu she knew it was lust for May that made her valuable to Master Jackson. She would never allow him to own or touch her own sister, not as long as she was alive. No one would ever own May. No one could ever take May away from her. She needed May just as she needed blood in her veins. She couldn't live without her.

With this newfound knowledge, April regained her strength and left quickly to find May. She knew just where to look, for today the women were making lye soap. Soap was made only twice a year, in spring and in fall. May never missed a chance to help; she would surely be there now. They both loved to hear the stories that were passed around the fire, as the women stirred the large kettle with the bubbling soap. With each turn came the chance to top the story told by the previous person. April was allowed to hear the tales, but never stir the soap.

As she ran around to the back of the house, the wind carried the sting of the lye soap to her eyes. April had to stop and wipe her face. When she was able to look again, she saw May sitting with the others. April quickly walked to her shoulder.

"May, we need to talk," she whispered as she tugged May. "Come with me."

"Not now April; sit and listen to this story. It's about a slave whose daddy was his Master. They say it be a true story. Y'all go ahead, finish the story. I want April to hear it too," May said.

"May, come with me now. It's important, we must talk."

"April, we talk all the time. I never get to hear stories this good. Sit here till she finishes this one, then I'll go with you."

"No May, come with me now."

"April, whatever it is will have to just wait. I want to hear the rest of this story. Now sit down for a few minutes and listen. Then and only then will I leave!"

"Promise."

"Yes, now please let her finish. Go-ahead Sudie finish your tale. We're listening."

"Well, y'all knows I's don't lies. Dis here be true as me and you be black. I's seen dis here boy with my own eyes. He don't look black, and he don't look white. He's got one eye blue and da other eye brown. His hair be blonde like the sun, and curly like a pig's tail. Dey says he's got a great big black mark right on his back, where his soul wants to be black. But the rest of em is the color of a pecan shell. He don't share a cabin with no ones but his own mammy. He won't never have to work da fields, and da master won't let no one ever beat him. He does whatever he wants all days long. But he don't know da master be his daddy. He thinks the master is just real nice. Dat master be real mean to all the others, though. He likes to beat all da mans and whoop all da children's. But not dis here boy and his mammy. No, nots dem. And dat be the truth," finished Sudie.

It was easy to be caught up in the storytelling of the women, their tales hard to believe but fascinating. They had a way of making the people seem real, almost as if you knew them. When a woman received the ladle, she was to stand and stir the soap as she spun her story.

"Okay, let's go. Sudie's finished." April said as she pulled on May's apron.

"Wait April, the soaps ready now. Let me at least pour one mold. Can't this wait for a few more minutes?" May said as she resisted April's pleading.

A table had been set out with the molds lining it from end to end. Each woman would take turns carrying the ladle of boiling soap to the molds.

"May now, we must go."

"April, why don't you pour some soap. You've watched us do it for years. Go ahead, take the ladle from Sadie." May said as she pushed April towards Sadie.

"Lord no," cried Martha, "da master would tear us apart for letting her do dat. Dis here ain't work for no white woman. You best sit yourself down, and let us do our work. You could gits burnt doing dis. Lord child, don't even thinks about it."

"Let her try," said May. "Y'all know she wouldn't get you in trouble. She's April; she won't tell on you. She done baptize y'all for heaven." May plead.

Against the others' judgment, they gave in to May's pleas and handed April the ladle. April was shocked to be given a chance to pour soap and have the ladle in her hands.

So much had happen in such a short time, April begin to feel it was a dream. April looked down at the ladle and then at May.

"Go ahead April, you always said you wanted to. Pour up some soap." May said grinning at the visible shaken April.

April walked up to the kettle and dipped in the ladle lifting it running over with boiling soap, and carefully raising it into the air. She looked up at May and saw her smiling with the sun glowing off her face. May was truly beautiful. It was then that the answer to their problem came to her. Master Jackson wanted May for her beauty, and that was all. April looked down at the boiling soap, and once again at May. The solution to their problem was right in her hands. Without another thought, she slung the boiling soap all over the left side of May's face and arm. May hit the ground screaming so loud, April had to cover her ears.

The women took off running in all directions. April stood above the screaming May, frozen with fear of what she had done. May was rolling back and forth, the steam still rising from her face and arm. Suddenly Master Jackson and her papa appeared.

"What in the hell has happened here? What has happened, April?" demanded David Cothran as he gently scooped May up in his arms.

May then passed out and lay limp against his body. April snapped out of the frozen state of shock and began to scream. After a few seconds she began pleading.

"I tripped Papa, and spilled soap on May. Help her please, help her. I didn't mean to hurt her. I tripped Papa, I tripped," April began crying.

Master Jackson could be heard cussing up a storm, and yelling as he followed David and April.

"The contract is no more David, do you hear me? I did not buy a damaged slave; I was buying a healthy slave. She's all yours. I'll go fetch the doctor, but that slave is still yours."

April followed her papa all the way to their house, pleading that it was just an accident.

" Don't let her die! Help her, I didn't mean for it to happen. They let me pour soap. It's not my fault. Save her Papa, save her." The others were still hiding from April. None could believe the horrible event that they had just witnessed. April had gone mad.

Chapter 5

April's Sent Away

May was carried into April's bedroom and gently laid on her mahogany bed. She began to drift in and out of consciousness. When she would come to, she began to scream out in pain. Master Cothran ordered cool towels placed on her burns, whereupon May started shaking as though she was freezing. Master Cothran sent for Lilly, her mother, to be by her side. When the towel absorbed the heat, Lilly would hold it between two fingers and spin it in the air, instantly cooling it.

April kept trying to get into the room with May, but her parents refused to let her enter, being afraid April would blame herself for the pain May was in. If May died from her burns, it would be too much for poor April to endure.

When the doctor arrived, he was shocked by May's condition. As he lifted the towels off May's face and arm, he saw that the soap had hardened and that the skin was falling off in pieces. He had never dealt with such serious burns, and found himself unsure how to begin treatment. Much disturbed, he excused himself from May's side, and went outside to regain his thoughts. May awoke and began screaming, bringing the doctor back to her side.

"Lord, have mercy on this poor girl," he whispered as he began to examine the wounds.

April sat on the stairway crying out May's name over and over again. When May screamed, April would try to run past the house slaves to reach her, but she was never allowed into the room.

Late that night it was decided that April should go to the Jacksons' plantation until the situation with May was resolved. Master Jackson had offered to take her when he returned with the doctor, but April refused to leave May. Finally Master Cothran gave her no choice.

"April, you must leave this house until I send for you. This crying is doing nothing to help May; you are only keeping yourself upset. What happened was not your fault; there is nothing we can do now but try to help May. You must go to the Jackson's' until I send for you."

"Papa, please let me stay. She doesn't understand what happened. She doesn't know that it was an accident. She will hate me, Papa. I must explain to her, and be with her while she's hurting. Please don't send me away."

All the pleading in the world would not change his mind. April was sent kicking and screaming from the house in the middle of the night and placed into the Jackson's' carriage.

The ride to the Jackson plantation took over thirty minutes. April's screaming turned into silence as she sunk deep into grief, reliving the throwing of boiling lye soap on May, and trying to convince herself it must have been an accident.

"Oh sweet Jesus, what have I done. What have I done? Be with May, don't let her die. I didn't want to hurt her...I just wanted to keep her. Forgive me Lord."

The upstairs slave who was riding with her to the Jackson's' kept her arms around April's shoulders and tried to comfort her. She had helped raise the girls since they were six, and could not understand what had taken place. Those girls were bonded.... and inseparable.

When they arrived at the Jacksons' plantation, Master Jackson and his wife Elise stood waiting. Elise ran to the carriage and helped April get out, then wrapped her arms around her.

"April sugar, I'm so sorry to hear what happened to your favorite slave. But don't worry, everything will be all right. Your papa will get you another. It's going to be fine."

With Elise's words, April looked at her. She felt no one truly understood how much May meant to her.

"I don't want anyone else, I want May." April tearfully said.

"April, listen to me child, this is not your fault. Accidents happen all the time. Those slaves should have known better than to let you pour hot soap. Women of our kind should not be doing things like that. It's really their fault. Now stop your crying and don't worry about it. That slave is probably going to be all right. If not, you'll get another one."

When they walked into the house, despite her tears, April began to look around at her new surroundings. She had always been impressed by the elaborate fashion in which the Jackson home was decorated. The Jackson's had imported all their furniture from Europe. Their windows were covered in rich velvets and satins. April was in awe at the beauty that surrounded her.

The guestroom to which April was taken was as impressive as the rest of the house. It had a heavily carved cherry bed, with faces of angels carved onto the massive headboard. There were wooden beams that formed the canopy from which heavy lavender drapes hung. The whole room was done in the color of lavender, even the sofa and chairs. The covers were pulled down showing beautiful lace trimmed linen sheets.

"Mrs. Jackson, I must go back home. May needs me. Please get someone to take me back, it's a mistake that I'm here." April said looking at Elise with pleading eyes.

"Your papa knows best, April. This is where you need to be right now. That slave will be all right soon, then you can leave." Elise said with great compassion.

"Don't call her slave, her name is May."

"Well then May will be fine without you, the doctor is there. There's nothing you can do for her now."

When April was finally alone, she turned out all the oil lamps and crawled into the bed. The fire that blazed in the fireplace lit the room with strange shapes. She began to re-think the events of the day once more.

"I hope papa doesn't find out what really happened. I'm sure May will realize the pain I saved her from and she'll understand why I had to do it. She'll know I saved her from Master Jackson's hold," thought April.

With a heavy heart she closed her eyes in prayer.

"Please hear me Lord, and save May. Please keep her alive. I can't lose her. I'll have no one who understands me. I need her, please be with her. Please forgive me."

The room was silent except for the crackling of the fireplace. April had cried so hard that sleep easily found her. She began to dream of May and her running away with May uninjured and beautiful. They were headed to the free states, and were looking for the Underground Railroad. In her dreams the trains of the railroad ran in great tunnels under the earth, so they were looking for a cave to gain entrance to the tracks. The cave they found was dark and full of bats, but they held onto each other and went deeper into the darkness. Finally they could hear the whistle of an approaching train. Suddenly April heard someone calling her name. It was a voice she didn't recognize calling her over and over.

She opened her eyes, shocked to find herself in a strange room. It took her a moment to remember where she was.

"I'm at the Jackson's," she thought. "Oh no, now I remember," she said and her heart began to sink.

"April, are you awake now?" the strange deep voice called out.

April looked towards the doorway. It was then she first saw him. Looking in at her stood the most gorgeous man she had ever seen. He called out her name once more, this time playfully.

"April, do you hear me?" he asked with a smile.

"Who are you, and what are you doing in my room?" she stammered, pulling the covers up to her shoulders.

"Why April Cothran, you really don't remember me. I'm Jewel. We used to see each other at parties here, even played together as children. Can't you remember? How about the time when we were five... we left a party at your house and went swimming in your lake? One of your slaves told on us, and we got in trouble for swimming without clothes. It was you, a slave girl and me. Surely you remember that." he said with a big grin.

"Jewel Jackson?" she said. "I can't believe it's really you. Why you're a grown man now." April realized how stupid she sounded and her face turned blood red.

He cocked his head back and let out a roar of laughter.

"Why Miss April, you are grown up too. And I must say you've turned out to be charming and lovely. I hope we see more of each other, now that you're located next to my bedroom," Jewel said with a mischievous smile.

With that comment, April pulled the covers up tight around her neck.

Jewel let out a mischievous giggle.

"I'm sorry if I embarrassed you. Mother asked me to tell you it's time for breakfast. So if you'll hurry and dress, I'll meet you in the dining room. And by the way, good morning!"

He shut the door, and April heard his footsteps going down the stairs.

"Jewel Jackson," she thought, "have you ever grown up. What a fine looking man you become. I wish May were here. She wouldn't believe it. A skinny little runt like you."

Chapter 6

Through May's Eyes

May felt the pain to be unbearable. She did nothing but scream out for help. Lilly stayed right beside her day and night. The doctor didn't leave the plantation for two days. He slept on the cot at the foot of April's bed. He wouldn't leave May in such pain.

He didn't care if she was just a slave, her strength and will power to stay alive amazed him. He gave her medication for pain, along with strong whiskey. Only sleep seemed to bring her comfort. The bandages were changed every four hours, which caused her great pain. The task had to be done to help prevent infection.

When May slept she dreamed of being with April. Sometimes in her dreams, they would run through fields of wild flowers. They would rest by the lake and talk of things they would do together in their lives. When tired of talking, they'd jump into the lake holding hands. When the water would splash on May, she'd begin to burn. She'd awake screaming and realize the pain was real.

"Oh mama, what has happened to me?" cried May. "Why am I hurting so bad? What's happened to my face? Why am I wrapped in bandages? Somebody stop the pain, I can't bear it any longer. Where is April?" screamed out May.

"Hush now child, your mama's here, and I ain't leaving. Mama's gonna make sure you be okay. Don't worry about Miss April, she be fine. She be real fine! Rest child, you gots a lot of healing to do. Your body needs sleep," said Lilly as she stroked May's head.

Doctor Albright came to May's side and gave her more fluid to drink. It eased the pain a little, and she drifted back into dreams. The dreams were peaceful and full of laughter. She and April would be playing and having so much fun. Then as soon as something or someone would touch her face, she would awake screaming. It felt like fire racing through her body.

May stayed in this condition for three weeks. The doctor came every day to check her progress. Sometimes, when she was having a bad day, he would stay through the night. He was proud of the progress May made, and felt that he had performed a miracle.

Lilly did not trust the doctor and his medicine. She made secret arrangements to have a Grisgris performed and given to May. This form of spiritual healing and protection was passed down through the Marabout tribe. Verses of the Koran were written on wood with charcoal then washed off with water. The water was captured and given to the sick as a cure.

To ensure full protection from evil spirits that caused pain and illness, verses of the Koran were written on paper and placed in a leather pouch worn around the neck.

The night the Grisgris was performed May was tormented by pain.

"Child, drink this water and feel the protection of your ancestors flow through your veins. Only they can ease your pain, only they will carry your burdens."

May looked wide-eyed at the dark black man who now lifted up her head, to hold the cup under her lips.

"Mama," May said, looking fearfully at Lilly.

"Drink child, this be our ways. This be medicine I'm sure of," Lilly replied, leaning closer to May and taking hold of her hand.

May drank the smoky colored water and coughed. She didn't have the strength to argue about the strange event-taking place around her.

After she drank the Grisgris, the wood used was placed into the burning fire in the fireplace.

The man who performed the Grisgris was a Marabout high priest. Several people in the cabins had given money and convinced Lilly to send for him. He came late at night while the master slept. The ceremony was performed in silence while Lilly and May watched. He whispered blessings upon the leather pouch that held the Grisgris, then slipped it around May's neck.

He stood by May's side and raised both of his hands towards heaven. Slowly he lowered them and waved them about May's face and arm.

"It is done. Tell no one of what took place here tonight. You are now protected by your ancestors."

He smiled at May and she closed her eyes. When she opened them again, he was gone.

"Mama, what just happen? That man dressed in white, who was he?"

"Don't matter who he was, just matters what he done. That man just saved your life; I feel it in my soul. I still pray to my Jesus, but child; you needed all the healing you could get. Now rest, soon it will be a new day," Lilly said, gently kissing May's forehead.

The mirrors had been removed from April's room. No one wanted May to realize the fate that April had placed on her. The master was doing everything he could to save her. If it had been any other slave, she would have died. David Cothran didn't want April to feel like she caused May's death. He felt it would be too much of a burden on her.

The slaves talked about the event of lye soap every day; it constantly stayed on their minds. The women who had been present seemed to change the event daily. Some felt April was jealous of May's beauty, some felt that April had just gone mad. But everyone realized that it couldn't have been an accident, because April had taken direct aim on May's face. No, it was surely not an accident.

Many were glad April had been sent away. For years she had been around them and they treated her just like she belonged. No one could ever trust her again. They had all been warned that you couldn't trust a white, now they knew why.

After three weeks May begin to stay awake. She was confused by what had happened. She couldn't remember anything beyond April picking up the ladle and walking with the soap. She slowly began to realize what had taken place, but couldn't understand why. They both had been raised and nursed as babies by Lilly. April hadn't acted mad that day. She joined in and listened to the stories being told. May had never loved another like she did April. She knew April better than she knew her own Mama. How could she have done this to her? What made her turn against her?

One day Lilly had a long talk with May. She decided it was time May knew the truth about why it happened.

"May, you know I'm your mama, and I wouldn't be a lying to you. That Miss April done throw that soap on you for purpose. She be aware of what she do. I says she don't like it that you be purdier than her. She don't like you acting like you her sister neither. She's the master, just like her daddy be. She owns you May! You her slave, not her sister. I be afraid someum gonna happen like dis. She wurn't gonna always be nice to you. She grown now, and want you to be in your place."

"Oh mama," cried May, "that can't be true. April loves me mama. Just like a real sister."

"Child, listen to me good," said Lilly with more firmness. "That April is your master. She done took away the bestest part of you. She took away half your face. You ain't never gonna be a beauty again. April done seen to that. When she comes back, remember, you her slave! One day we be free but till that day comes, you a slave. Do you hear me child?"

May started a hard cry that came from deep within. She was a slave. Yet it was only at that moment she realized what that meant. She could not control what was done to her, she couldn't fight back. Her body was not her own, it belonged to the master, and the Master was also April.

"April," she cried out, "How could you have done this to me. What changed? What happen to you."

These thoughts would haunt May for most of her life.

Chapter 7

May Looks Into A Mirror

It had been eight long weeks since May was burned. The bandages were removed from her face, so that air could help in the healing process. May begged to see a mirror, but was terrified at what she might find.

"Please mama Lilly, let me see. You keep telling me it's going to be all right, and that it's not as bad as it could be. You've got to let me see for myself. It's my face, and I need to know." pleaded May.

"May, the doc be coming by today. When he gits here, we ask him to let you see. He will know what to do. Now hush up, and wait." said Lilly.

May sat near the window and awaited the arrival of the doctor. Finally late afternoon he arrived. May pleaded to see her reflection. She promised that she could handle her appearance. She had to know the truth.

"May, I don't think this is the right time. You still have a long way to go. Your face should heal more before you look at It." replied Doctor Albright.

"Please, I must see what everyone else sees. I have to know. I have to see."

Finally, everyone gave in and brought in a mirror. May was made to sit in a chair and take deep breaths.

"Are you ready?" asked the Doctor.

"Yes, I'm ready." replied May.

May stared at her reflection for a few moments. She couldn't believe what she saw. It looked as if half her face had melted. Her left eye was pulled down and you could see inside the bottom lid. Her skin was drawn tight and pinkish in color. She wished to be dead. The mirror began to shake in her hands. The voices around her started to sound like the buzzing of bees. Her reflection seemed like that of goblin. Something to fear and hide from.

"No---no." she said softly.

She saw her mouth move and realized the face was really her own. She dropped the mirror and it shattered at her feet. She tried to stand and felt her body struggling for balance. Everything became dark and silent.

"May, can you hear us? Quick, someone bring some water! This poor child has passed out. I knew it was too soon. Where's the water? " called out Doctor Albright as he lifted May onto her bed.

The depression that followed was great, with no end in sight. Forever the image was etched into her mind. May had always treasured her beauty as a special gift from God. She loved the attention beauty had brought her. Now she wanted never to show her face again.

After staying in her room for two weeks, May confronted Doctor Albright.

She stood up from her chair when he walked into the room and stood face to face with him.

"Why did you save me? Don't you see how horrible I look? No one shall ever love me. I am in constant pain with no relief. Why don't you shoot me and end my suffering!" she said through tears.

It was then he sat her down firmly and knelt, looking into her eyes.

"May, you have inspired me with your will to live. Something deep inside you would not give up. I'll be honest with you, I never thought you'd live through that first night, but you did. You cannot give up now. The outside of you is just a shell, with the real person lying deep within. You still have great beauty and charm, but now it lies deep within. Don't ever give up. God in heaven has great plans for you. You have to carry on." speaking slowly and softly as he held onto May's shoulder.

May trembled at his touch. He had spoken to her almost as a father. No white man had ever spoke to her like April did. As if she were important and more than a slave. His words invoked hope. Something she had not felt since the burning.

"Thank you." she replied.

"With all my heart, I mean it." he said.

He checked May over and noted the improvements in her eye. The puss that had puddle inside had almost disappeared. The eyewash and drops were working. Neither said another word as he finished with the treatment.

"May, I'm proud of how well you've done. You are a strong young girl. Life is worth living. I will return to see you in four weeks. If you need more for pain, send someone. Try to go outside as much as you can, but stay out of direct sunlight. Good-bye." said Doctor Albright as he picked up his hat and headed for the door.

Soon after, May begin to accept her appearance and began taking short walks to regain her strength. She'd hide the left side of her face with her long dark hair. All the others wanted to see the outcome of the event. Rumors were spread that her whole face was affected. One day a group of children ran up to greet her from the children's cabin.

"Hay May, you all better now. We heard you were sick. What's that on your face? Is somepun on it?" they asked.

May knew this day would come and felt it was time to face their reactions.

"An accident happen awhile back, burning my face and arm. Do you want to see my arm."

They nodded yes.

May lifted the blouse that covered the scared arm and watched their eyes widen and mouths open. Then she slowly lifted her hair and watched the horror that filled their faces. They took off running without looking back.

"Mama Lilly, what's wrong with all of them? Can't they see it's just me? Don't they understand how bad they make me feel? I know they're just kids, but so am I." May said as they turned to walk back to the plantation.

"May you gots to knows, they just plain slaves. They be a little scared when things change or people change. They knows it's you, but just don't knows how to act. Gem em time, theys all will come around. Its just gonna take time." Lilly said reassuring to May.

"May I's got news for you today. April be coming home tomorrow. Master done told me to tell ya. He says he wants you to act like you all right, and be kind to Miss April. He says she done had a hard time bout what happen to ya. He don't want her to hurt no more. I can't believes he says she been hurt. It was you she liked to killed. Don't dat beat all." finished Lilly shaking her head in disgust.

May stopped walking up the steps and just stared at her mother. April was coming home. The emotions that overcame May had not been expected. She began to cry and reached for her mother.

She cried for the sister of her past. The one who could never be again. April was coming home and she was her slave. Nothing more, nothing less.

Chapter 8

April Returns

April stayed at the Jackson's for the winter, with May never far from her thoughts. She prayed that May would be healed, and all would be forgiven. Everybody continued to call the incident an accident. April was beginning to believe that it was.

April found staying at the Jackson's enjoyable. Jewel Jackson showered April with attention, and she begin to grow fond of him. She found him especially funny when he'd been drinking. She wished her spirit could be as free as his seem to be. He took life easy, and didn't seem to worry. No matter what happened, he would just smile and say, "Well, so be it."

Jewel was also an excellent dancer. He took April to many parties while she stayed with them and insisted she be his partner, leaving her dance book with only his name in it. He danced with skill while April stumbled and stepped on his toes. She felt like a duck dancing with a swan. Jewel was full of life, and April thought living with him would be heaven on earth.

Jewel had all the ladies charmed. As they danced across the room, April saw them lower their fans and give pouted looks with their lips. Some would lower them and flash smiles or toothy grins his way. He was a ladies man, no doubt about it. He would just laugh and pull April closer to him, and then she'd pull away. She had no plans of being just another conquest. She wanted more, much more.

Finally the day came when April received a note from her father: it was time for her to come home. The note read, "May is doing well. She is happy to hear that you will be coming home. We all have missed your cheerful smile, and look forward to your return. Love, Papa and Mother."

April had mixed feelings about going home. When she left, Jewel would no longer be near her. She hungered just for the touch of his hand on hers. She yearned to hear his laughter, and to be near enough to smell him. He had a musk smell about him and reeked of manhood. Desires were beginning to be stirred in April. Something deeper than friendship was being formed.

Jewel teased April and was always looking for reasons to stand close to her, or to touch her. With each touch April's heart would beat faster and she'd tingle all over. Was this love, she thought? Could he possibly be feeling the same way about her, she wondered.

The accident had happened in late October, during harvest, and it was now the first of March. April had begun to think it was truly just an accident. No one would burn another on purpose. It just had to be an accident. April decided to tell May just that: it was a horrible accident. She had tripped on a rock and the lye soap just fell out. That was just how it happened, plain and simple. Surely May would understand and forgive her.

April's parents came running down the walkway to greet her. Her mother cried, "Oh April, darling, we're so glad you're finally home. It has been so lonely here all winter without you. I hope you'll forgive us for sending you away. Everything is fine here. May is back to normal and holds no hard feelings towards you."

"Mother, do you mean that. Where is May? Why isn't she out here to greet me?" said April. "There is so much I've got to tell her. My stay at the Jackson's was refreshing. They are really such good people, and they have a son that is my age. Mother, do you know him?" she asked.

"Now where is May? I've just got to see her, I cannot wait another moment!" April looked over the shoulders of her parents.

"Wait a minute young lady! You'd better give your old papa a hug and kiss. It sure is good to have you home!" April flung herself into her father's arms and he twirled her around and around.

"Papa, it feels so good to be back. But I must see May. You can't imagine how much I've missed her." said April.

"Okay, I'll take you to May. But we must talk first. May is doing good now, but there are problems from the accident. Come on in, we will talk in the library." He placed his arm around her shoulder and led her in.

If she had looked up, April would have seen May looking out the window at her arrival. But she wouldn't have seen the tears that were rolling down her cheeks. For May had promised herself, that April would never get the satisfaction of seeing her cry. April would never know from her lips how deep her scars truly were. It was not only her face and arm damaged forever, so was her heart. Never again would she openly allow herself to love April; love for her sister was now buried deep within. It could not be destroyed, but it could never grow again. NEVER!

For April, it felt good to walk into her own home again. She had forgotten the smell of the house, an aroma of rich wood freshly polished. She stood in the hall and savored the feel of the place. She didn't realize how much this house meant to her until she had to leave it, she promised herself she would never leave again.

Her father took her hand and led her in to the library. She sat on the sofa and he placed himself in a big wing back chair.

"April, there is something you must know about May. Everything is not as grand as your mother told you. May has changed. She doesn't act like she used to, and I'm afraid she will be different around you. The accident heavily scarred the left side of her face. Doc saved her life, but he could do nothing to stop the scaring. May will look the way she does now for the rest of her life, and it has not been easy for her to accept her appearance. Her scars might make you feel sick when you first see them, and I am concerned about your feelings of guilt over the accident. At no point must you blame yourself. Things happen in this world that we have no control over, and there is nothing we can do to change the outcome of an uncontrollable event once it happens. We must learn to accept what happens in life. Do you understand why I'm saying this to you? You must not blame yourself for any of this!"

He leaned forward and looked into April's eyes. "It wasn't your fault, it was more an act of God."

April leaned back on the sofa and tried to take in all her papa was telling her. She hadn't been told of the horrible scarring until now. She found herself repeating over and over in her mind that it was just an accident. The truth was just too hard to handle. Tears started streaming down her face. Her heart was breaking for her sweet beautiful May. She couldn't bear the thought of May blaming her. She said through her tears, "Papa, I'm sorry for what happened. I wish it had been me that was burned, and not May. She is so beautiful."

"Everything is going to be all right, April. May will get her spirit back, and things will be as they were. Now if you are ready, I will send for May and you two can spend some time alone in here, away from the rest of us."

April wiped the tears from her face and said, "Okay Papa, I'm ready to see May. Please send her quickly to me."

Chapter 9

The Sisters Meet Again

April sat quietly in the room, waiting for May. She found it hard to grasp the events that had lead up to this moment. If her father had only kept his promise, this accident would have never happened. It was he who made plans to sell May. He knew she could never live without her. May was as much a part of her life as the limbs of her own body. She felt sorry for the pain she had caused May, but it wasn't all her fault. If things had just remained the same, everything would have been as it should be. May was her sister; they belonged together.

April could hear May's footsteps coming down the stairs. It struck her as odd that she could still remember the sound of her sister's footsteps, but there was no mistake, it was May coming to greet her. May came into the doorway with her head down, and her hands grasping each other. Right away April could see the scars on May's hand and arm: they didn't look as bad as she expected. Had her Papa misjudged the appearance of the scars?

"May, I'm so glad to see you. I've missed you so much." April said running to May and wrapping her arms around her. May stood stiffly, not moving a muscle.

April pulled back from her and asked, "May, what is wrong with you? Are you glad I'm back? Didn't you miss me?"

There was no reply from May; she just stood there with her head hanging down.

"May! Can't you hear me? Why won't you answer?"

May replied, "Yes Mistress, I hear you."

"Yes Mistress!" April said loudly. "What are you talking about! It's me April."

"Yes mistress, whatever you say mistress." replied May again.

"May, this is not funny. You stop this right this moment. You know I'm not your master!" April said with her hands on her hips.

"I know now you are my mistress," said May.

"Stop that right this moment! May look at me! Look at me right now!" she said with her voice raised and the words sharply spoken.

"Yes mistress." replied May as she slowly lifted her head up towards April.

April felt the room begin to spin. The scarred flesh she saw was so unreal it couldn't be part of May. She hit the floor with a loud thud, and May run to the door to call for help.

"Leave now!" shouted Master Cothran as soon as he reached April.

May lowered her head and slipped silently out of the room.

"April darling," cried her mother, " Are you all right? Speak to us April. Speak to us!'

April began to come around under the gentle shaking of her parents. They all knew that seeing May for the first time would be hard for April. It was hard for them to look at May, and they'd been with her since the accident.

April was confused when she came to. Every time the image of May came to her she would feel sick to her stomach. She wondered how she could ever get used to seeing May in this condition. She still needed her and wanted her for a sister, but didn't think she could get used to her.

May was told that evening that it would be best for her to go live at the cabins with the other slaves. April would need more time away from her to adjust to what had happened.

"May, don't be upset over being sent to the cabins. It will be temporary," said Master Cothran. "When April has adjusted to what happened, we will send for you. I need you to begin working in the fields until then. You are well now, and we have crops to plant. I'll make sure all your needs are met. Now you and Lilly go, I will send for you later."

Chapter 10

May's Life At The Slave Cabins

May being sent to live in the slave cabins only proved that what Lilly had told her was the truth. She was just a slave, like all the rest. It would be hard living among the others; many didn't like her. Once their dislike arose because they felt she thought she was better, now they were afraid of how she looked.

The hardest part for May lay in the fact that her feelings did not change with the burning of her skin. Inside she was still the same May. She wondered if that was the way older people felt: trapped in bodies that weren't appealing anymore? She could still close her eyes and hear in her head all the comments that used to be spoken of her great beauty, making her proud. Now she tried to hide her face from everyone. Sometimes she wondered if God really cared, and if great plans had really been laid out for her life as she had been told. Right now she didn't see how anything good could come from her.

May was frightened as she and Lilly approached the cabins. She had never truly lived with anyone but April. Everything was different now, and she feared that the other slaves would turn away from her. Lilly went in first, and told the others what the master had done to May. May was outside scared and trembling.

Out the door came her mother Lilly and all eight slaves who shared her cabin. One by one they embraced May and welcomed her home. May was overcome by the deep emotions that arose within her, and broke down. Never did she expect so warm a welcome into a home of strangers. Not with the scars on her and the past that she was now leaving. So, on the first day of March in the year 1836, May begin her life as a slave.

May had been sheltered all her life at the plantation house, not realizing what a hard life slaves had to live "No wonder they all resented me," thought May. "They have almost nothing, and I had everything I every wanted. God, please help me adjust to this new life. Help the others see that I am a good person, and worthy of their friendship."

Everyone in the cabins was required to arise at daybreak at the ringing of a large bell attached to the trunk of a tree. The bell could be heard throughout the cabins every morning, except Sunday when no fieldwork was done. May had heard it all her life, but it never held any meaning to her. To May it was just like the crowing of the roosters.

The overseer at the plantation, M.J. Perry, was a huge man. He was pleasant enough most of the time, but he didn't care much for foolish behavior. Mr. Perry always rode on a beautiful stallion that he called "Good Enough". When it was necessary to whip a slave, he always summoned the master to watch. Often he would warn a slave several times before he would whip him. If it ever came down to an actually whipping, the slave usually deserved it. Mr. M. J. Perry had long dark hair that he kept pulled back in a ponytail. If you didn't know any better, you would have thought he was an Indian. He lived alone in a cabin in the woods near the fields, where he kept watch. Three poor white men helped him patrol the workers in the fields. The slaves called them the patty rollers.

As soon as the first bell would ring, everyone would get up and start fixing the morning meal. They loved to eat hoe cakes, sowbelly, and drink their coffee. You could smell that meat cooking all around the cabins. The workers would take food left over from breakfast in metal pails out to the fields for their mid day meal. When the bell rang the second time, it was time to line up by the shed. Each worker was given a hoe and pick at the tool shed. Several of the male slaves were in charge of the mules and the plowing of the fields. You could hear them calling out pet names of their mules all day long, as they urged the animals to pull faster.

"Gertude, move gal!"

"Come on Sugar Stick, plow."

At midday, M.J. Perry would blow on the ram's horn he kept on his saddle and everyone would try to find a shady spot to sit down and eat. There wasn't enough time to go back to the cabins, a worker had to rest and eat right in the fields.

The first day May worked the fields; she felt she would die. When the crews stopped working that evening, May went straight to the cabin to sleep, and her housemates couldn't even wake her to eat. Next morning every muscle in her body ached. The other slaves, noticing her difficulty, stayed near and took some of her workload.

In March, slaves had to start preparing the land for planting. Fields were to be plowed and large stones removed. Some of the land was used for planting rice. To grow rice required flooded fields at planting time, and preparing the paddies seemed an endless labor.

"I'll never learn to be a good field slave," cried May. "The work is too hard, and the sun hurts my face. Oh Mama Lilly, what did I do to deserve this treatment."

"Now you just hush you mouth. Ain't none of us done nothing to deserve dis here hard work. We are slaves, and black. Dat's all you has to be. You just were living easy for the first part of your life. You's git use to it soon enough. Soon enough you be just like da rest of us. It ain't as bad as it could be. Least we don't git the same treatment as some do." said Lilly as she helped May back to the cabin.

Every evening for the first month May could barely make it home. Eventually, she discovered there were many jobs on the plantation besides fieldwork. Some of the women worked all day on the spinning wheels, and weaving to make fabric from cotton.

When sheep were sheared, others would work as carders, manipulating and softening the wool so that it could be spun on wheels for yarn and cloth. The fabrics made were used on the plantation to clothe all the slaves. Seamstress slaves would cut out the cloth and make all the clothes that were worn. Nothing was every wasted on the plantation. Clothes that were too torn to wear were used to make patches to fix others, or made into beautiful quilts.

Then there was the job of the shoemaking. The shoemakers had to make footwear for everyone at the cabins. Plantation-made shoes weren't fancy, but they served their purpose. Slave children mostly ran barefoot, except for the coldest months. Socks were treasured in the wintertime, and many fights broke out over them. People always seemed to believe that others were stealing their socks, and they were usually right.

Saturdays and Sundays were the slaves' favorite days. One needed to work only half the day on Saturdays, and every Sunday was a full day of rest. The people of the cabins would wash their clothes in the afternoon, and play music for dancing in the evenings around a large bonfire. On Sundays, after church, slaves would tend their gardens and do their visiting. Lucky people could get a pass to visit other plantations, and seemed everyone had kinfolk scattered everywhere. A person had to be careful who he jumped the broom with, for more than once a slave would find out he or she had married his own brother, sister, or cousin. If a romantically inclined pair looked alike, the two had better do a lot of talking about where they came from, since slaves sometimes had wives and husbands on other plantations.

The Sermons heard on Sundays were by white preachers who would tell the slaves that God had cursed them years ago, and their lot in life was to be slaves. If they listened to their masters and obeyed them, God would be pleased. To some it sounded like God wanted them to be slaves at His place too. This was something they couldn't accept.

They much preferred what April had told them years before. That God loved them and wanted them to be free one day, if they were baptized.

May found herself becoming a treasure to the others. She brought with her a Bible that April had given her, and she read it to them often. They loved the stories about God setting the slaves free with the help of Moses. They understood why they had to wander the Sinai wilderness for forty years because of lack of faith. When God released them from bondage, they would be faithful. Their prayers always included a plea for a Moses to be born for them. The

Sermon on the Mount was another favorite reading. Some of the people where still a little afraid of May's face, but with time she became accepted by all.

May received notes from April almost daily. Sometimes when she was working in the fields, she'd see April ride up on a horse and watch her from a distance. She didn't understand whether April did this because she missed her or because she wanted to torment her. From April's notes, May learned that April spent a lot of time with Jewel Jackson, and it sounded as though she might be thinking of marrying him. May knew that if Jewel were like his father, April's life would be hell, but she also knew this was a lesson April would have to learn on her own. May still loved April, even if others said she shouldn't. There were too many good memories that couldn't be erased.

"One day," thought May, "April will understand what it means to suffer. I don't wish it on her: she will make it so herself."

Meantime, May continued to hoe the field she was working in with sweat running down her face and back.

May learn much from the people of the cabins. She never realized how important herbs and plants where in keeping one healthy. Lilly and Cecil taught her of many herbs and what they were used for.

Mixture of pinetop, mullein and salt treated swollen feet and legs, as a tea mullein was good for heart dropsy. Barefoot root and lard made a salve good for Rheumatiz. Jerusalem oats worked well for worms in children. Tansy tea, red shank, and hazed roots were good for female problems. May apple root is good to make slow bowels move. Cherry root is good to make tea to increase someone's appetite. Punsley made a good tea for dysentery.

Elderberry, pokeberry and mulberry made good wine. Poke salad was just plan good to eat when made with fat back or lard. May love to add wild onions for extra flavor.

"Child, I can't believe you don't knows herb's and greens. We always been doctoring ourselves. We got our own peoples called medicine men. Dey knows all about what it takes to get ya better," said Thomas one of the cabin mates.

"I still wear my Grisgris around my neck. Don't know if I understand what it's for, but I still wear it." May said as she pulled out the pouch and showed it to those in the cabin that day.

"I members da night you got it. After dat night, you took a turn for da good." Lilly said.

May learn many of her ancestor's traditions. In winter the young teen boy's were circumcised at what was called the February Feast. They believed the Devil Ho-re would take uncircumcised boys and keep them in his belly for 9 to 10 days. When the teens where circumcised they weren't allowed to speak for the same amount of days. The elders of the slaves performed this. Once the boys were circumcised, they were considered men.

May had heard men talk in a tongue unknown to her. Everyone called it Mumbo-Jumbo. May learned it was a society that only men could join. They would talk to each other in a chant language. She learned that in Africa if a woman learned Mumbo-Jumbo, she would be killed. May then heard the story of a great king.

"Once a King loved his wife so much, she convinced him to teach her da secret language, and he did. Da Queen was beheaded and her head displayed in da village for all to see. Den the King protested her death, den he was beheaded. Both der heads was kept in the village on tall poles." said Old Bald William.

William was the oldest slave on the plantation. He didn't know his age, but he remembered Africa.

On Saturday nights, near the bonfire, all would gather to hear Old Bald William speak. He'd tell many tales of the motherland. They learned of many tribes, of their customs and the wars that had been fought. Gold was plentiful in some tribes giving reason for wars. There were kingdoms, with great and fair kings that protected their people. People captured in battle were turned into slaves. Most tribes treated slaves as prized possession and treated them as family members. In the Mandingo tribe selling a slave was considered a wicked thing, unless slaves committed a crime. Only then could they be sold without consent of the other slaves.

"Now dey be some mean Kings too. Kings dat would order his men to sack one of his own villages and sell all da peoples to da white slave traders for supplies. Kings dat would condemn people to slavery for minor crimes like theft, and unpaid debts," said William with his hands making motions in the air as he spoke.

Everyone leaned in close to William and hung on to every word he said. The only way to learn of the motherland was listening to those who still remembered. "Da tribe named Dahomey's eat peoples. Da wear da teeth of who da killed around dey neck. Dey kills and eats da enemy thinking dere soul and strength would become part of dem. Da bodies were boiled to eat. Neber did meet one of dem, but I's knows de be real," William said shaking his head up and down.

"I's members da day I's was captured! Done heard how white traders be cannibals. I's working a field for cropping, all da sudden, I's hears screams coming from da forest. I's first thoughts, lion done gots another man, den da screams get louder and coming at me. I drop my's hoe and took off running. Everyone in dat field did same. We run right into men's wif big brown nets. Da threw dem on us, and we trapped!" using his hands he acted as if he were fighting the nets.

"It pains me to members da rest." he said holding his head down.

"Tell us! Please tell us!" several called out.

"We's needs to hear. De be hard memories, but we need to know," said Jacob as he rubbed William on the back. "Please tell us old man."

"Dem white mens was yelling and screaming at us. Da had long whips and guns. We all scared as dey shoved us together. Some young'uns tried to run; dey shot em in da back. I was near da edge of da group and dey grabbed my's arm. Dey put irons on my's right leg and hooked me to another man's left leg. Dey tied us gether wif two mo mens wif ropes around our necks. Barely could walk." William had stood and was acting out his entrapment.

"What happen next, did dey put you straight way on a boat?"

"Naw, we's walked like dat for two days. At night da throw fruit and breads at us for eating. Not much water for drinking, thank God for fruit. Dey was a fortress full of people's dey put us in. Tribes from all over was dere. We found some people's who spoke like us and stayed near dem." shaking his head back and forth.

"Dem white mens took young girls, and had dey way with em. Dem girls pleading for help as dey was dragged out, but we could do nothin. Daytime de makes us walk in circles and sing. Strangest thing I eber saw. Dey be some dat just sits der and stares at da ground. Dead ones be left in der for days. Don't know how longs we dere. Seems like forever. Den ships come. We's all cry as de load us. Put so many in dere we lying toe to toe and head to head. Couldn't move much. Everyone be quiet at first in dat dark hole of da ship, den it starts moving. Everyone panicked. So much noise I covered my ears. It hurt. Still I's can close my eyes and be back der. I's can still hear dat day," William said wiping the tears from his eyes.

"What happen next? Did dey start eating on people?"

"Naw, but dey shore killed a lot. You be sick de geb you medicine, if dat don't work, de throw you in. Ain't neber saw so much water, no land, just water. Sometimes dat water be angry, knocking dat ship every which way. Felt like it tries to make em give us up. At day we had to stand on da ship and jump up and down. No room da run in circles. We's eat slop put in cans at night. Least it be food. It be hot at day, and cold at night. Sometimes da wind blew hard and we's barely could jump. It blew salt water in our eyes and da swell. Most time we stayed in da hole. Felt like being buried." William said then he grew quiet.

No one said a word. They continued to look at William who jerked a few times, as if experiencing the event.

"When we's lands, we's bathed, shaved and oiled, den branded. Den marched in front of bunch of white people naked. One by one we's was sold. Babies taken from da mamas, and mamas taken from da husbands. Lots of crying dat day

We's all knew den, we neber could go home. We's lost forever from our people. Once I had me three sisters and two brothers. Now I be a slave. But all you be my family now, and dats enough."

"Dis proves my story is true," he said as he pulled down his shirt and showed the brand of WB on his shoulder. The brand was a raised scar of white. Motherland was a real place called Africa.

Chapter 11

News Of The Steam Boat Trip

In the year 1838, April's parents came to her to discuss their upcoming trip.

"April darling," said her papa, "your mother and I have asked your Uncle Andy to come and stay with you for awhile. Both of us are going away together on a Steamboat Trip. Your mother and I will be celebrating our life together, for we have been married now for twenty years. Andy has agreed to run the plantation while we are away. What do you think of our second honeymoon plans?" he said as he put his arm around her.

They begin to walk in the flower gardens. Some of the flowers were just beginning to bloom.

"Oh Papa, it sounds so romantic! I think it's a great idea for a second honeymoon. I miss seeing Uncle Andy, it's been a long time since he was here last. It will be good to spend some time with him. But do you think he will be able to run the plantation?" April looked up at her father.

"April, your Uncle Andy has been running a plantation twice as big as ours since he was 16 years old. I'm sure he will have no problems. Besides, Mr. Perry takes care of the slaves for me and my brother will be here to make sure there are no problems. Plus, he will have my sweet little April to watch after him," said her papa, bending down to kiss her forehead.

"Well," said April's mother, "I'm glad you two feel like everything will be fine. I'm not sure about leaving here for weeks on end and leaving April with your brother. What if something happens to us? What would become of April and our beautiful home? I still don't like the idea of leaving like this." she said.

April reached out and took her mother's hand, "Mother, stop worrying! You and Papa deserve this trip. Everything here will be fine, and I will not allow anything to happen to you and Papa. You'll have the time of your life, and then come home with lots of gifts for me!"

"You can tell whose child you are. You think just like your Papa!"

"Oh mother, you know I'm just teasing. Please go and have fun, everything here will be just fine." said April embracing her mother in a playful hug.

"I'm glad you feel good about us leaving. It has been hard to convince your mother that it will be good for us. She thinks if we leave, we'll never come back. You know how your mother loves to worry," said April's father.

"Mother, you worry too much. Go for me and enjoy yourself. I'm not a little girl anymore."

"Well, I'm glad that's settled. My brother Andy will arrive next Friday. Mother and I will leave the following Friday. I want to spend a week with him, to make sure he feels comfortable here."

The next few days were filled with preparations, getting everything ready for her Uncle's arrival. April and her mother helped in cleaning the house. The plantation truly was beautiful; April understood why her mother was afraid to leave. The front of the house had six large columns that stood to the second floor. There was a huge porch on each floor, each with lots of white wicker furniture to relax on. April's bedroom had a door that opened right onto the upper porch. April could still remember summer nights May had spent with her sleeping out in the cool breeze. They would make pallets on the floor, and bring out all their feather pillows. April remembered all the dreams they shared there. Some nights April stayed out on the porch in the large swing and cried for all the dreams that might not come true.

There were four large bedrooms upstairs, with a long hall. The walls were of beautiful wood, that was always cleaned and oiled. The smell of wood hit you when you entered the front door. There was a wonderful staircase, with wide smooth rails, that April and May would use to slide down the stairs with great laughter and screams. Once they caught her papa coming down the same way, laughing when he didn't slow down and hit the floor.

Downstairs was the Library, also called the Gentlemen's Smoking Room. It was large and was filled with heavy red mahogany furniture. There was even a pump organ that April's mother could play beautifully. April was learning to play it, spending many evenings with her mother.

There was a covered walkway that led to the kitchen. The kitchen was separate from the big house in case of fires. The kitchen had a huge fireplace that was used for all the cooking. It seems to always smell of fresh baked breads. When meals weren't being prepared, April loved to talk to the kitchen help. She would ask them to tell her anything they knew of May. She was happy to hear May was doing fine with the others.

It had been a long time since they spoke face to face. April preferred sending May notes. She felt May had been unfair by calling her Mistress.

Near the kitchen, was the dining room. They had a long table that could seat twelve people. April loved to help with dinner parties. She'd get to help with the menu and decorating the house. The Jackson's had been coming to dinner often, because Jewel and April were speaking of marriage. April felt it odd that he never spoke of loving her or proposed marriage to her. He just started speaking in terms of " when we're married". She wished he were more romantic like her papa treated her mother. All she wanted was to feel loved and treasured.

The time passed quickly, and soon it was Friday. Uncle Andy was to be there by supper. It would be nice to sit and talk of the past with him and listen to his great stories. He was a never-ending book of strange and exciting tales.

She was sitting on the porch when she saw a rider approaching. She didn't think it was her Uncle Andy because it was a rider on a horse instead of a carriage. Then she realized it was him.

"He's here. He's here!" she screamed as she ran out to greet him. He looked so dignified on his horse, with his gray hair showing under his hat. And of course there was his pipe. He used to joke it would have to be buried with him, or he'd come back to haunt them all.

Andy's face lit up as soon as he saw April.

"Well good afternoon madam. I'm here to see my brother and his wife. And of course their little girl April." he said with a sweep of his hat.

"You get off that horse Uncle Andy and give me a hug. You're not fooling me none, you know who I am." April said placing her hands on her hips.

Andy let out a roar of laughter as he dismounted his horse, and gave April a big hug and a twirl around. He lifted her feet all the way off the ground.

"My, oh my, what have we here. My little April has done turned into a woman before it is time," said Andy still laughing.

"Well, you certainly are no good with time, because I've grown up right on schedule. It's you who seem to be affected by time. Look at all that gray hair, is it a wig?"asked April jokingly.

"No, I got this head of gray from two daughters just like you. Now don't you make any plans to add on to it, just because I'm staying for a few weeks. I have just the right amount to make me a mature man! Now where is that brother of mine, and his beautiful wife?" asked Andy as he took April's arm in his and headed towards the house.

"Papa's rode out to the fields. He wasn't expecting you for a couple of hours. Let's go wait for him and surprise him. Look, here comes mother now."

April looked up at Uncle Andy and smiled. She knew right away that she would enjoy her time with him.

Chapter 12

April's Parents Bid Farewell

David Cothran was glad to find his brother Andy sitting on the porch when he arrived.

"Andy, it's good to see you. My, you're looking more like an older brother! Where did all this gray hair come from?" said David, embracing his brother.

"One more comment about my gray hair, and my services will be quickly withdrawn. You, my chubby brother, do not appear to be much younger than I. The crops must be coming in really heavy, for you're showing the reaping of the harvest." replied Andy as he patted David's belly.

Both men broke into loud laughter. It felt good to be able to tease each other again.

"Andy, you will never know how much your coming means to me. Betty and I have been wanting to make this trip a long time."

"Well, I plan on taking the first born son of all your slaves, when I return home. That would be a fair trade." smiled Andy, raising his unlit pipe to his lips.

"You are still the dreamer, I see!" replied David.

The slaves had really outdone themselves with the evening meal that followed, and Andy ate like a trencherman.

"David my brother," he said, "If I had known the fine meals you serve here, I would have come to see you much sooner. Maybe I'll carry one of your cooks home with me."

After dinner they retired to the sitting room where Uncle Andy, over Port and cigars, began to weave such a huge tale.

"You all have asked me how my hair got this gray in such a short time. I've decided to share with you what happened. It all began with a crazy dream I had about two years back."

"I dreamed that all the slaves would be made free, but not until a Great War happened right here in the south. In my dream, the northerners tried to make us free our slaves, and we, of course, refused. Next thing you know, we are in full-scale war with them. A far greater war than our Revolutionary War. Some of the slaves joined the south, with some joining the north against us. The worst part though, was that we lost. All the slaves were freed. Every last one of them. I woke up in a cold sweat and in the morning light found all my hair had turned white. You know my plantation has over three hundred slaves, the backbone of the plantation. Without all my workers, I wouldn't be able to survive. All my money is tied up in slaves and land. I can't have one without the other. So that, my family, is what happened to my hair."

Everyone grew silent for a few moments. Then David burst out laughing.

"So let me understand what you are saying, my dear brother. So as far as you are concerned, the north turned your hair gray?"

April and her mother burst out laughing too.

Keeping a straight face Andy said, "Laugh all you want, but that's what happened. My hair had just a touch of gray, but after the dream, I had what you see now. And that my family is the truth!" There was no smile on Andy's face.

April loved her Uncle Andy, but sometimes it was hard to tell his stories from the truth. She had mixed feelings about slavery, but to dream of a war was hard to believe. Slaves were personal property, and law protected property. Of course it was different with May. May wasn't a slave.

The week seemed to fly by. April didn't get to see much of her uncle, for he was always with her papa. David took him to introduce him to lawyers, bankers, and tradesman making sure everyone knew his brother would be taking care of the plantation. Plus Papa loved to go to the town of Cainnoy, and to the neighboring city of Charleston. To April, her papa seemed to know just about everyone in both.

On the day before her parent's departure, they held a huge party. Everyone who was anyone was there, so many people that they flowed from the house onto the lawn. It reminded April of the Jubilee.

Uncle Andy had a grand time that night. His tall tales of adventure drew people to him. As far as April knew, he'd only been off his plantation a few times. But he could make you think he'd been all around the world. He seemed to know about everything.

Jewel Jackson was charming that night. April took notice that it was not just her he was charming. All the young women seemed to be falling at his feet.

"You just keep on looking Jewel," thought April. "You are just trying to tease me and make me jealous. Well, it's not going to work. Tonight I will dance the whole night through. With or without you."

Soon after midnight, the party was over. All the guest departed, and everyone went off to bed. April began to get a little concerned over her parents leaving. She wanted them to enjoy themselves, but she wished she could go with them. If something happened, at least they would all be together.

April didn't sleep well that night. She could hear the least noise the house slaves were making, cleaning up after the party. Her parents would only be gone for three weeks. But now that seemed like a long time.

When she finally awoke, it was with her mother on the bed gently shaking her.

"Get up sleepy head. Are you planning on rising today? Your papa and I are ready to leave, so get dressed and come down to see us off. It's already half past one."

April gave her a sleepy smile, and arose from the bed. She wasn't about to tell her mother about the fears she was having. Her mother and papa were the only family she truly had; besides May.

When she arrived downstairs, the trunks were already loaded onto the carriage. Her parents would be catching the ship in Charleston, and they both seemed so happy. The Pulaski was the largest vessel of its kind. It was June 13, 1838. Her parents would be on board and leaving the next day. Her mother had tears welling up in her eyes, so April knew she was feeling fearful. She ran to embrace her mother, and assured her everything would be just fine.

"Oh mother, I'm so happy for you. Please don't worry about a thing here. Just go with Papa and have the time of your life. You deserve this trip."

"Now don't you two start crying, and acting like you are never going to see each other again." said April's papa. "You two know we will only be gone for three week's. Then home we will come. Now young lady, you come on over here and give your papa a hug."

David whispered in April's ear as he hugged her tightly.

"You are the finest gift the Good Lord ever gave me. There are two pieces of my heart. Your mother holds one, and you hold the other. I will miss you darling, but I promise to bring you back a gift to remember."

April smiled at her father's comment.

Uncle Andy embraced both his brother and his wife. He begged them not to worry about a thing. The plantation would be kept well and running smoothly, on this they had his word.

Once again before her mother was helped into the large black carriage, April ran to embrace her. Deep inside, her fear of losing her parents was almost overpowering. She began to cry.

"April, where are these tears coming from?" her mother said. "You are the one who talked me into this trip. Please don't frighten me into staying."

"Oh mother, I'm sorry. Sure I want you and papa to go; I'm just a little nervous. Please forgive me and go have fun."

Uncle Andy came to the rescue.

"Ah, pay her no mind, she's just crying because she knows I will only be here a few week's. But don't worry, she'll calm down as soon as you leave. She's got a lot of stories to listen too. Why she doesn't even know about the time I was in Africa and got attacked by a pack of monkeys." said Andy with a big smile. The beginning of that tale made them all laugh, for Andy had never been to Africa. April and Andy stood on the dirt road watching them ride away in the carriage.

April still couldn't shake the feeling that they were riding right out of her life. Andy held her shoulder as they waved farewell.

Two days after the departure, a rider was seen charging down the dirt road to the plantation. He was kicking up dust as he sped towards the big house. April and Uncle Andy were sitting on the lower porch when he rode into the yard.

"What in the tarnation is going on? " Andy said loudly as he stood and walked towards the rider. April arose and followed behind him.

"Sir, is this the Cothran Plantation?" asked the rider as he panted for breath.

"Yes, what do you want?" Andy replied as he stopped the horse so the rider could dismount.

"Sir, there's been an accident with the Pulaski and I need to speak to the relatives of David and Betty Cothran."

"We are them, what has happen?" demanded Andy.

"Where are my parents? Are they all right? Tell me! Tell me now!" April said with a shaky voice.

"May we sit down?" he asked.

"Certainly young man, but tell us what kind of accident." Andy said as they headed towards the porch. "Where is my brother and his wife?"

They all took seats facing each other on the porch. April felt the hair on her arms stand up and chills run up and down her spine. She held back tears as she spoke.

"Please don't tell me their dead!"

"Sir, ma'am, it is painful for me to tell you this sad news. The Pulaski blew up 12 hours after it departed from Charleston."

"Dear God no." said April as she sunk deeper into her chair with tears filling her eyes.

"Blew up. How can a ship just blow up? Did it sink? Were there any survivors? Was it on fire? What happen man, speak up!" Andy said as he stood.

"Sir, the wood burning boiler's that powered the ship blew, best we can tell, the gages malfunction and exploded. The ship was mostly wood, so it caught fire. They found some survivors, but 110 passengers and crew perished. David and Betty Cothran are unaccounted for. They are believed to be lost at sea.' finished the man named Frank, reaching up to wipe the sweat from his brow.

"So are they dead? Is that what you saying? What does lost at sea mean?' April asked as her hands began to tremble.

"Ma'am, they are believed to be dead. The ship sank. Other vessels went to investigate the smoke and explosion and rescued people in life rafts. There was an opening Ball that night, most had no time to prepare. The survivors claim the fire spread quickly." Frank reached out to touch April's hand. " Your parents were not among them… I'm so sorry."

"Uncle Andy, what am I to do? My parents, gone. What am I to do?" April said as she ran to Andy. He wrapped his arms around her, and let her cry.

"Is there more you need to say?" asked Andy as he looked at Frank.

"Sir, I was sent by the Pulaski ship line with deep regrets. They will soon send papers of the deaths at sea for the Cothran's estate. If there is anything they can do, please feel free to ask. Once again, I'd like to say I'm sorry."

"Will you please leave now!" said Andy as he led April into the house. "This is a hard day for us all…. Come April, you must rest."

April felt her body drifting down the hall that led to her room as if she were in a dream. She allowed Andy to lay her on the bed and drank the brandy that he made for her.

"Hon, I can't believe this has happened. But don't you worry; I'll stay until you're ready for me to leave. I'll send a messenger home and explain what has happened. I won't leave you alone. I promise." Andy said as he kissed her cheek.

"Please send for Jewel. He must know. I need him." April said through her tears.

"I'll send for him this moment. He'll want to be here. You just lay here and rest. Everything will be all right."

"No it won't. It will never be all right again." April said raising her forearm up to cover her eyes as she cried.

Andy reached down and held April with tears running down his face. He had lost his only brother and now held his brother's only child.

Soon April fell asleep.

April was awaken by a knock on her door. It was Jewel.

"They're gone!" she cried out when he walked in.

"Hush, my darling, everything is going to be all right," said Jewel, " I'm here now and I'll take care of you from this day forward. Don't worry about anything."

He sat there for hours holding April and stroking her hair. She clung to him tightly and whimpered and cried like a small child. He kept repeating his love for her, and his desire to take care of her. Finally she drifted into a heavy sleep.

It wasn't considered proper for a gentleman to be in a lady's bedroom. But this was different…very different.

Jewel thought of things he would change about the plantation. It was certain that he must marry April. There would have to be some kind of ceremony for her parents, then soon after, they would marry. There wasn't any way a young girl could manage such a large plantation. Jewel thought her Uncle would try to take it away from her. He had to protect April; all she had was him now. Jewel stayed until dark, then told Andy he would be back the next morning.

All during the first night April awaken and began to scream. It was as if her whole body was protesting her parents' death. Each time Uncle Andy would run to her, giving her brandy to calm her nerves. At his order, the servants tried to keep the house quiet, so that she might sleep. There wasn't much more anyone could do.

When May heard of April's parent's fate, she cried as if they were her own. She had loved them ever since she was born. They had been good to her until she was sent away. She cried for April, and the pain she must be feeling. Of all the plantations that May had now heard of, the Cothran Plantation was considered the kindest.

She begins to fear the fate of all the Cothran slaves. If April married Jewel Jackson, there would be hell coming to them all. She knew of the cruelty the Jackson slaves had to bear. If they weren't good breading stock, then they were whipping stock.

May reached up and touched the scars on the side of her face, knowing she wouldn't be good stock. No man would touch her. If April married Jewel, she knew what would happen to her. She would receive scars on her back to match the ones on her face.

"Sweet Jesus, be with us all. Protect us from the evil ones. Guide the ones who control our lives. Give us strength to carry on. A men." May prayed loudly so the others could hear.

Everyone on the plantation was in mourning. The workers were frightened not knowing who their new master was to be. It didn't seem possible to them that April, still a young woman, could run the plantation. Her Uncle Andy owned a plantation; he couldn't be master of both. The slaves' future always seemed certain with Master Cothran. They were his and he fed and clothe them.

May tried to calm everyone that first night. They had gathered around a large fire talking of their future. The young men wanted to run; the women and children were too terrified to run.

Master Cothran had been fond of a lot of his slaves. When unable to work at hard labor, he would find something useful for them to do. Mothers were frightened their children would be sold away from them, being the practice at most plantations. Master Cothran had always understood a mother's love for her child. He wouldn't separate families if he owned them all. After two days of talking to different slaves and soothing their fears, May convinced most just to stay put.

It was strange to see what was done in the Master's honor. Two normal size wooden caskets were placed side by side in the parlor. On top of one stood a painting of Miss Betty . On Master Cothran's there stood a painting of him with his hunting dogs. Inside each casket lay a set clothes and a pair of shoes. People were invited as if it were truly a wake. Everyone walked by the caskets and spoke kind words to April. There wasn't a dry eye in the room. Slaves stood at the back door and waited for their turn to mourn. Then one by one passed by the caskets and cried softly. Slaves could be whipped if they didn't mourn properly for their masters, but Master Cothran's slaves were truly in mourning. April removed hair from her mother's brush and made a mourning necklace.

The hair woven and shaped like a small flower, then placed into a locket. A custom followed by most.

The caskets stayed in the house for three days. On the fourth day the paintings were taken out of the frames and placed inside the caskets with the clothing, then nailed shut. Then they were carried to the family graveyard.

A black funeral buggy pulled by two white stallions carried the caskets to the graves. A line of mourners followed behind on foot. The plantation grounds were covered with people dressed in black and weeping. April, Jewel and Andy followed first behind the funeral buggy. Almost everyone carried flowers in their hands. It was strange, but lovely. The preacher gave a short sermon on death and on the life of Master Cothran and Miss Betty, and then the caskets were lowered into the graves. When they were covered with earth, everyone came and dropped their flowers onto the graves. Flowers were piled up to your knees on both graves.

Several weeks later, the stone master finished their tombstones. They read:

David Leroy Cothran	Betty DeBower Cothran
Born: Dec.4, 1798	Born: Aug. 13,1800
Died: June 14 , 1838	Died: June 14, 1838
Here lies his memory:	Her lies her memory:
Good husband & Father	Good wife & Mother
Master to Many	Loved by All

Above each name were carvings of angels and hearts. It was hard for April to see the tombstones, for it made her parents' deaths seem real. For the rest of her life,she prayed that one day they would come walking down the path to home.

When the will was read, everything had been left to April. She inherited 1220 acres of land and 202 slaves of various ages and sex. Uncle Andy had been willed his brother's Revolutionary guns and swords, weapons that once belonged to their grandfather. Andy was greatly pleased, not expecting to receive anything.

April felt overwhelmed by it all. She was confused by what to do. Uncle Andy told her to wait one year before making any big decisions.

"April, I know you've been through a lot this past week. But it's important that you wait at least one year before making big decisions about your life." said Uncle Andy.

"Uncle Andy, please promise you will stay until fall. I don't believe I can make it by myself. If you would stay and show me how to run the plantation, maybe I could." said April.

"Don't fret April, I will not leave until you are prepared for me to go." said Andy, placing his arm around her shoulder.

"April, have you considered when you would like to open the trunk that was returned? I believe it may be your father's. The salt water might have destroyed the contents, but there may be something to keep."

"No Uncle Andy, maybe tomorrow." said April. She stood and walked over to her writing desk. " Uncle Andy, I'm sending for May. I don't know if she has forgiven me, but I need her here with me. I know you're here, but I need her."

Andy saw tears rolling down his niece's cheeks. He found himself agreeing that May's return would be the best decision she could make for now.

"I will take the note to May myself." he said. "I'm sure she'll be glad to be with you again. Enough time has passed for her to have forgiven you. Hasn't it been two years? She'll be glad to leave the cabins."

As he walked out the front door, he slipped his pipe into his mouth. He lit it and the smoke came out of his mouth in big billows. The smell of cherry tobacco filled the air around him. April prayed the note would be welcomed news for May.

Chapter 13

May Returns To The Big House

May was sitting outside her cabin on a bench when she saw Master Andy approaching. She went inside not knowing how he would react to her scars, she hid from people she didn't know. She knew who Master Andy was, but he had never spoken to her.

Andy walked up to the cabin door. "I'm looking for a girl named May, she lives in this cabin. Can you tell her I'm here?" said Andy to Lilly.

"Here I am Master," she said walking out of the shadows.

Andy looked at her, and didn't react.

"I've a note from Miss April. She said you could read. Please comply with it as soon as possible," said Andy.

He then simply turned and walked away.

May went outside to sit on her wooden bench. She carefully unfolded the letter and began to read:

My Dearest May,

My parents have died. I'm all alone. I need you with me. Come right away.

Your Sister, April

May lay the letter on her lap, not believing what April wrote. "I need you with me, come right away! Your Sister, April." She'd been working with the others for two years. She'd adjusted to her new life, being with people of her own race and who truly loved her. Now, out of nowhere, April wanted her back. April needed her!

It was never of any importance if she needed April. It was only important that April needed her. Yes, she was truly her slave. May fumed that April had this power over her, up rooting her at will. The sorrow she felt for April's parents passing was now filled with anger. May hated being a slave, being at the master's beckon call.

May slipped the note in her apron pocket and went to pack her bag, only having a few belongings, packing didn't take long.

May's mother was upset. It was good to have May living with her again. May meant a lot to them all. She was secretly teaching them to read and write. She read the Bible to all who gathered outside her cabin in the evenings. To the others, May was a lifeline of hope making them think one day, they'd be free.

73

One day, God would free them as he had the slaves of Egypt. Freedom would be known to all.

May hugged everyone in her cabin good bye. She had always thought she'd be called back to the big house but with the passing of time, she had begun to doubt it.

May begin her walk to the big house as evening was sitting in. The crickets began their night music and bullfrogs had started their lonely calls. All around her where the sounds of life.

Some of the children of the cabins came running to ask May where she was going.

"Ain't you gonna read to us tonight Miss May. Where you going wif dat bag?"one of them asked.

"Got no more time for reading," said May. "The master done called me back." she finished without stopping to speak with them. She didn't want them to see she'd been crying.

When she told them of her return to the big house, they ran off in different directions.You could hear them yelling as they ran to their cabins, " Y'all, come quick! Miss May's going back."

May tried to hurry down the long row of cabins. Many ran to their yards to bid her good bye as if they wouldn't see her again.

May's heart swelled knowing the great respect and love they held for her.

"Bye now," she said in a tearful voice.

As May approached the big house, she saw April's figure on the lower porch looking frozen in place. Finally she began walking towards May with her arms out stretched.

"Oh May!" she cried out. "Welcome Home!"

"May, I've missed you so much. There hasn't been a day that I haven't thought of you," she said as she wrapped her arms around May.

May stood with a gunnysack in her hand, and a great urge to hug April back. For a moment she was carried back to her childhood with love for April creeping in, but only for a moment. Then she was in the present with all the hurt and pains that came with it. April wasn't her sister; sisters would never hurt each other in such a horrible way. They were slave and master, nothing more.

May took a deep breath and replied," I'm here Mistress, what shall I do?"

April ignored the word mistress.

"Please come inside with me May." as if everything was all right.

As May walked inside she stopped and looked around. Everything looked the same. She had forgotten how wonderful it was. Fresh cut flowers were in vases set about everywhere. She felt a cool breeze flowing through large open windows. There was no stuffiness of the cabins. Here there was room, and you could smell the wood mixed in with the scent of flowers. The cabins smelled of human sweat due to long work hours in the fields. Flowers would not and could not hide the scent of sweat.

April stood beside May and placed her arm around May's shoulder.

"Welcome Home May!" with tears welling in her eyes.

"I do hope you're glad to be home. Please forgive my parents, God rest their souls, for not sending for you sooner. I never wanted you to go. Your place has always been with me. They tried to protect me from pain. I begged them to bring you back. They always said it wasn't time... now surely it must be." finished April.

May was confused. She wondered if April had really tried to get her back. She slowly turned to look April in the face. April did not look away.

"Mistress, is that the truth?"

"Yes May, I swear it. Please forgive them, I have."

May didn't reply, she stood there looking around, being confused over her own feelings.

Finally she asked, "Mistress, where do you want me to sleep? What do you want me to do?"

"Please stop calling me Mistress, you know my name. I am not your Master," replied April. "Of course you shall sleep in my room. Just as it always was, until that horrible accident that damaged our lives."

May couldn't believe what April said. How could her burning have damaged April's life? April hadn't felt any pain, which was certain. May was the only one who suffered. April had enjoyed her life, surrounded by riches and pleasures. It was her suffering and hers alone.

April reached down and took May's gunnysack.

"Let me help you. I'm so glad you're finally home. It's been lonely here without you. I do hope you forgive and forget the past. All that matters now is that we're together again."

May didn't believe what she was hearing. Welcome home? This was not her home; it was the master's. As a child it was home, but now she knew it could never be again. Not as long as she was a slave, and could be up rooted at will. Now, April herself was the master.

April led May into her bedroom. She had placed another bed by hers. It was nice, but not as fancy or large as April's.

"I hope you like having separate beds. I thought now that we are grown ladies, that you might want your own. I so enjoy sleeping by myself, I hope you do too." she then placed May's bag on the smaller bed.

May thought of the cabins with straw mats and rope beds. The beds were shared with others, only when sick did you sleep alone.

"Thank you Mistress." she said without sharing her thoughts.

April reached out and took May's hands into hers, looking into her face.

"May, I beg you to stop calling me mistress. You know I'm not your master. I shall always be your sister." April said sadly looking at May.

May turn her head from April's graze and looked through the large window at the cabins down the lane. From April's room she could see her true home.

Chapter 14

The Opening Of The Trunk

For May it felt odd to be back in the big house. She'd forgotten how it felt to sleep on a feather bed; it was a strange comfort. She lay for hours listening to the sounds of the night, thinking she heard the laughter of the slaves in the distance. It had been a hard life, but she'd grown use to it. It was strange to be, once again, separated from them. She prayed nightly for them all.

Sleep finally found her late at night. She awakened to the first sound of the work bell. She jumped from her bed, and began to dress for the fields.

Her movements awaken April and caused her to laugh at May hurrying around the room.

"What on earth are you doing? Get back in bed, it's not time for us to get up. You don't work the fields any more, remember. Things are back to normal. You're home."

May stood looking out the window, watching the cabins bustling with life. She could see people out stretching and carrying in wood for the fires. She felt like a traitor.

"May, did you hear? You don't have to rise with the bells anymore. Why don't you go back to bed?"

"I can't sleep. I'm not use to much sleep. It you don't care, I'll go downstairs now." said May as she turned towards April.

"Do what you must, but you'll never get use to sleeping if you rise with that bell every morning." replied April as she lay back down and pulled the covers up, May quietly finished dressing and went downstairs.

She was surprised to find April's uncle up and sitting in the pallor. He turned and looked her way when she reached the bottom of the stairs.

"Good morning May. I hope your first night back was restful. Please come in and sit, I would like to speak to you."

May looked around being confused, scared and nervous by his request.

"Please don't be scared. I just want to talk about April," he said as he motions her to sit in a chair near him.

She walked into the room with her head down following his request. She was visibly shaking.

"I'm sorry if I frightened you. I don't mean too. April has spoken of you often. I'm glad we've finally met. These past two years have been hard on April. First you were burned then the death of both her parents. I'm concerned for

April's well being. It's almost too much for one person to carry. How does she seem to you?" asked Andy leaning closer to May.

"She appears fine to me, master. I think she is of good health." May nervously replied while fidgeting with her hands.

"Good, I'm glad you think so." he said sitting back in his chair. "You know these things can change a person. I guess you know, you must have went through a lot of changes after you were burned."

"Yes master."

"May, I'm not going to beat around the bush. I think it's a strange relationship between the two of you. Never heard of anything like it. It used to worry my brother. But after getting to know April, I can understand why he couldn't change things. She's a determined young lady, when she sits her mind on something."

"Yes, I know master."

"I've heard she's always claimed you for kin, taking on anyone who begs to differ. I think she would die for you, if that need be. What I'm getting at is; April needs you right now. If there is any love in your heart for her, please find a way to forgive her. She needs your help to get through all this. I believe you can help her."

May held her head up and looked Andy in the eyes.

"Master I do love Miss April, but I don't understand her. If she truly loved me like kin, how could she leave me when I was burned? How could she send me to the fields to work sunup till sundown? In my heart, there is love. But I can't understand her kind of love. I loved Master Cothran and Miss Betty too. I cried when they drowned. I cried for them and April. It's hard to forgive April and all the pain she gave me. But I'll try, for I want Miss April to be okay. I want the pain for everyone to stop."

Neither one spoke for the next few minutes. Andy just sat there looking at May.

"May, I've never spoken with a slave like this. Your answer has surprised me. You are a very smart and caring young lady. I now see why April says you're special. I feel much better now. I'm glad we had this talk."

"Me too Master." replied May. "Me too."

May was excused and she went to the kitchen to help prepare breakfast.

When breakfast was ready, April was summoned to eat. April insisted May eat with them in the main dinning room.

"May, today is a special day for me. Now that you're here, I want to open the trunk that was sent from the ship." April said. " Uncle Andy thinks its Papa's."

"And I hope you'll find something in the trunk that will warm your heart." Andy said as he reached over and squeezed her hand.

"Uncle Andy, you've been so kind to me, a real blessing. I'm so glad Papa asked you to come. I don't know what I'd do without you," she said patting his hand.

When breakfast was finished, May and April left the room to go to the library. The trunk was sitting in a corner.

"May, I'm glad you're here with me. I've waited to open the trunk with you. I know you loved papa as much as I did. I still can't believe they're gone. To me, it will be like being with papa one last time."

April had searched the house and only found one trunk key. She sat down in front of the trunk and motioned for May to sit next to her. Her hands were trembling when she placed the key in the metal lock. She gently turned it to the right and heard a click. The lock popped open in her hand. She looked at May with amazement. It was if the key had been left behind on purpose.

April slipped the lock off and lifted the latch. The smell of moldy salt water filled the air around them. Her papa's gray over coat lay on the top. She picked it up and held it to her nose. She tried to find a scent of her papa.

"I can still smell him. Oh --Papa." she whimpered.

She held his coat for a few minutes more, then handed it to May. She saw tears welling in May's eyes, touching her deeply.

Next were stacks of his shirts, slightly damp but neatly folded. Under the shirts were his trousers. April took each one and gently handed them to May, who neatly stacked them on the floor.

May thought of all the good things about Master Cothran. How he took care of her during the burning, the way he had played with her as a child. In her eyes, he had been a good master.

Near the bottom of the trunk was a heavily craved box. It had etchings of Greek dancers on the sides and top. The women where dancing and singing in flowing garments with birds above them.

Neither April nor May had ever seen anything as beautiful as the box. Lifting the lid April found a large round music disk that shined like gold. The inside of the lid was lined with purple velvet. She ran her hand over the velvet, then felt the tiny spikes over the disk. She found a crank on the side of the box and turned it. The room was instantly filled with a sweet melody. April closed her eyes and pretended her papa was there and they were waltzing.

When the music stopped she opened her eyes and looked at May.

"This was for me. Papa was going to give it to me. I know he was," said April with a soft smile.

April found several disk stuck in velvet-lined pockets. Each disk was played as they quietly listened. April closed her eyes and tried to imagine her parents at a ball dancing. Every disk proved to be more beautiful than the last.

May started to hand April the last disk to play. "Miss April, I see a book stuffed inside this one."

"Let me see."

April reached for the black book and sat back on her knees. Opening it she stared at the first page. It read:

"Journal of the life of David Leroy Cothran"
Born: December 4, 1798
Savannah, Georgia

April recognized the hand writing… it was her papa's.

"May, this is papa's journal. This is the story of his life. Oh May--it's the greatest gift he could give. The disk must have kept it dry. Look May, it's not even damp. This is wonderful."

"Uncle Andy," she called out loudly. " Come see what we've found."

Andy rushed in the room thinking that maybe they found gold.

"What you got there? Is it a book of treasure maps? What's all the commotion?" Andy said as he rushed into the room.

"Look, it's papa's journal. We found it among the music disk. It's in perfect condition, not the least bit damp." exclaimed April, holding up the book.

"My oh my, how wonderful. I've never thought about it before, but that would be a great treasure to leave others. I'd like to read it when you are finished."

Uncle Andy rubbed his chin in thought. "If you read anything stupid in there involving me, I had nothing to do with it. You know you're father always was a story teller."

With this statement, they both began to laugh. Each aware of whom was the true storyteller. May just sat with a puzzled look on her face, not understanding why they were laughing.

"Look at this music box. I know they bought it for me. I can't believe the treasures I've found. If only they were here." April said looking down at the journal.

"Yes my child, it looks like a true treasure trunk. No amount of money could equal its worth." Andy said as he knelt down to look at the disk.

Chapter 15

Papa's Journal

April waited till evening before she began reading the journal while alone in her room. He began by talking of his childhood, and being raised on a large southern plantation. His childhood sounded much like her own. He had a wet nurse that cared for him when he was young, and he'd played with the children at the cabins.

He spoke in detail of his childhood. He'd had many exciting adventures being brought up with Andy. Most of the stories made her laugh at loud. It seemed like she was back in time with them, watching through a window their pranks.

There was one tale of a foxhunt involving most of the county men. The brothers found a dead fox and skinned it. They attached the fox skin to a stick and dragged it around a field in a very large circle. When the hounds where released the next morning they took out chasing a fox, then they picked up the fox scent in the field. They began to run round and round in one large circle. The men just sat on their horses looking puzzled at the dogs' behavior. The best foxhounds had been brought for the grand hunt, who now where behaving wildly. The boys sat on their horses laughing hysterically. They never admitted to anything, yet their father knew they were involved.

The hunt was tried again with success the following day. The boys had been locked in their rooms until the hunt was over.

Reading the memories of her papa made April wish she'd spoken more to him of his past. She'd never thought it important before. Now everything about him was important…everything.

She read further and found out how her parents met. Her papa had stolen her mother from another man. He met her at a church social and knew right away that he wanted her for his wife; Betty didn't feel the same way. She thought she was in love with a man named Adam... David decided to win her over. He showered her with gifts and flowers. He picked arguments with Adam in front of Betty, trying to show Betty the true side of Adam, knowing that he was the better man. Finally he bought her a Persian cat. Adam was allergic to cats, and Betty loved them. Within four months time, Betty broke up with Adam and married David.

April sat back and remembered her mother's cat. She remembered the day it had died and how upset her mother had been. She'd stayed in her room crying for two days. The cat had lived for 14 years. If only her mother would have shared the story with her. If only she had known.

April always felt her parents were deeply in love. They would dance in the flower garden with no music playing. They always hugged and kissed each other softly in front of her. They always slept in the same room. The Jackson's did not.

He then spoke of April's birth. He had been terrified that Betty would die. She had lost blood and had many complications. She was told the next night that she could never bear another child. April never knew the pain her mother had suffered.

The birth of May was mentioned next and the emotions David felt of having April raised with May. He wanted to make Betty happy, so he allowed it. He spoke of the day she arrived at the plantation with Lilly. He felt shame for causing Lilly to mother at such a young age, herself being just a child.

Many times in the journal he spoke of how much he loved April and the great joy she brought into his home. He had no regrets of not having a son. April was all he ever needed in a child.

There were details of May's burning that she had never known. He wrote daily of the struggle May made just to live. He spoke of the infection that attacked her body and how close she'd came to death. April never realized the depth of her pain.

After reading this, she laid the book down and wept. She finally understood. May came into the room to prepare for bed.

"May, I'm truly sorry. Papa spoke of what you went through. I didn't know. No one ever told me. They always sent word that you were improving. Can you ever forgive me?" April said as she crawled into bed.

"I'll try." replied May.

The girls spoke no more that night. They each had a lot to think about.

After breakfast the next day, April continued reading the journal.

She was shocked to learn her papa had mixed feelings about owning slaves. He spoke of many by name, and was fond of them. He had been around slaves and the business of owning them all his life. It was all he knew. He believed they were intelligent, thinking them smart and capable of learning despite what others thought. He wondered if it was a sin to own others. Hadn't there been slaves in the time of Christ? He hated the abolitionist because they wanted to force the issue and steal slaves to freedom. He felt it should be a decision made by their owners.

April laid the book down in disbelief. Why hadn't he spoken to her of his feelings. Did he think she was too young to understand? Her papa's words made her reflect on the issue, but she knew no other way to run the plantation. The keeping of slaves was a necessary evil. How else could the south grow.

After an hour, she came to the last pages. Her papa spoke of finding the music box in a shop in Charleston on their arrival. They both thought it would be the perfect gift for their daughter who loved to dance. Her mother couldn't wait to get back and give it to her. It had belonged to a young lady who had died from the fever, who had purchased it in England. The shop purchased it from her brother. She had died at 21.

Finally she came to the last page, the night of the opening gala Ball.

The last words written in the journal were these;

"Tonight we are going to the Ball. My bride looks as lovely as the day I married her. We shall dance till we can dance no longer, then I'll hold her in my arms until the sun comes up. This night will be etched in our hearts forever. I have truly been a blessed man."

April closed the book and held onto it as if she were holding onto her parents.

Chapter 16

The Greatest Gift

It was July 15, 1839. May had been back at the big house for a year. Their relationship had improved with time, but far from their past relationship. April was aware that when Jewel came to call, May would slip off to the cabins. She never raised a fuss about it, for she knew May's visits kept her happy. May had stopped calling her mistress but continued to call her Miss April. Uncle Andy had left in the month of June. April was capable of running the plantation alone. Her uncle had taught her how to keep the books and things flowing. M.J. Perry handled the fields and the workers. At first it was hard for him to work for someone so young, but he'd grown to respect her. She carried many of her papa's ways and she was the most intelligent woman he knew.

It was a hot sweaty night. Jewel and April were sitting outside on the porch. April was drinking sweet tea and Jewel his usually bourbon. May was visiting down at the cabins.

"April, you know I love you. It's great how you've taken over this place. This is a large plantation. Why, it's almost as large as ours. Sugar, it's really too big of a job for someone as young and sweet as you are. You need a man, a husband to stand beside you and make sure everything is taken care of."

"Jewel Jackson, what on earth are you talking about? I can run this plantation with my eyes closed. This is my life. I love this land and my home. I love you too, but I don't have to have a husband. I'll wait until somebody really loves me. Not just my land and home. You know what I mean."

"Ah April, stop teasing me. You know what I'm getting at. You know I love you. I started falling for you when you came to stay with us. I hated when your folks called you back. I asked your papa for permission to court you; he approved of me. He'd want you to marry me; him and father were good friends. "

"Jewel, are you asking me to marry you? Is this how you propose to one you claim to love so dearly?" she said with a smile.

"No, this is."

He walked to where she was sitting and pulled her up from the chair. He held her face and kissed her passionately. Then he gazed into her eyes. "April Marie Cothran, will you be my wife? Will you let me hold you forever and make all your dreams come true?"

"Jewel, do you mean it?"

"Yes darling, I need you as much as I want you. No other woman has ever made me feel this way. I promise to make you happy, if you'll marry me. Say yes, say it for us."

April laid her head on his shoulder. "Yes... yes. I've waited for this day, I knew we were meant for each other. I knew the day I first meant you."

"Then it is settled. Soon you will be Mrs. Jewel Jackson. Then we'll fill this house with children."

He pulled her away from him and looked seriously at her.

"You do want children, don't you?"

"Oh yes, lots of them."

Once again he kissed her. Then he pulled out a box from his pant's pocket.

"This was my grandmother's ring. Mom and I both wanted you to have it as a promise of our marriage." He then slipped it on her finger.

"It's beautiful." She said holding it up to the light to see it sparkle.

It was a silver ring with a red ruby surrounded by diamonds. Her fingers were thin and dainty, making the ring look large.

They sat out until the sky darkened and the stars began to shine. It was time for Jewel to leave.

"One day soon, my love, it will be just you and me. Then when darkness creeps in, we shall lay together and find each other. I yearn for that day."

"Jewel, stop. You're embarrassing me. You're shameless." April said as her face turned red.

"One night, my love, you'll know my passion."

"Jewel!" she said as she pushed him away. "It's time for you to leave, before I faint dead away. You with all this talk of passion. You know ...I've never."

"Yes, I know." he said with a sly smile.

He then walked off the porch, jumped on his horse and rode out with the moon to light his trail, turning around once and glancing back at April. She held up her arm and waved good-bye.

As soon as he disappeared she called out loudly for May, then took off running towards the cabins.

"May, where are you, I need to talk to you."

"Here I am Miss April. Are you all right? Has something happened? I'm over here with the others."

April saw May sitting with a group with lanterns lighting the circle they were in. The cabins glowed with the lights hanging from the rafters. April never realized how peaceful the cabins appeared at nightfall. Children were out and about playing hide-n-seek. Babies were being cuddled by their mothers. The air was filled with the smell of honey suckles and ripe peaches from the trees scattered about the cabins.

"Yes, something wonderful has happened. Please come home, I need to show you something." April called to her.

"I'm coming. See y'all later, the mistress wants me." May said leaving the group.

April went back to the big house, with May not far behind. She waited in the parlor where the light was the brightest.

"May, you won't believe what happened to me tonight. Jewel proposed marriage and I accepted. Here is my ring. It belonged to his grandmother, his mother wanted me to have it. Isn't it lovely?" she said holding it out for May to see.

May took April's hand and looked at the ring. She wept.

"May, what on earth is wrong with you. Aren't you happy for me? What are you crying about? Nothing will change between us. I will give you your on room. When I have children, you can help me raise them. We'll raise them together, won't that be wonderful! Think about it May, it will be a great new life for us!"

"Miss April, your Jewel, he don't like me. I know how the Jackson's treat their slaves. They beat them and work them to death. They beat them for no reason at all. He'll put me back in the fields. He don't like colored people, you know this is true." May said as she wiped her face with her apron.

"May, what on earth would you have me to do? Don't you want me to be happy? As my sister, you should want what's best for me." she said with her hands now on her hips.

"As my sister, set me free. Give me and my mama freedom, then marry Jewel."

"Freedom!" screamed April. "What in the tarnation are you talking about. I brought you out of the fields, which was the only time you've ever had to work. I can't believe you even made such a statement. How dare you!" April said as she turned and ran up the staircase. May heard her crying as she slammed the bedroom door. May sat down on the bottom steps and leaned against the handrail, then slowly drifted off to sleep.

When she awakened, all the lamps had been turned off except for one left near her. She picked up the oil lamp and slowly climbed the stairs. Her heart heavy for the future she knew would be hers. For the first time in her life, she thought of running. She opened the door to their room and quietly climbed into bed. April was sleeping soundly.

With the breaking of dawn, they both awoke. They didn't speak as they dressed. Finally the truth was placed in April's hands. Like most slaves, May dreamed of freedom. April had never thought May would consider leaving her and never considered May as a slave. She thought May was happy.

"Miss April, its Sunday, may I go to the cabins for the day. I want to visit mama."

"Yes, of course. Go on."

April had decided to spend the day alone. She needed her papa's guidance, so she pulled out his journal. She began to read again his thoughts on slavery, questioning herself on her relationship with May. She heard many horrible tales about the Jackson plantation, but she was bound and determined it wouldn't happen to hers. She was sure she could control the situation. The stories might have been made up and passed around by the slaves. No one could be that cruel. No one.

She laid her papa's journal down and began to think of her past with May. They were close growing up. She was lucky to have a sister like her. Then for the first time, she tried to imagine what it must feel like to be May. She finally faced the fact that it wasn't an accident that had caused May's burns. It was her own need to keep her. Not just to keep her safe, but to keep her. Now it was possible she might be putting May into the hands of the ones she tried to save her from.

"Oh Papa, what am I suppose to do. I love Jewel and I love May. If only you were here. If only we could talk this out."

She read over his words one more time, then made her decision. There was only one way to correct the entire harm she caused May. She'd have to give her up. May would receive her Freedom.

She called for a horse to be saddled and headed for Cainnoy.

A law had been passed in 1800 that required the master of a human chattel to seek a permit from a magistrate to grant emancipation. The magistrate had to be convinced of the character of the slave and his or her abilities to make a living. Then the clerk of court recorded the certificate and deed of emancipation and a copy of the deed was made for the freed Negro.

April's father's dearest friend was the magistrate in Cainnoy. She rode to his house in town and told him of her decision, requesting a permit and deed for both May and Lilly.

"April, I'll be glad to help you. Don't get many requests for freedom deeds. Yours will be the first of the year. Last year I only received one. It's a strange thing to set property free. But I reckon it's like turning a faithful mule to pasture. You reward them when it's time."

"Yes sir, I guess it's like that. I never really considered May property, still don't. But she'll need papers to travel. It's going to be hard without her, but I'm getting married soon."

"You and Jackson's son Jewel?"

"Yes sir. He asked me last night. See my ring, it belonged to his grandmother."

"Well congratulations young lady, I wish you all the happiness in the world. I know your papa would be proud of you. I'm proud of you myself. You have been doing a fine job with your plantation. I really hate all you been through. You deserve some happiness."

"Thank you sir. You're right, I do."

He went to his desk and filled out the papers.

"Here you go. Everything is ready for some very lucky slaves. Freedom is a big step. I hope their ready for it." he said.

Chapter 17

May's Introduction To Freedom

May arrived back home later that evening. She found April sitting alone in the library reading over some papers.

"Miss April, you all right?"

April looked up and May saw she'd been crying for her eyes were beginning to swell.

April stood up and motioned for May to sit on the sofa. Then she came and sat next to her. For a while they just sat there, neither one speaking. Finally May broke the silence.

"Miss April, I'm sorry I can't be happy over your marriage plans. I know some of Master Jackson's slaves, and they tell the truth about him. I'm sorry, but it's all true. He's a mean man. I don't know about his son, but I do know about him. They say the apple don't fall far from the tree."

"May, I'm not upset over you not liking Jewel. I understand. I'm bothered by what I know I must do. But first I must talk to you, and I need you to really listen. I have never thought of you as a slave. You probably don't believe me, but I swear it's the truth. You told me you wanted your freedom and I always felt you were free. The only hardship you ever knew was those two years in the fields. I would give anything if they hadn't happen."

May turned her head from April in anger when she suggested she didn't know hardship. What did April know of hardship? She'd never worked a day in her life.

"May, please look at me. This is hard enough for me to say."

May turned her head back towards April.

"It really shocked me to hear you wanted freedom. I felt like you were happy being here with me again. Now I realize that we both have changed. I really need to marry and start a family and fill this house with laughter once again. I realize you may have the same desires. All my life I've been blessed to have you. You have given me such happiness and filled my heart with wonderful memories. For this alone I thank you."

April reached over and took one of May's hands and squeezed it tight.

"Many nights I've laid awake replaying the accident in my mind. I prayed one day I could make it up to you. It hurts me that I'm responsible for your scars. I still remember your great beauty and how everyone raved over you. To me, you are still beautiful, and always will be. I've been praying all day for answers to many questions. I feel there are two things I must do. I must marry Jewel

Jackson, and I must give you papers of Freedom. May, if you promise to always keep in touch, I have your freedom papers. I'm giving you and your mother both freedom, but please promise you'll always keep in touch." April finished with tears in her eyes.

May sit frozen staring at April, not believing what had just been said.

"Fre... fre... freedom," she stammered. "Did you just say I'm free?" May said with disbelief.

"May, if that's what you truly want, you're free. I have your papers and I'll give you supplies and a wagon to move north. But you must keep in touch; I must be able to talk to you, even if only by mail. I'll always need to know you're okay."

May started to cry and reached over to hug April. April began to gently rock her from side to side. They sat there as they had when young, comforting each other. Knowing exactly how the other felt.

Finally they were to be separated, possibly for life.

"May, I'm giving Lilly her freedom to watch over you. You are special and I want you to always be safe and happy. If it takes freedom for your mother to assure your happiness, then so be it." April said softly.

"I don't know what to say. I won't know how to act."

"You'll be fine May, you're just like me. We'll make it through everything."

"May, it will take at least four days to prepare for your departure. I will give you a wagon and supplies for a new home. I've decided to give you two mules, a plow and a horse. We must do this quickly so that no one can question my decision. Call your mama here to give her the news. I would like to be part of her happiness. Just tell her I have a request to make of her. Why don't you go now, and get her. I don't believe it's too late."

May was out of the house before April could finish the last word. April sat smiling, feeling her papa would be proud of her right now. She could almost hear him saying: "That's my Princess and I'm sure proud of you."

Within a few moments, May returned with her mother Lilly in tow. Lilly was still a young woman, hardly looking like the mother of May. She was slim and had a lighter complexion than May. She was pretty, in a normal sort of way.

"Miss April, here's mother. I fetched her like you said." May said smiling from ear to ear.

Lilly had no idea why she was standing in front of April. May had told her April had said for her to come quickly. She was frightened because it was late and she thought she'd done something wrong. She kept her head down as she stood in front of April.

April asked Lilly to look at her, for she had a very important request to ask of her.

Lilly slowly raised her head to look into the eyes of Miss April. April could see Lilly's eyes start to water. Fear was written all over her face.

"Lilly, I need you to go with May on a long trip. You shall never return here again. It will be to ensure May's happiness and safety. I need to know if you are willing to do this. If so, you will be leaving here in a matter of days. Are you willing to leave?" April asked smiling.

Lilly stood with a confused look on her face. Finally she started talking rapidly.

"Miss April, I don't understand. You want me and May to go on a trip? We sold to another plantation? Miss April please don't sell us! We belong here!" Lilly began to cry.

April and May began to giggle. Lilly was confused that they would be happy by something to painful to think of. Maybe, she thought, they'd both gone mad.

"Let me tell her. Please let me be the one!" begged May to April.

April nodded.

"Mama, Miss April is giving us our freedom. Do you understand? Freedom! Mama, from now on, you and me, we be free. We belong only to God and ourselves. No more slaving no more masters. Mama we free, we freeee!" May said joyfully.

Lilly watched May in disbelief.

"Free?" she whispered turning to look at April.

"Yes Lilly, from this day forever more, you and May are free."

"Sweet Jesus," cried out Lilly, " Thank you sweet Jesus."

Lilly reached for May and hugged her with all her might.

She turned to April and asked her, "Miss April, is it all right dat I hugs you too?"

"Yes Lilly, it is very all right."

Lilly ran over to April and hugged her like she'd never let her go. Then kissed her cheek and whispered, "Thank you."

Chapter 18

The Departure

It was July 20, 1839. It had been four days since May and Lilly had received their freedom. Lilly had been staying at the big house as a guest. It seemed like overnight everything had changed. Today was the day of departure. Everything was ready for May and Lilly to leave.

Outside the big house a wagon stood loaded with furniture, supplies and food. It was enough for two women to get a fresh start. They were not sure where they would go, they only knew they would head out for the free states.

The blacksmith had made them a few tools to garden with, and a large knife for protection. Some of the workers had gathered to give them gifts. Cecil gave them a quilt she made from clothes cast off for rags. It was colorful and would be a prized procession.

"When eber y'all miss us, just wrap up in dis. Den you know you wrapped in our love and prayers." said Cecil as she handed it to May.

"Thank you Cecil, we'll use it often. You know we'll miss you all," said May.

They also received canned jars of various vegetables and fruit. The shoemaker made them both a fine pair of leather shoes. April had told him to hold back no expense.

Another gift that proved to be their favorite was given by a young man named Joseph. He was an artist. He'd taken a large piece of bark and managed to pound it out flat. He used charcoal to draw a perfect likeness of the big house with people standing about it.

"Dis is so you neber forget were you came from. Here is where people love you." he said as he handed the drawing to Lilly.

"Thank you Joseph, you'll never know how much this means to us." May said as she hugged him.

Finally April appeared with their papers and belongings she wanted them to have. She had their papers of freedom in a leather carrying case. She gave May a metal purse and told her to keep it safe.

"Inside you will find three hundred dollars. This should buy you a small cabin with land. May I taught you all I know about money. Don't let anyone trick you into giving up one penny. This is a lot of money, so keep it hidden. Never tell anyone you have it. Buy a place to live with it. You might meet people who will come as friends, but don't be deceived. Be careful on the road. I'm putting this note on your shirt. If anyone stops you, let them read it. They'll bother you no more.

The note read:

Anyone who reads this, be aware these two women are freed slaves from the Cothran Plantation. They are to pass to the free states unharmed. Any harm put on them will be punished by death.

It was signed by the magistrate and April and carried the Cothran seal. After April pinned it on May, she helped her crawl onto the buggy board. Another worker helped Lilly up the other side.

To April and May it seemed like they were acting out a dream. Never had April fathomed giving May freedom. She had thought life would always remain the same. With the death of her parents she realized life was just a series of changes. Nothing ever remained the same. With time, all things must change. Time brought growth and growth brings change.

Most everyone in the lane was crying as they bid farewell to May and Lilly. April handed May the leader rope attached to the mules.

"May, distance cannot change how I feel about you. You are my sister and will always be. Every night I'll pray for your safekeeping and happiness. Remember that you agreed to let me know where you are. I'll write you as soon as I hear from you. Never forget me May. Please, never forget me!" cried April.

"April, I shall never forget one thing about you. I'll keep the memory of you and this place in my heart. One day you'll realize what a great thing you've done on this day. One day, you'll see what happens here is wrong. We'll always be sisters. Always!"

With those final words, she jerked on the line for the mules to go. She headed out down the tree-lined lane that led to a new life. The others in the field ran as close to the road as they could to wave good-bye. You could see April waving as they traveled down the road.

The air was now filled with the sweet smell of freedom.

Chapter 19

The Wedding

The wedding was set for January 1, 1840. April wanted to start the new year by starting her new life. It had been over four months since May's departure, with no word of her safe arrival. April prayed that they made it north before winter approached.

Jewel had become furious when he heard of April's decision to set them free.

"Woman, are you mad. You don't release slaves like that. They were in good health and capable of reproducing. There's no way they could have made it north on their own. I heard you sent two mules and a horse with them. I can't believe I'm about to marry you," he said as he turned his back to her.

April was upset over the possibility of losing Jewel too, and promised never to make decisions of such importance without his approval.

"Jewel, I'm sorry. You've got to forgive me. I was thinking only of my bond with May, and the pain that I've caused her. I was trying to set things right, so that we could be happy. I didn't mean to upset you." she tried to turn him back towards her.

"If you promise to never take on such decision making again without speaking to me about it, then I'll forgive you."

"I promise."

With this, he came to her side and embraced her.

April wasn't sure why she wanted a winter wedding, it just felt right. She planned on having the wedding at the plantation. It was to be a small wedding party, with a best man and maiden of honor. April asked Jewel's sister to be her maiden of honor. Jewel was pleased, although it felt strange to April, for she hardly knew her. Jewel's sister was married in lived in Athens, Ga. She had met her on a few occasions in the past. After May left, April realized she didn't have any friends. Jewel had suggested his sister.

April learned to never bring May up in conversations with Jewel. It never failed to cause a fuss. She prayed time would ease his hate for May, and that one day he would understand. Jewel began to spend more time at the plantation once the wedding was announced. April allowed him to go over the books with her to see how she'd been running the plantation. He promised her the only changes he would make would be for the benefit of the plantation. He began drawing up plans to gain more profit, and to cut back on waste.

April often wandered to the family cemetery and stood over the tombstones honoring her parents. She wished they were with her. She wanted to be sure of their approval of her marriage. Jewel would be stepping into the shoes of her papa.

"Papa, mother, how I wish you could answer me. I think it will be good to marry Jewel, but I wish I knew for sure. I don't know what to do. I don't know how to be a wife. Mama, I wish we could talk. You too, Papa. I wish there were someone to talk to. I just want a marriage like yours. I want children."

April talked knowing they couldn't answer nor hear. Just being close to their graves brought comfort.

That day after her visit to the graveyard, she found her mother's wedding gown in the attic. She had been looking for her Grandmother's silver tea set, when she came upon the lined trunk. She took it as a sign that she should go on with the wedding. She tried the gown on and it fit her perfectly. It was of ivory white lace, with a chiffon sash and bow. The sleeves had white beads going up each side, which continued around the neck. It was perfect. She gazed at herself in the mirror.

"Mother, why did you leave me? I need you. I miss you so. Thank you for guiding me to your gown. Oh, how I miss you." April said out loud. Then she began to cry.

No one came to comfort her, because there was no one left that cared.

April was 18 and alone. She pulled herself together and carried the gown to her room. She would need for it to be cleaned and pressed for her wedding. Daily she prayed that God's hands would guide her down the right path. When she was with Jewel, she never questioned their marriage. She felt secure and safe. When she was alone, the doubts came. One thing she knew for certain was she wanted children, and so did Jewel. This much she knew they agreed on.

Jewel had shown some concern for the depression April was in. She assured him it was due to her parents' death. It was hard to handle the wedding plans by herself. She yearned for a mother to help, but it was not to be.

April enjoyed taking care of the plantation. There was so much she hadn't realized her papa had to do. She enjoyed going to Cainnoy and bickering with the stores to lower their prices for her. She personally went with M.J. Perry to buy the seeds and equipment needed for crops. People in town were amazed how a young lady could run a plantation so well. She was firmer than her papa, with no one able to pull the wool over her eyes.

"Well if that's the best you can do, I'll just ride over to Charleston. I'm sure to get a discount there. If you can't be fair, someone else will."

"Okay Miss Cothran, we'll let you have the seeds for $10.00 dollars and I'll throw in a basket of plums. There is no need in you riding to Charleston. I'll take good care of you," said Duffy, the owner of the feed store.

"Thank-you."

Jewel was beginning to drink more around April. April felt it was due to the up coming wedding and him being nervous. She was sure after they were married he would calm down. He was funny after a couple of drinks, doing crazy things to make her laugh. She found him to be adorable in his antics. It was hard to say anything about his drinking access.

"Jewel, my love, sometimes you act plain crazy." she said with a laugh.

"I'm crazy for you, and crazy in love. What do you expect?" he said with a grin.

Jewel wanted them to share her parents' bedroom after they married.

"I cannot stand the thought of sleeping in the room you and that slave had. I think of her every time I see it. Her scared face and the way she controlled you. I can't stand it."he said as they discussed their future together.

"Okay, if you feel that way, we'll take their room. But what if they are found? What if they come back?"

"April, my love, your parents are never coming back. They're dead. You have me now. I'll take care of you."

The wedding day had arrived. The hall was decorated in strips of linen, with large bows hanging from lamps and the chandeliers. The staircase was draped in lace and satin wrapped around the rails. On several tables were large vases with white winter roses. The fireplaces were all lit. It was warm and cozy. Everything looked perfect. April had spent two days getting it ready. The housemaids were eager to help, feeling the excitement of the wedding. The kitchen maids made a beautiful three-layered wedding cake. All the silver was polished and two long tables were set with the finest china from both houses. A huge hog was cooked for the wedding feast. The hog was cooked outside in a pit for two days. Everything was perfect and ready. It would be the finest wedding ever held in Cainnoy.

Jewel's sister Anna came that morning to help April get dressed and do last moment task. She was impressed with the transformation of the house. The wedding was set for 1:00 p.m. The guest starting arriving at 12:20.

April became nervous when she heard the chatter of voices downstairs. The guest were being served wine as they waited.

"I look dreadful. How could Jewel possibly want to marry me!" she exclaimed as she looked at herself in the mirror.

Someone knocked on the door, and said it was time. Music began to fill the air. Anna hugged April.

"Sweetie, you look beautiful. Actually stunning. Jewel is lucky to found such a lovely wife. I'm sure you'll both be happy. Don't worry, I was scared too on my wedding day. Once you start down the stairs, I promise you'll be all right." Anna said. Then she kissed April on the cheek.

April trembled as they walked out of the room and towards the stairs.

"If only my parents were here. If only May were here." thought April.

As April approached the stairs everyone stood and looked up at her. She could see Jewel standing proudly near the minister. She began to relax. When she neared the bottom of the stairs, Uncle Andy was there to take her arm. He led her down the center of the chairs with all eyes watching her.

When they reached Jewel, the pastor asked, "Who gives this woman in holy matrimony?"

"I, her father's brother." Uncle Andy replied.

Then he stepped back and let Jewel take her hand. Before he moved away, Andy leaned over and kissed her cheek. April gave him a grateful smile.

Then everyone was asked to lower their heads in prayer.

"May God bless the union of these two families, and fill this house with love and laughter. Forever more let only goodness and grace pass through the doors of this home. A-men."

The wedding vows were exchanged; the union was sealed with a kiss. Jewel whispered in her ear before they turned to greet the guest.

"At last you belong to me. You shall never regret this moment. Never!"

Chapter 20

April's New Life

Jewel and April honeymooned in Savannah. Uncle Andy stayed at the plantation for a couple of weeks while they were gone. Jewel was sweet and gentle with April. She had much to learn about being a lover and a wife. All too soon, the trip was over.

As soon as they arrived home, Jewel began drinking heavily. April couldn't understand the need for so much liquor. After only four weeks, she had grown frightened of his behavior. She decided it was time to confront him and get to the bottom of his problem.

They were alone in their bedroom; April had prepared for bed. Jewel was sitting on the side of the bed fully clothed and drinking straight from a bottle of vodka. April was at her dresser brushing her long brown hair.

"Jewel," she said. "Are you happy? Are you still glad you married me?"

"What's with the questions? Are you regretting the fact that you married me? I married you, didn't I? Isn't that enough? What more do you want of me?" grumbled Jewel.

April was shocked, not expecting so much anger. "I'm sorry if I angered you. I've just noticed that you've been drinking a lot since we've been home. I feel like something is bothering you." replied April.

"Bothering me, you say! You want to know what is bothering me! I'll tell you what's bothering me!" yelled Jewel.

He stood up and walked over to where April was sitting and stared at her through the mirror.

"To start with, you have the laziest bunch of slaves in this state. They do what ever they want, and get away with it. I'll tell you right now that it's going to stop. No slave of mine is going to rule my house. They'll do exactly what I say, at the exact moment I tell them to, or they'll learn a lesson for daring not to listen. I am the master of my slaves, not the other way around. And my darling wife, how dare you question my drinking habits. You knew my passion was drinking! So don't start acting like I'm some big surprise!" screamed Jewel.

April turned around to face Jewel.

"Jewel Jackson, those are my slaves too! They are all good! You shall never lay one hand on them while there is one drop of life in me!" yelled back April.

April felt a sharp sting against her face as he slapped her. Then she gasped for breath as he used his large hands to squeeze her neck. He used his thumbs to apply pressure to her windpipe. She tried to pull his hands away, pleading for him to stop with her eyes.

He bent over and began talking slowly into her ear.

"Don't you ever talk to me like that again. I am the master of this house, you are my wife. Do you understand me? Just my wife! What I say goes. Never defy me again! Never forget I'm the master!"

When he let go of her neck, she fell to the floor coughing and gasping for breath. He stormed out of the room and slammed the large wooden door. It sounded like a gun going off.

April crawled onto their bed and began to cry. All she wanted was a marriage like her parents. She prayed silently before she drifted off to sleep that she would not wake up. The man she married was not the man she had fallen in love with. It had been a perfect deceit. She was now the master's wife, nothing more.

At dawn, April awoke to the smell of barn animals. She raised up to see Jewel laying fully clothed next to her, still holding his empty bottle of vodka. He had been in the barn, but the cold made him wander back to their room. She tried to slip out of bed without waking him. She felt his hand grasp her wrist.

"April, darling April," whispered Jewel. "I'm sorry, so sorry. I don't know what happened last night. I just blew up. Please forgive me. I promise to never lay another hand on you. I can't believe what I did. I've never behaved like that before. I'd rather hurt myself than to ever hurt you." cried Jewel.

He began to sob. He took the empty bottle and slung it across the room, shattering it against the wall. He swore in God's name he'd never drink again. April couldn't stand to see him crying. She reached over and held him in her arms. He wept like a baby. Now, she felt, I have the man I married back. He wasn't a monster, just confused by drink. He behaved now like a wounded child.

"Hush Jewel, it's okay. I forgive you. We'll be all right. I understand, you didn't mean it."

He reached up and kissed her fully in the mouth. April almost gagged from the taste of vodka and vomit. Jewel slept until late that evening.

Things appeared to be going well until late one evening in March. Jewel had gone to Cainnoy early that morning to see about a banking dispute.

April heard screams coming from the cabins. She ran down the stairs, put on her cape and grabbed an oil lantern. She then ran as fast as she could to the cabins. Everyone was standing around someone on a horse. They all had their lanterns held high, and were pleading with the man on the horse.

She screamed for them to move and let her through. Then she saw what the screaming and pleading was about. It was Jewel, almost falling off his horse drunk. Then she looked behind him on the ground and saw the tattered and torn body of Joseph. Jewel had him attached to a rope by his hands, and dragged him. You could see rocks and sticks stuck into Joseph's body. Joseph looked dead.

"Please, no more. Please!" he called out as he looked towards April. April trembled.

"Someone cut him loose! Do you hear me? Cut him loose now!" she screamed.

"The first person that comes to the aid of that slave shall receive a musket ball to the head, administered by yours truly." said Jewel as he took his hat off in a sweeping motion towards April.

"I caught this slave in Cainnoy without a pass. That means he didn't have permission to be there. It is better that he is caught and punished by his own master. Let them all see what comes when you defy your master. Let him die on the ground where he lays. He'll never leave this place again." Jewel said with slurred speech.

"I gave Joseph a pass!" lied April. "He must have lost it. He went to Cainnoy for me. Do you hear me? Now let us cut him loose. I beg you! Let us cut him loose!" cried out April.

Jewel was drunk and couldn't keep his balance on the saddle. He was swaying from side to side. He leaned down towards April.

"My darling wife, you wouldn't be lying to save this stinking slave would you? You know how angry that would make me. You don't want me angry now, do you? Did you give this slave a pass, the truth! " Jewel said in a hissing tone.

"Jewel, I swear on the graves of my parents that Joseph had a pass. He went to buy me buttons. Now cut him loose, Please!" April said knowing it was the biggest lie of her life. She would later run back and tear buttons off dresses so that Jewel would never know.

"All right, take him. I don't think it'll do any good. He stopped running behind me a while back. The fool's just been dragging behind and slowing my horse and me up." laughed Jewel.

When Joseph was cut free, Jewel slapped his horse and took off. He slowed down long enough to yell for April to get home. She cried as Jim picked Joseph up and carried him to his cabin. He turned to April before he stepped in.

"Dats a mighty fine thang you done for Joseph. Mighty fine thang."

April stood staring at his cabin not believing the cruelty that was committed on Joseph. He was a quiet young man who never caused a bit of trouble. God had given him a great talent. April had a drawing of May and herself that Joseph had made when they were young. He surprised her and May by giving it to them for Christmas. She prayed that his life would be spared and her lie forgiven.

You could hear Jewel screaming her name down at the cabins. She headed back down the lane to home. Her papa would have killed a man for doing that. It was beginning to sound like a good idea.

As she reached the house, she saw Jewel sitting on the front swing.

"Help me April. I feel sick. That stupid slave upset me so much I drank. It wasn't much. Help me inside, and bring me a wet towel," Jewel said as he tried to stand.

April walked over to him and let him put an arm around her shoulder. She considered taking him up the stairs and pushing him down. If he died, it would be ruled an accident.

He smelled like a saloon. No one would ever blame her. She could say he walked up by himself and fell. April prayed God would let her keep her sanity.

Chapter 21

The Long Road To Freedom

Lilly couldn't believe they were free. She asked May as they traveled down the road if she could hold the leather case that held their papers. She untied it and looked inside.

"Lordy, da eben smell like freedom. Smell'em May, ain't dat be da finest smell you eber did know. Ain't neber in my life feels as good as I does on dis day." Lilly said smiling from ear to ear.

Lilly began to sing. She started making up songs about freedom. Some of them were down right funny, and they'd both laugh.

"I'm free-like a bumble bee-ain't gonna cry-ain't gonna die-ain't pickin cotton no mo-ain't cropping no mo-spend my days like I please-look at me be a bumble bee."

When Lilly grew tired of singing May began talking of where they should be heading.

"Miss April told me Pennsylvania was a good state for freed slaves. She said they're lots of us there. I think we ought to head out for Pennsylvania. What do you think, Mama."

"I's think if da Lord take me now, I's die happy. It don't matter much where he decide we should go. Iffin da Lord done put it in your heart, den dats where we goes. You ain't gonna hear no fussing from dis free gal, no fussing at all. It looks like da sun done got brighter on us. From dis day forward, thangs gonna be just fine, I's feel it in my bones. Penny vania! Dat suits me just fine. Penny vania! Look out, we's on da way!" yelled Lilly standing up in the wagon almost failing out.

May and Lilly both burst out laughing. May had never seen her mama talk so much, or be so happy. Freedom fit her mama well.

May knew she had to be careful. April told her to watch out for slave prospectors. They were men who would steal slaves and sell them in other states. They even took freed slaves, selling them back into slavery. That was the main reason April told May to keep the note pinned to her shirt. May didn't tell Lilly of all the things that might happen to them for fear that Lilly wouldn't go.

May remembered all the tales of the Underground Railroad, knowing that some whites would help slaves. She prayed God would lead someone into their path to guide them. The roads were beginning to get tough.

They traveled once for two days without seeing a soul.

"May, you shore we be going right? We still heading for Penny vania?" asked a worried Lilly.

"Mama, I think we are still heading in the right direction. Don't worry, we'll see someone soon." assured May.

Soon they saw four men coming up the road. When the men saw them, they made their horses gallop to approach them. They stopped the wagon.

"Where you two think y'all heading with that wagon full?"

"We freed slaves, heading north. We got papers, and this note." May said holding the note on her shirt.

The tall skinny man leaned over to read it.

"Let these colored gals pass y'all. We don't need to be messing with them. Someone thinks they're important. They got all the right papers."

"Y'all better git out of North Carolina and never come back!" yelled the red headed man as he rode past them.

May looked over at Lilly who was still trembling.

"Well mama, it looks like we've in North Carolina!" May said with a smile.

"Lord child, you so brave. I's thought those men would hurt us for shore. I's figured at least I was free a little while." Lilly finished as she wiped the sweat from her brow and breast.

"Mama don't worry. Ain't nobody taking our freedom. Nobody." she said firmly.

Sometimes they saw slaves working fields near the road. If they didn't see an overseer, they'd holler out greetings to them. They'd usually holler back and asked them where they were going. May yelled they'd been set free and where heading north. You could hear the word passed around, then the workers would take off their hats and wave good luck to them. May and Lilly felt the joy of being free, but great burden for leaving so many still in bondage.

The road was hard to follow. The snow and rain from the past year left holes and branches to deal with. They had to go slow to keep things in the wagon from being thrown out. They were afraid of losing a wagon wheel. They had a long pole that May used when they became stuck in a rut. Lilly would take the lead rope while May used the pole to push the wagon wheel up. It was back breaking work, but she managed.

At night they set up camp next to the wagon. They never pulled off far from the trail that led north. They had a tent, and oil lamps. It was dark in the mountains at night. Every night they'd look for the drinking gourd, a star formation, to be sure they were heading north. It was sign runaways depending on for the direction of north. Every night they'd thank God for their freedom and asked for guidance the coming day.

One day a white man in a beat up wagon stopped to check their papers and warn them of the road ahead. They told him they could handle the mountains, they'd passed over several.

"Mountains, you say. I'm sorry to tell you what you've passed over was nothing more than hills. The mountains are yet to come. Let this be a warning, the road will vanish from site in some places. Just go with your instinct and keep following where it should be. You will have to pass over some fast waters that will drag you under if you go the deep end. Ride in first with your horse, then carry the mules and buggy across. If I didn't have work waiting, I'd take you through the first one. Good luck to you both. God speed." the man named George said as he tipped his hat showing respect and rode past them.

"May, should we try to go on?" asked the worried Lilly.

"I'm sure not turning back now. I'd rather die free." May said as she whipped the mules into moving again.

Late that night as they sat around a small fire near their tent, they heard someone walking towards their campsite. Both were frightened.

"Who goes there?" yelled out May as she grabbed a large knife and stood.

They saw the shadow of a large man come out of the trees. He walked towards them with his hands raised above his head. It was George.

"I'm sorry to frighten you. I was hoping you hadn't gotten far. I had a strange feeling come over me that I should help you both. There is no way two women can pass through these mountains alone. I promise to God, I bid you no harm. I just want to help you pass over to your freedom." George said keeping his hands raised.

May looked at her mama.

"Mama, what you think? Should we trust him? We did pray for help. Remember?" May said while keeping the knife raised towards George.

Lilly stood up and gave George a long hard look. He smiled back at her. Then she looked at May.

"I's thinks dis be a good white man, not white trash. You be hungry?"

May lowered her knife and invited George to share their food. He gladly accepted.

"I ain't never in my born days seen slaves, I mean free slaves, as smart and tuff as you two. You have to be wise and brave to travel this far by yourselves. Your papers say you're from Cainnoy, South Carolina. That's near Charleston."

"Yes sir, we've come a long way. We're heading for Pennsylvania. We appreciate your kindness. Excuse our fear, it's hard to trust whites. My sister April warned me to watch out. But you seem to be decent."

"What I find strange ma'am is that you don't speak like a slave."

Lilly started laughing.

"I was raised in the big house with the master's daughter. We were raised as sisters. My mama here nursed us both. Didn't work the fields but two years; that was after I was burned. The master and his wife drowned on the Pulaski, the ship that exploded."

"Yep, I heard about that. Sure was a terribly thing. His daughter, was she rescued?"

"April didn't go with them. She stayed at the plantation with her Uncle. Now she owns it all. She set us free, and gave me what you see here."

"She must have thought a lot of you," he said reaching for more coffee.

"April is the reason I'm burned. She spilled lye soap on me."

"She done thrown it on you. It weren't no accident," exclaimed Lilly.

"So that's what happen to you! Don't mean to be fresh, but that's why I came looking for you two. I figured you suffered more than your share, and deserved to be helped." George took a sip of coffee and rubbed the hot cup.

"Ain't never owned slaves. Never wanted to get one. I travel from town to town making iron gates. I rent blacksmiths stales, and pay when I'm done. I've gone as far as New Orleans making iron gates. My favorite are the ones that look like corn stalks. They're real fancy. The gates I make will out live me. I'm proud of what I do. Kinda like a traveling artist or something." finished George.

May and Lilly found George likable. He was the kindest white man they ever met. It was apparent that he was poor by his shoes and dress. But he was sure proud of his gates. George pulled his wagon closer to theirs and they settled in for the dark night. The small fire was kept to ward off animals.

The trip through the mountains proved dangerous. Once they almost lost both wagons to a rock slid after several days of rain. One fateful day, Lilly met up with a polecat. She was washing her clothes out in a mountain stream. She didn't notice it till its tail was raised and the deadly smell was out. She began coughing and her eyes burned.

"May, help me, a pole cat done squirt me down. Lordy, I can't stand it."

May rush to help her mama. They both gagged and coughed as they striped her down. Lilly had to wash in the cold stream with lye soap. The clothes where burned in a fire. Lilly wrapped up in a blanket when she was finished.

"Mama, you ride in the back of the wagon. You still stink to high heaven."

From then on, if they wanted Lilly to hurry up, they'd holler they seen a polecat. Lilly always would take off running.

They were lucky crossing the rivers. George spent hours finding the safest places to cross over, and they never lost anything to the raging rapids. George was truly a Godsend.

When they finally made it through the mountains they were weary. Thanks to George, they were safe and alive. They reached Danville, Virginia. There

George told them the best way to Philadelphia was by train and ferry boats. The train had cars to carry their wagon, mules and horse. It was time for him to move on.

He took them to the train depot and helped them buy passage to Alexandria. Then they were to cross the Potomac River by ferryboat. Once they made it to Washington, they could catch a train ride all the way to Philadelphia, Pennsylvania. The total trip would cost them eleven dollars and twenty cents.

"George, we cannot pay you enough for all your help. But here is what we can give." May said as she extended her fist with some money in it.

"No ma'am, I don't want your money. You just go on now and have yourself a good life. When you settle, just remember my gates. They the finest in the world, guaranteed."

George then handed them a calling card and rode away as they waved goodbye.

May read the card.

"Bowling Green, Kentucky. Mama, they sure raise fine men there."

"Da shore do." she replied.

Chapter 22

The Freedom House

The train ride proved to be easier than the rugged trip through the mountains. They rode in a passenger car for people of color. It was the first time they saw a China man. Lilly was amazed at the length of his hair. His hair was a braided ponytail they went down to his knees. His clothes looked more like a sleeper, and he wore a round white hat. When he walked past them, he looked at them and smiled.

On the train they met other former slaves. All were amazed at May's story, and how far they had traveled. They found the white man's kindness to be unbelievable. Lilly enjoyed sharing the story of May's burning. Each time she told it, the tale grew. It was hard for the others to understand April. They all shared their lives on the long journey.

Two freed slaves were the children of the master. His wife had given them their freedom and paid for their passage. She wanted them away from the plantation. Their mother had died. They were both green eyed.

In Gordeonsville, Virginia a large group of Indian Chiefs boarded. The Chiefs all had a regal air about them. They seemed to be more than just people. They stayed together and talked very little. Their faces showed much sadness and discontent. May knew that America had once been their land, theirs alone. She hoped to one day meet and speak with Indians. She knew they had many stories to tell.

When they reached Alexandria, they caught the ferry to Washington.

Washington was a fine town. Lilly saw a black man sweeping the dirt streets and asked him what he was doing.

"Well, it's my job ma'am. This is how I care for my family. Been doing it seven years now. Pays good."

"Da pay you?"

"Yes ma'am. They pay."

Lilly couldn't get over street sweeping being a job.

They decided to spend the night in Washington. They found a hotel that accepted freed slaves and rented a small room. It contained a large soft bed with clean sheets. They didn't realize how tired they were until they lay down. They both sleep for fourteen hours.

In the morning they were awaken by a knock on the door for wake up. They had requested it so they wouldn't miss their train. The hotel cost them eighty-nine cents, and was worth every penny.

As they headed toward the train in their overloaded wagon they once again saw the Indian Chiefs. The Chiefs were standing under a blooming tree. Several of them nodded at them in recognition. Indians seemed not to have a problem with the color of ones skin.

The train was loaded with people of color. Most had been free for some time. All were friendly and eager to share their stories. They were interested in May's burns and how she had gotten them. Once again she shared her story. May defended April, with Lilly still angry at her. Lilly was sure it wasn't an accident.

"Well, least she set us free. Dat be one good thang she done."

On September 23, 1839 they reached their destination. "Philadelphia, Pennsylvania. It had taken over two months of rocky roads, trains and ferry's to realize their dream. A chill was in the air, winter felt like it was trying to set in. They needed to find a place to live quickly.

They set their tent up on the out skirts of town, and began to look for land with a small cabin. May soon encountered people trying to sell overpriced land and cabins. April had warned her. May stood fast and refused all that she was shown. May kept her money hidden and never let anyone know how much they had. Most people thought she had a meager amount.

One day while riding in the country, Lilly saw a small log home that appeared empty. She fell in love with it. They rode up the road one-mile until they found a small white washed church. Tying their horse to a hitching post, they went up to the door.

"Is anyone here?" May called out.

The door was partly open.

"Can anyone hear me?"

A tall light skinned black man came to the door.

"Welcome, please come in. You are at "The Chapel Of The People". Everyone is welcomed here. Please, come in." he said.

"Come up front. The wood stove is heating and I have a pot of coffee on. It will soon be ready. Please come in." he stood to the side and motioned for them to enter.

As soon as Lilly got in she started telling him they were freed slaves from South Carolina.

"Yes siree, we's free as da burds. Nobody owns us but da Lord. All we needs now is a home for ours freedom. You knows bout da one down da road. I sure likes it."

May was shocked to see the boldness of her mother. Freedom sure suited her. She was no longer afraid.

The man smiled and told them his name.

"My name is Rev. Redbone. The log cabin you speak of belonged to my uncle, who recently passed away. The place has been empty for three weeks. The will has just been read, and the cabin belongs to my cousin. He lives in the city. I believe he's looking to sell it. I have the key to the lock if you'd like to see inside."

"We's shore do."

They rode back down to the cabin with him. He unlocked the door, and they went in.

"Dis is it, dis is my Freedom house. Thank ye Lord. Thank ye." Lilly said with her hands clasped. "We's now standing in our future."

"Mama, we haven't talked to anybody yet. We might not be able to afford it. It ain't ours yet. This might not be our freedom house."

"Child don't fret. Da good Lord done whispered in my ear. Dis here is our freedom house. Ain't no question bout it. Just go git dat cousin of hisen to sign da papers." Lilly said with a huge smile on her face looking around.

Rev. Redbone smiled at May and offered to carry her to his cousin's. He lived in the city not far away. He felt his cousin would be there.

"How could he refuse to sell, after the good Lord done told your mama it was hers."smiled Rev. Redbone.

"See what I means. He knows what I's talking bout. Y'all go ahead, ain't leaving my new home." Lilly said with a determined look on her face.

Rev. Redbone laughed and said it would be fine for Lilly to stay. They could pick her up later.

When they left, Lilly found wood and started a fire in the fireplace. She then found a broom and started to sweep.

Redbone's cousin was an educated black man who worked for a lawyer in town. He owned a large house in the city. May was shocked when his cousin Alfred agreed to sell them the cabin. He offered to let them move in right away, and they could keep the furniture that was inside.

"Dad never would move from that place. I was born and raised there. Dad said my home was to fancy. He would come to visit, but never spent the night. Said he preferred the woods to the smell of the city. He was proud of me though, he told me often. I was his only child; Mom died when I was 12. I'll be happy to know you live there."

"I'll sell you the cabin and fifty acres for two hundred and fifty dollars. Can you afford that?" he asked.

"Yes sir, I sure can. I thank you very much for selling. Mama and me will be real happy there. We couldn't even get her to leave. She claimed it was ours right away. I'll take good care of it, I promise."

They exchanged the money and he signed over the deed.

Moving into the cabin was easy for all they owned was in one wagon. The cabin had three rooms downstairs and two rooms upstairs. There was a large shed that needed repair in the back of the cabin. On one side was a spring well and shed. On the over side were several small sheds, with one being the outhouse. They even had a root cellar made under the cabin.

There were a total of four fireplaces. In the kitchen the fireplace took up half the wall. It contained metal rods sticking out for hanging pots for cooking. Nothing was fancy, but to them it was beautiful.

That first night they made a roaring fire and pulled up chairs to sit in front of it. Lilly had found and claimed an old rocking chair. As they were sitting there watching the fire, Lilly began to cry.

"Mama, what's the matter? Aren't you happy? Everything worked out just like you said it would. Why are you crying?" May asked concerned.

"I's happy. I's real happy. But feels like I's don't deserve it. I ain't done nuten to git all dis happiness. We's done left our peoples. Da all still slaves. You and me just sitting here being happy and free. It just don't feel right," she said sniffling.

"Mama, don't cry. We can't do anything about them being slaves. They'd want us to be happy. Wait, I know what will make you feel better." she stood up and left the room.

She came back with the large quilt that Cecil gave them, and the picture that Joseph had made. She placed the picture on the mantle and lovingly wrapped the quilt around her mama.

"Remember what we were told when they gave us these gifts. Cecil said with the quilt, you would know all their love and prayers are with us," she said rubbing Lilly's shoulders.

"Joseph said we could look at where we came from and never forget with his drawing. Now mama, we're starting a new life. We'll never forget the old, but we must go on. One-day mama, everyone will be free. I just know they will," she said as she sat down in her chair.

"I'll tell you what we need to do, lets talk about all the good times we had at the plantation. Let's remember everyone as happy, not slaves. I'll go first. Do you remember the Jubilee, and when Cecil met Henry. Boy, she sure loved to dance!"

For the rest of the evening, that's just what they did. You could hear their laughter all the way down to the road.

Chapter 23

Child Of Mercy

At dawn April was awaken by loud moaning and cries coming from the slave cabins. She knew instantly that Joseph had died. She removed Jewel's hand from her shoulder, and silently slipped out of bed. Dressing quietly she slipped out of the room without waking Jewel. It was Sunday, and the slaves were not required to work.

When she arrived at the cabins, she tried to calm them by assuring them this would never happen again. Cruelty had never been a part of the Cothran plantation. Everyone was in shock by the actions of Master Jewel Jackson.

Joseph's mother was with his body in their cabin. Joseph's body was laid out on the wooden table, having died during the night. His body was washed and he was dressed in his Sunday best. Someone had painted two small stones, which were placed on his eyes. It was still apparent the torment his body had taken. Even in death, his face showed pain. Lying around him where his prized possession. His quill pen and ink, unfinished drawings, and glass marbles he had since childhood. His drawings covered the walls. Candles were lit, but it still felt dark and cold.

April stood at his feet and wept. Joseph's mother came to her side and thanked her for trying to help him the night before.

"Miss April, thank ye. I knows what you did fer my Joseph."

April yearned to tell them of her anger towards Jewel. She knew if she only asked, several would be willing to kill him. Then another life would end because of Jewel. If a slave killed a white for any reason, the punishment was death by hanging.

April promised them she would do everything within her power to keep anything like this from happening again. Joseph was the youngest son of Mertda's. His older brothers had married and asked to be sold to the plantation of their wives. Mertda now had no one, and April's heart ached for her. Before leaving she placed a few bills into Mertda's hand

"I know this will not bring Joseph back, but I hope it will in some way help you. Joseph was special, I want you to know that." April said with tears in her eyes.

Mertda thanked April and asked if Joseph could be buried on Tuesday. It was custom to have a wake before a funeral. Many slaves believed that if a person wasn't mourned properly, his spirit could not rest. Mirrors would all be turned to face the wall for the fear of one's soul getting stuck inside. After the burial the mirrors would once again be turned out.

When April returned home, Jewel was awake and downstairs.

"Just where in the world have you been? You didn't tell me you were going anywhere."

"Jewel the young boy you dragged last night, he died."

"Well it serves him right! Laws are laws, and he should have shown me his pass!"Jewel snarled.

April couldn't believe how quickly Jewel had changed. She didn't know him anymore.

Soon it was spring, April's favorite season. Her own mother had loved it so much; she named her daughter after it. Spring gave the feeling of a fresh start. A chance to begin everything all over again. April prayed her life with Jewel would soon change. She yearned for a marriage like her parents.

Jewel went to Cainnoy with M.J. Perry to buy supplies needed for the fields. He returned with two letters for April. One was from Uncle Andy; the other was from May. April was excited when she saw the letter stamped Philadelphia.

"They made it!" yelled out April to no one at all. Jewel had walked back out the moment he handed her the letters.

May's letter was short and to the point. It read:

Dear Miss April,

We made it to Philadelphia, Pennsylvania. We purchased a log cabin with fifty acres of land with our money. Thank you for our freedom. Freedom feels good.

May

That was all that was written, then she had simply signed her name. April wanted to hear of her new life. She was glad they were safe, and prayed that they were happy.

Uncle Andy's letter was long. He wrote of his first grandchild, swearing he looked just like him. He said it made him feel good to see how happy April was when he left. He prayed they would be happy. After reading his letter she laid it down and cried. If he only knew, he would surely come to her aid.

In the middle of spring, April became sick. She wasn't able to hold anything down. The worst attacks came in the morning. Finally Jewel summons the doctor. After he checked April over, he talked to them both.

"What's wrong with my wife?" asked Jewel, placing a protective arm around her.

"She has an aliment that only time can cure. She'll need a lot of attention and will have to stay off her feet when possible. I suggest you assign a slave to help her in all her needs. Then I suggest you should both be thinking of a name."

"A name for what?" asked April. "I have a sickness so rare it doesn't have a name?" looking puzzled at the doctor.

All of a sudden, Jewel began to laugh. This made April furious.

"So you think it's funny that I have a rare disease? How dare you!" she said with great fury, pulling away from his touch.

"No my love, I think it's wonderful that we're going to have a baby. I can't wait to tell mother. She'll be so happy. April, we're going to have a baby. That's what the doctor is trying to tell you, in a amusing way." Jewel said with a big smile on his face then kissed her cheek.

"A baby?" she whispered. They both nodded yes.

"A baby!" she screamed as she got up and started jumping around.

"Calm down April. This is your first; you need to take it easy. We don't want anything to go wrong," warned the doctor.

"Okay." she said, " Give me a moment. I'll calm down. I wish my parents were here. They dreamed of having grandchildren."

Jewel stood up and walked over to where April was standing and wrapped his arms around her. He kissed her like no one else was in the room.

"You've just made me the happiest man in the world. From this day forward, our life will be perfect. I promise. I love you April Jackson." Jewel said softly.

April shed tears of happiness. She'd prayed God would give mercy to her. She never thought it would come through a child. She requested for Cecil to help her, remembering the childhood friendship, and she needed someone near that she could trust.

"Me, to da big house. Why I'm a darkey! Dat suits me just fine though." Cecil had said when a house worker went for her.

Cecil always heard only light skinned people ever worked in the master house, and she was darker than May. From that day on, she never worked the fields again.

Two days after she learned of her pregnancy, she wrote May a long letter. She told her everything that happened. She spoke of Joseph's death and the beatings she received from Jewel when he was drunk. She shared her dreams of the birth changing her life for the good. She told of Jewel's promise to make their life better. The baby was due in December, and she hoped to have it before the Christmas.

April received her wish. Five days before Christmas, in the year of 1840, April gave birth to a 7 lb., 2 oz. baby boy. She named him Samuel Joseph. Jewel picked the name of Samuel, to honor his father. April picked the name Joseph, to honor the slave. April told Jewel it was her great grandfather's name. He had smiled and told her it was a fine name. He never knew anything different.

The slaves felt respect and love for her. In her own way, she had avenged Joseph's death, and his name received new life. She would call the baby Samuel; the slaves always called him Massa Joseph.

Chapter 24

April's Family Begins

Samuel was a wonderful baby. From the moment of his birth, he never gave April anything but joy. The doctor had been amazed at the easy delivery, yet he still made her lay in bed for weeks before he allowed her to get up.

Cecil was a great comfort to April. She'd had a baby not long after her marriage to Henry, but he died with the fever when he was one year old. Henry was sold to another plantation, and they lost contact. Cecil wasn't even sure if he was still alive.

Together April and Cecil spoiled Samuel rotten. Samuel learned everything at an early age. He walked when he was only 10 months old. He never took to crawling, just stood up and started to walk on his own. Jewel loved him dearly. He had his father's light blue eyes and blonde hair, and his mother's temperament.

Jewel took Samuel horseback riding sometimes when they'd go to check the fields. He swore Samuel would make a fine horseman. He gave Samuel a pony for his first birthday. Samuel cried for hours when he couldn't bring it into the house.

Two months after Samuel turned one; April was found to be with child once again. The morning sickness returned, yet this time she wasn't frightened. She knew the cure.

Before Samuel turned two, he had a little brother. April named him Benjamin David. Benjamin proved to be different from Samuel. He was a demanding baby who never could get enough attention. Without Cecil's help, April wouldn't have been able to handle the two together. Benjamin looked just like Jewel. He even had his temper. April loved him, but Samuel loved him most. He didn't want his baby brother out of his sight.

April treasured how close her two sons were. They reminded her of May and their childhood. She knew that in the future her sons would need this great bond.

The boy's grew quickly. April's dream of filling her house with joy and laughter was coming true. Jewel controlled his drinking habits, and was kinder to April. When he did go to Charleston to drink, he would stay over night. April asked him early on not to drink around the boys. When he did he would play too rough, and she was afraid he'd hurt them.

Once they had a huge fight because Jewel felt April was turning the boys into sissies. He claimed they needed toughening up with rough play. April became like a female bear when it came to protecting her sons. Jewel proved no match for her when their welfare was concerned. So when he decided to drink, he'd just leave.

April prayed that one-day Jewel would see that she was a good woman and give her the love and respect she needed. She was the mother of his sons. Sometimes it seemed that was all she was to him.

April went to Jewel's mother to see if she could get advice on how to react to Jewel's temper and drinking.

"April, he is a grown man and has the right to drink if he so wishes. It's a wife's duty to stand by him no matter what. Jewel is just like his father. He strikes me sometimes when he's mad, but not too often. Over the years, I'll learn to take it. Once you have been joined together by God, only death can undo the ties. You'll be all right. Just give it time. Try giving in to Jewel more. Do as he asked." replied Elise, Jewel's mother.

April was shocked to learn of Jewel's mother's fate. She acted as if it were a natural part of life. April's parents had never shown violence. April felt doomed to an un-happy marriage. She prayed God would touch Jewel's angry heart.

April tried to keep everything running smoothly, not giving Jewel a reason to go into a rage. Sometimes no reason was necessary.

"You just wait, Miss April, da be's better days a coming. I promise dis be da truth. Better days will come." Cecil would tell April when she was upset.

Together Cecil and April waited for the better days.

In the year of 1844, April gave birth to her last child. She was a beautiful baby girl they named Carolyn Betty Jackson. She had April's features. Everyone who saw her swore she looked like April as a baby. The slaves had their own saying.

"Miss April done spit dat one right out."

"Cecil, I'm so happy. God has blessed me with three beautiful babies. I don't know what I'd do without you. You have become more like a friend. I'm so glad you are here to help me."

"Been my pleasure Miss April. Be bad though dat May can't be here."

April kept Carolyn dressed like a little doll. Carolyn was a quiet baby, having a sweet nature.

Not long after Carolyn's birth, Jewel regressed back into drinking heavily. Not only did April have to suffer abuse, but so did the people of the cabins. For no reason at all he'd drag one to the whipping post and give them 20 lashes.

One evening April confronted him.

"Jewel, stop this. Jake has done nothing wrong. You cannot do this."

Jewel stopped long enough to slap her into silence. The slaves waited for a signal from April to stop his aggression upon her. April began crying and ran back to the big house, leaving the others to watch Jewel's madness. She was now powerless to stop him.

One day he told April he was moving from their bedroom into one of his own. April pleaded with him not to leave their marriage bed.

"Jewel if you refuse even to talk to me, we shall never be able to repair our marriage. Jewel, I still love you. The children need to believe that we love each other. If you move downstairs, away from me, they'll know you don't love me. Please don't do this to us. We can make it, I know we can."

"I'm sick of you. You're always trying to make me give up something or the other. I am a man, do you hear me? " He began to scream and the veins in his neck protruded.

"A man does what he wants, when he wants! You are not turning me into a sissy like you are trying to do my sons. I will not stand for it. You have whimpered and whined long enough. Now I'm taking control of my life!" he said throwing things around.

He stormed around a bit more without speaking, then started again.

"This is how it should have been from the start! I will drink when I want! I will leave this house when I want! I will see other women when I want! And there is nothing you can do about it! Further more, I will take complete control over my slaves. They don't even understand the meaning of Master! They will learn, and they'll learn it from me!" yelled Jewel just inches from her face.

"Jewel, please."

"Shut up and listen. You asked me too much, and you make too many demands! I run this plantation now, you do not! I am not the wimp your father was! You are nothing but my wife! You stand behind me, not beside me!" screamed Jewel with his finger in her face.

"Until you learn that, I want nothing more to do with you! I am a man! You need to realize what that means and respect me!" finished Jewel.

April stepped back in fear that the finger would turn into a fist. She never tried to say another word. She stood against a wall and watched him storm around the room, gathering all that he decided was his. The house workers carried his things to his new room.

"I wash my hands of you! If you decide to be a decent wife, I'll come to you. Never come to me unless I send for you. Do you understand what I'm saying?" screamed Jewel again, with the workers coming in and out of the room.

April just nodded her head. There wasn't anything else she could say or do. All her dreams had just been thrown on the ground and trampled.

Chapter 25

With This Ring, I Do Wed

Lilly and May had settled into their new lives. The money left over from the purchase of their home was spent on wood to repair the many sheds that surrounded their cabin.

"Mama, doesn't this feel good. All our work now goes to making our lives better. Now we'll finally see the fruits our labor can bear. I swear through, chopping this wood is the hardest thing. Don't know how the men use to make it look easy, cause it shore ain't." May said as she swung the ax.

"You shore got dat right. But smell dat sweet wood. It shore gonna keep us warm dis winter, it shore will." Lilly said as she stack the wood in rolls.

Together they had cut down small trees and dragged them by mule to the back of the cabin. On a large existing stump, they split the large pieces to fit the fireplace.

Pennsylvania winters were cold, and it would take many cords to heat the cabin. They had packed mud into cracks that had formed between the logs of the cabin. May had climbed onto the roof and repaired the rotten pieces of wood. They'd proved to each other that they were capable of taking care of themselves. After the trip through the mountains, they knew nothing was beyond their reach.

Lilly and May joined the little church of Rev. Redbone's. It felt good to worship God without being watched over by whites. Rev. Redbone preached of a God that loved all people, a God that created people different for reasons other than hate. To his God, the color of your eyes held no more importance than the color of your skin. He preached that Jesus was a savior for all, and that he died for everyone. Through knowing his love, we could know God. By believing in his birth, life and death… we could reach heaven. By forgiving the whites and praying for freedom of the slaves… we would all be saved.

"Forgiving is easily said, but hard to mean." May thought to herself.

The stares May received that first Sunday overwhelmed her. Children where frightened when they'd glimpsed her scar. Then next Sunday morning Rev. Redbone asked her to share her story with the members. She agreed, hoping it would help others to accept her.

May told of her relationship with April, the lye soap burning, and her life at the cabins.She shared April's parents death, her call back to the big house, and their eventually gift of freedom. She finished with the trip through the mountains and finding the freedom cabin.

In closing, she asked for everyone to pray that one day she could forgive April for her suffering. Many of the members had tears in their eyes as they listen.

When May finished she pulled the hair back that covered the scar so all could finally see the result of the burning. Little gasps could be heard.

Lilly got up and went to the front of the church and embraced the now crying May. Bearing her scar for all to see was the hardest and bravest event of her life. Then everyone began leaving their pews and walking up to May. They took turns hugging her and biding her welcome to her new home.

May never had experience so much love and acceptance. She'd shared her life with everyone, and by doing so she'd become part of them.

Lilly began to notice the Rev. Redbone was spending more time visiting them.

"I's thanks dat Rev. Redbone got a eye for someone in dis here house. I's purdy shore it ain't me. Whats you thanks May?" said Lilly with a smile.

"I believer Rev. Redbone is out to save souls. I don't think his visits mean anymore than that. Why would a good looking man like him be interested in a scar face like me?" said May as she wiped the flour off her face. She and Lilly were preparing biscuits for the evening meal because Rev. Redbone was coming.

"Well, I's do know a little bout men folks, and I's thanks dat thar man's wants to see someone in dis here house. And dat shore ain't me. He ain't looking just to save souls. Dat man be looking for a wife."

"Oh mama, I think you been out in the sun to long. He could court any young lady around. He don't have to settle for me, or an old coot like you. Now help me with supper, I'm hungry, and he'll be here soon." finished May as she placed the biscuits in the coals of the fire.

"Marks my word, I's not as dumb as you wants to thank. I's don't know much, but I does know men." said Lilly as she began cutting up potatoes.

May looked at her mother and started to laugh. Lilly started giggling too. May wouldn't admit it, but she was thrilled at the thought that Rev. Redbone might be interested in her.

May received a long letter in March from April. She couldn't believe what Master Jackson had done to poor Joseph. She later held the drawing of the big house and cried. Joseph had been such a gentle spirit. It was unbelievable that someone would torture him.

May read on of the madness that seemed to be brewing in Master Jackson's soul. She felt sorry for April for the second time in her life. She'd tried to warn her. The apple doesn't fall far from the tree.

April opened her heart to May, and told her of the pain that had came into her life. She wrote of thinking about pushing Jewel down the steps. May thought it might have been the best thing April could have done.

May felt her letters from April were private, and kept them in a wooden box she hid under her bed. She shared with Lilly some of the contents but not all.

On a bright beautiful day in the middle of April, Rev. Redbone invited himself to supper.

"Lilly, I've something important to say to you. I'd be happy to come to dinner with you and May, if you'd like."

"Why shore, supper will be at 6:00. We fix ya up someum good."

May was happy for her mother, but a little jealous. She had hoped he had a little interest for her, but her mother deserved to be happy.

"What was I thinking. Men want to be proud of their woman, no one could be proud of me. I let mama led me on. It's her he wants," she thought to herself.

Looking at her mama she realized she wasn't that much older than her. Lilly had very good skin, and a nice body. You couldn't see age in her face; she looked fresh and young. No wonder Rev. Redbone was attracted to her. Maybe he really was looking for a wife. Lilly had never been married and deserved to be happy. May tried to feel happy for her.

"Here I've been pretending my scars weren't visible, and he saw through them. How could I be so foolish?" she thought.

The meal they prepared that night turned out perfect. Rev. Redbone praised their efforts and thanked them for such a fine dinner. Living by himself he didn't cook often. He said the main reason was he couldn't cook.

Lilly and May both laughed.

"You may think I'm kidding, but I tell you this is true. Once I tried to cook a big meal, it all looked pretty good but tasted bad. So I fed it to my dog. Well, my dog almost died." he said pulling away from the table and leaning back in his chair.

"Now every time that dog sees me in the kitchen with pots and pans, he runs outside. Can't say I blame him much. I'm afraid of eating my cooking too." finished Rev. Redbone laughing at himself. Lilly and May were rolling in laughter at the thought of the dog running out of the house when he tried to cook. They could just imagine that old dog making a beeline for the door.

It was a dark and wonderful night, so they all decided to go outside and sit under the stars. It seemed like God was putting on a show for them. They could clearly see all the star groups and the little and Big Dipper. They talked of how runaway slaves always followed the drinking gourd to find north. The stars glowed and made the night seem like magic. They saw three separate stars shoot across the sky.

They sat there enjoying the evening and sharing stories. Each would try to top the other by telling a funnier story, or more dramatic one than the others did.

May decided to excuse herself after a while. She knew Rev. Redbone wanted to speak in private to her mother Lilly.

"Well, it's getting late. I best go in now. I've got a lot of things to do tomorrow. You two enjoy the evening. I'm sure you both have a lot to talk about. See you in the morning mama." said May as she got up to go inside.

Just then, the Reverend grabbed her arm. "Please, don't go in yet May. I need to ask your mother something very important, and it will involve you too." he spoke gently.

May felt the blood rushing to her face. She didn't think she could handle the Reverend asking her mother to marry him. She had feelings for him the first time she laid eyes on him, the first time he came to the church door.

She sat back down in her chair, and looked at her mother. Her mother looked so happy. She wanted to feel joy for her, but felt her own heart breaking. Tears began to form in her eyes, with no way to stop them. She thanked God for the darkness; maybe they couldn't see her pain.

"I don't really know how I'm going to say this, so I'll just start with things you probably don't know about me." said Redbone as he nervously rubbed his hands.

"I was engaged to be married once, to a wonderful woman named Molly Few. She died two weeks before our marriage from the fever. I've never had feelings for another woman after she died. It's been years. I thought God would never place another in my heart. But the day you both came riding up, everything changed. Now I have a woman that I know God has sent me. It's why I've come here so often, just to be close to her. I'm afraid I'm in love. When I get up in the morning, she's all I see. I'm not a man of great wealth, but I'm a good man."

Redbone got up and walked towards Lilly and took her hands then knelled at her feet.

May begin to tremble. She should be happy for her mother, but the pain was too great. The pain was worse than the day of the burning. The pain was within her very soul.

"Lilly I'm begging you, if May would allow, to one day consider my hand in marriage, to your daughter May." he finished as he looked longingly at May.

"Well glory be," said Lilly. "It's bout time you asked. I's thought you'd neber get round to it. I's been telling dat girl you had eyes for her. I's knows it shore weren't me. I's had you pick for my sons and law since first seen ya May, what's you feels bout Reverend standing here. You thanks you'd grow to love him. He shore seems to love you."

May sat there staring at the Reverend. He walked over to her and bent onto one knee looking into May's face. He then pushed the hair from her scar that she kept hidden and stoked her face. May leaned her cheek towards his hand and closed her eyes.

"May," he spoke softly, "Is there any hope for this love sick man who is before you now. Do you think you'd ever love me? I can't get you out of my mind. Please allow me to court you, and with time, maybe you will share the same love."

With that, Lilly stood to excuse herself. As with custom, he'd asked her permission first to court May. Now it was up to May to decide.

"I's better go in now, for I start bawling. All dis love stuff is gitten to me." she said as she wiped the tears in the corner of her eyes. Lilly thought if anyone deserved to be loved, it was her beautiful daughter May.

"Do you mean it." she whispered. "What about my face, my scars?"

"What scars?" asked the Reverend as he moved closer and his lips softly touched May's. It was the first time she had ever been kissed, the first time she'd been touched by a man, the first time she'd ever been in love.

Chapter 26

The Broom Jumping

May was swept away with all the attention she received. They talked for hours when they were together. She found out he was of mixed blood. His mother was full blood Choctaw Indian. His father and grandparents were the first freed slaves in his family. His people were from New Orleans, Louisiana.

"When my grandfather was a child he was sold at the slave markets of New Orleans. His mother was sold to a plantation in Georgia, and he never saw her again. My grandfather was sold to a plantation in New Orleans. I know this is hard to believe, but my father and grandfather received their freedom in a poker bet," said the reverend.

"In a poker bet? How in the world did that come about." May said watching his facial expression.

"Grandfather's master was a big gambler. He lost all his money one eventful evening to an English man he was playing against. The English man placed a bag of gold and all his earnings on the table. The master was eager to win the bag of gold and his money back.

The English man told him he would consider anything of value in the game. The master put my grandparents and my father up as a counter bet. The English man asked to see them, and they were sent into the room. He excepted."

"Don't stop now. Tell me more. If he won them, how did they become free?" May said completely caught up in the tale.

"To my grandparents surprise, the master lost the game. The master said he didn't have a bill of sale to pay off his human bet, but the Englishman did. The master then signed them over to him. When the papers were signed, the Englishman pulled out another group of papers. It was freedom papers. He then signed them, and handed them freedom papers and two pieces of gold to move north." he said acting out the papers being given.

"My father said the master began cussing up a storm and slung his chair against the wall. He ran out of the room as if it were on fire, shaking his fist at the Englishman. The Englishman told them his name was Hillsberry and that he found slavery in any form disgusting. He took great pleasure in winning at poker and being able to free men from time to time. He bid them farewell and left. They stood watching him leave in a state of shock. That night they slept in the woods, and purchased a wagon and mule the next day. They left New Orleans with only the clothes on their backs."

The story had May and Lilly on the edge of their seats. They begged him to tell more.

"How'd you git Indian blood?" Lilly asked.

"How did you get to Pennsylvania. What is your Christian name? Where did the name Redbone come from?" May ask.

He laughed at their many questions. He'd never thought to tell her his first name. He was so used to being called reverend, and it had been a while since he heard his name.

"My Christian name is Phillip. I'm sorry I didn't tell you sooner. It's been a long time since anyone has wanted to know. As for the rest of the story, my father and mother met when he was staying with her tribe in Clarksdale, Mississippi. My grandparents and father became deathly ill on their journey north. The Choctaw Indians took them in and nursed them back to health. When father first met mother, he fell in love, like I did May." said Philip as he reached over and touched May's hand.

"Within a month, my parents had fallen deeply in love. When they were well and needed to leave, she pleaded not to be left behind. The tribe agreed to let them marry as long as he honored Indian ways. They were joined together in an Indian ceremony, which was said to join together two souls. They began their journey again and they traveled through Tennessee, Kentucky, Ohio and Pennsylvania. They settled in Harrisburg. That's where they still live." finished Philip

Lilly loved this story and wanted to hear it over and over again. It was if she were pretending it was her history and she needed to remember every detail. Philip was kind enough to feed her all he knew. He told her of some of the Indian ways he was brought up with.

"Mother will be glad to share more information with you when she arrives for the wedding. She can tell you of other tribes. She knows of most of them."

"You telling me da be just like Africans and have bunches of tribes. Well glory be, hows you like dat. I's gonna like your mama, yesiree." she exclaimed.

Lilly hoped the Choctaw woman would be her friend. She never knew an Indian before.

"We were a Christian home, but we kept mama's traditions. I lived comfortably in both worlds. When I was a young child, I felt the call to preach. I wanted to spread the word and help those in need. I always wanted a church for all God's people. We all belong to the same God, no matter what we call him. I came to Philadelphia to finish my schooling and saw a need for a black church here. God led me to the one I'm in now. Just as he led you both to me," he said with a smile on his lips and a twinkle in his eyes.

Philip and May decided the wedding would be on July 16,1841. It would be a great celebration for it was also the two-year anniversary of her gift of freedom. She was now 19 years old. As soon as the date was decided, Lilly began her campaign for grandbabies. She would walk around the cabin talking about their arrival.

"When my grands git here, dey's gonna be some changes around dis place." Lilly said dancing around the house.

"Dey be coming fore you knows it. I's can't wait to see dem. Dey shore is gonna love dis here free gal. My grands ain't gonna be no man's slaves. Norsiree. No, not dem."

May laughed at her mama. She realized her mama was young enough to have more children. All Lilly seemed to talk about was her coming grands. The way she carried on, you would think she already knew each one by name.

"Mama, just how many grands are you counting on. Philip and I aren't even married yet," she asked with a smile.

"Oh, just a whole cabin full. Dats right, a cabin full of grands!" she smiled stretching her harms out wide.

May and Lilly both fell to the floor laughing. Lilly had gone nuts on the idea of being a grandma.

"I's just got me one child. Everybody needs more dan one. Two boys and two girls, datta work for me." holding up four fingers.

"If you want more, have more. There's nothing wrong with you."

"Nope, it be your turn. I's just watch. Sides, I's ain't got no mans. You do." she said with a smile. Lilly was 32 years old.

May wanted the wedding to be outside. She wanted it out near the land she had grown to love, the land she worked with her bare hands. Chairs were brought from various homes and the church. They were set up facing the cornfield in the back of the cabin and sheds.

Flowers were sat out on tables that were brought for the reception. One of the ministers from the city, who went to college with Philip, was performing the ceremony. May made a lovely dress by hand. It was a long off white dress with white lace around the collar. The lace was in the pattern of small flowers linked together by a continuous vein. The dress felt smooth and soft, like a new baby's skin.

When May tried on the finished dress and placed the baby breath flowers in her hair, Lilly began to cry. Once again May's beauty was undeniable.

"May, you is beautiful. Ain't neber thought any of dis would ever happen. We's blessed May, we's blessed."

"I know mama.... I know."

Philips parents and grandparents arrived for the wedding two days prior. Lilly attached to them like they were her own kinfolk. She enjoyed Philip's mother most of all. They would talk for hours of their past. Lilly couldn't get enough of the tales of the Choctaw Indians and Izetta yearned to learn of plantation life.

Izetta's Indian name was Morning Star. She had taken the name Izetta from a missionary she liked who visited her tribe. She thought it sounded very white. Before Izetta left to go home, Lilly had her raving about future grandbabies. They both had now joined in the campaign. This made everyone laugh.

Guest began arriving for the wedding. Each had brought food to join in the celebration. The food was carefully laid out on the tables according to the variety. Lilly felt it was a "Mini Jubilee."

Philip walked up to the front to stand near the minister and waited for his bride. A light breeze was visible as it stoked the cornfields and made them come alive with motion. It was a calming effect, looking like waves on an ocean. The chairs had been set out in neat rolls with a walkway down the center. The whole church was there, and every chair was taken.

May walked down the center alone. Philip could barely hold back his emotions, watching her every move. She walked with grace and dignity, as if she were a Queen.

Her smile lit up her eyes, and the scar on her face seemed to disappear. She was stunning. Philip heart was full of love and desire for her. When she reached his side, he took both of her hands. He had to fight off the desire to grab her and press his body close to hers. His heartbeat quicken knowing that she would soon be his.

The minister began:

"We are gathered here today, in this beautiful display of God's world, to join together this man and woman in holy matrimony. This couple have declared their love for each other, and have made the decision to become one. One half is no greater than the other. They both have traveled different journey's to come to this point in time. God's will is not understood, but leads us where we need to be. I ask all here to pray for the happiness of this union, and to let it be fruitful."

"A men to dat." Lilly said out loud.

Everyone giggled.

"Let no man try to take apart that which is joined in the God's eyes." he then turned to Philip.

"Do you take this woman to be your wife forever more. To love and cherish above all others. In sickness and in health. Till death do you part?"

"In front of God and all those present here today, I do take thee May, as my beautiful wife." he said with tears welling in his eyes.

May 's tears were beginning to fall from her cheeks. It had been a long time since anyone had called her beautiful... and meant it.

"Do you take this man to be your husband forever more? To love and cherish above all others, in sickness and in health. Till death do you part?" he asked.

"With my heart full of love and joy, I do."

"Philip, you may now give the ring proving you great love for May."

"With this ring, I do Wed." then he gently slipped it onto her finger.

"May, would you now give the ring proving your love for Philip." he said.

"With this ring, I promise my love." she said as she pushed it on his finger.

"I now pronounce you man and wife. You may now kiss your bride." he finished closing the bible.

Philip took May into his arms and gently kissed her lips. He pulled away and smiled then pulled her to him again and kissed her once more.

They both stood smiling and facing the guest with tears on their faces.

Lilly had spent two days making and decorated a broom for their wedding ceremony. They all had decided it was necessary for their marriage.

"I ask you both now to hold hands and jump your marriage broom. This is done to honor our ancestor's and our people in bondage. Let us never forget that from hence we come to this great land. The broom is a symbol of starting a new life. Once the jump is made you have swept out the old life and your new life begins."

Philip and May both were laughing as they joined hands and jumped into their new lives. Everyone stood and applauded. Lilly even let out a shout of joy.

"Praise da lord."

After the wedding, the party began. People had brought their instruments and after eating they began to play. Music, laughter and the sweet smell of flowers filled the air. Everyone joined in on the dancing. The small children would dance with grownups by standing on their feet. Lilly got bold enough to ask Philip's minister friend for a dance. Philip had urged her to. The party went on for hours. It was one of the best days in May's life. When the party was over, Philip and May left for the city. They were spending a couple of days in a hotel for their honeymoon. Lilly stayed with his parents until they departed. She made plans to visit them the following spring.

"I's be coming to see ya." she said as they loaded into the wagon.

Lilly and Izetta cried at her departure. They were kindred spirits and felt a great connection to each other.

"Lilly, I 'm glad to know you. I'll wait for your visit. You remember more stuff to tell me then, okay."

"You betcha I's will. I's will indeed."

When Philip and May returned, Lilly went to stay with a widow woman from their church. She was planning on staying only for a few weeks, but liked it so much, she stayed.

"Y'all needs to be alone, and I's need to act available. I's reckon maybe I's git me a man too." she said with a sly grin.

"Oh mama!" May laughed.

Lilly came every day to help them tend the fields. She loved to haul the vegetables to market in the city. She enjoyed meeting with the other farmers and received far prices for her efforts. She'd carry the money back to May, and received her share. They now divided the money into thirds.

Lilly got her wish. Her first grandchild came 10 months after the wedding in the month of May. She had a beautiful baby girl she named Alicia Delane.

A midwife was used for the delivery. A doctor had been notified in case anything went wrong. Alicia had been an easy delivery. The only one excited and needed to be controlled was Lilly.

"De here. Oh lordy, de here. Whats I's gonna do. Is I ready." she said as she ran around trying to assist the midwife.

"Lilly, if you don't calm down, you gonna give yourself a heart attack. Your grandbaby is on the way, and you'll do just fine. Now bring me some clean towels and more warm water." the midwife said as she hurried about carrying for May. She spoke quickly with no sign of an accent.

"It be a girl May." Lilly called out as soon as the final push was over. "I done got me a grand daughter. Thank ye sweet Jesus, thank ye."

"Philip, do you see her. Is she all right." May said trying to lean up to glance the child.

Philip took her from the midwife and laid her in May's arms.

"She's as beautiful and perfect as her mother." he said leaning down to kiss May's forehead. "Are you all right my love?" he said softly.

"I have never felt this way before. I feel like God has personally laid a gift into our arms. One I never thought I'd receive. Thank you Philip. Thank you for loving me."

"The pleasures all mine." he said as he kissed her lips.

"Now hush dat mushy stuff, and let me git a good look at dat grand. My, she looks just like me, don't ya'll thank." she said smiling at them both.

They both laughed and agreed.

Lilly moved back in to help care for the baby. She had a problem in the beginning of not wanting to ever leave Delane alone. At the least whimper, Lilly would rush to her side.

"Mama, you're gonna spoil that child rotten. Why in the earth don't you let her fuss sometimes? It won't hurt her, and she's wearing us out."

"She shore ain't wearing me out. Shore ain't."

Lilly's idea of constant attention on Delane changed the following year with the birth of their second child. He was named John Anthony. The year was 1843.

"Can't let y'all spoil dis one. Dat girl bout wore me out. Ain't gonna spoil dis one." Lilly said as she held her grandson. Delane was crying in her room upstairs. They all laughed knowing who had spoiled who. Izzeta came to help after each child was born. Lilly and her together where a site to see. They bickered over who was the best grandma as they held the newborn.

Together the infants proved to be a hand full. When they were cropping, they tied the children in slings on their backs. May took turns nursing them under a shade tree on a stump. All three worked hard to get the small farm going. The growing seasons was shorter than in the south, for the fall frost came too soon and winter lingered.

When Anthony turned two, May gave birth to her second son. They named him Thomas Wesley. He was a chubby baby full of life and more curious than the others were. He always had his fingers in something when he learned to walk at 11 months.

"Lordy May, you done had us a fast one. Dis child is shore a curious fellow. He seems to have more dan two hands. Lordy, gib me strength."

Lilly's dream of having a cabin full of grands was coming true, and it was more than she bargained for. Izetta came for only one month at a time, the rest was hers.

In the year of 1846, May gave birth to her last child. They named him Joshua Joel. It had been a troubled birth, and the doctor was needed in the delivery. Joshua was very weak and they feared he might not survive. Philip and Lilly sat up with him night and day. May was weak from the complicated birth, and from losing too much blood. She had been given a pint of her mother's blood in an emergency transfusion after Joshua's birth.

"Dear father, don't take her." Philip had called out several times as the doctor worked on her.

"Take me Lord, I's ready. Leave dem both." Lilly had said.

It took four days before May was able to sit up in bed. It was decided all precautions would be made to keep her from bearing another birth. The cabin was full.

May was happy in her new life. The children kept them all busy. May yearn to share her life with April, and did so through her letters. May wrote April after each birth and shared the details of her children. The letters she received from April seemed to prove her life had become a living hell. April's children were all the happiness she knew.

Chapter 27

Carolyn, April's Joy

April was deceived by a clever man. The children were her saving grace. When alone at night April would cry for the love that would never be hers. April was beginning to believe he had just wanted her plantation and the children. Now he had them both.

Jewel was a good father. She knew Jewel was capable of compassion and love. She would see him playing and talking with the children, and sometimes she tried to join them. When she entered the room he would become silent and excuse himself.

"What are you doing? Can mama join?" she asked.

"Well, that's enough of this. I've got things to do. You children be good now." getting up and walking past April as if she wasn't there.

Jewel acted like the very site of her was repulsive.

Once April reached out to touch his arm as he left the room. He quickly jerked away from her.

"Why Jewel, why?" she asked herself.

One thing was certain, Carolyn was Jewel's little girl. He showered her with affection. April felt cheated that he held none for her, but never let this affect her love for Carolyn. Jewel worshipped the ground Carolyn walked on. When the buggy rode into town, Carolyn would usually be with him. The boys would beg to go, but Jewel only had room for Carolyn.

"Sweet Carolyn, where are you? I'm home." he'd call out when walking in from the fields.

If Carolyn heard him call, she would run like the wind to him. Carolyn was always eager to see him. To her he was loving and kind. He showered her with surprises and love.

"Papa!" she'd cry out. "Hold me, Papa."

April yearned to be part of his life and to share the joy of having the children with him.

She'd pray that May had found happiness. By the letters she received she felt this to be true. May's letters were full of stories of her children and the love of her husband.

April and the children loved to roam the woods near the plantation. Sometimes they'd venture into the swamps with the canoes that were kept there. April loved to share the stories of her childhood with May. They would beg to hear the stories because many were funny. The woods had been one of their favorite places as children.

"Once May and I climbed a tree trying to see who could go the highest. May won, but I was only one branch under her. We were so excited about climbing that we didn't think about coming down." April said with her eyes widened showing the fear.

"When we looked down we were terrified. You see that tall tree over there." she said pointing to a tall Oak tree. "We were almost at the top. We started yelling for help, but no one could hear us. It was then we saw the bugs. We hadn't noticed them on the way up, but sitting still, we saw them. They had little black bodies with red heads and were crawling all over us. We would knock them off, but more came. It was then we decided we had to try to climb down."

April said as they walked closer to the tree. "May climbed down to my limb and then together we came down one limb at a time. It was scary. I started crying and May got mad."

"Ain't no use in crying now. It was your dumb idea to climb up high. You can't cry and climb down at the same time, so you stay here and cry. I'm going down."

"May you better not leave me in this tree. Wait for me. I'm coming." I told her.

"I don't know how long we were in that tree, but when we got home our clothes were dirty and torn. Mother was mad as a hornet at us. She said she'd skin us alive if we ever acted so foolish again. We didn't know it was dangerous, we just thought it would be fun. Now y'all don't get any ideas, May and I were lucky not to get hurt."

They were now standing under the tree and looking up.

"I'd never try that. Mama, you telling us the truth? You climbed this tree?" said Samuel, who was now seven years old, as he pointed up to the top.

"Yep, sure did."

April loved to take the children to the beach. They would take the plantation ferry to a small strip of beach not far from their home. Cecil always went with April to help her. The children loved playing in the waves and building things in the sand. They'd take a lunch and would eat it on a cover thrown onto the sand. They'd spend hours there laughing and talking. Once Samuel asked April a question that broke her heart.

"Mama, why don't daddy love you?"

April didn't have an answer.

Jewel loved his boys, but showered all his affections on Carolyn. When the boys grew older they began to notice it more, and tried to get their father attention. He would become annoyed when the boys begged him to play with them. If they pushed him too far, they would be spanked.

Old Bald William was all the children's favorite. He walked with the help of a cane, holding it with both hands. When he'd see the children, he would smile from ear to ear. He loved to sit and carve them wooden toys. They would watch him as he told them old stories of animals that talked and acted much like humans. April remembered William as an old man when she was young, she thought he must be near 100 years old. He hadn't been able to work the fields in a long time. When the children saw him coming they'd run to greet him.

"Grandpa William." they'd call out. All the children on the plantation called him Grandpa.

"Grandpa, how old are you?" Benjamin asked.

"Don't reckon I know. Best to dis memory, I's could be's a hundred, maybe eben more. Des old bones done worked hard. Dey be tired all de times. I's still glad to be here though."

April had overheard him speaking to the children.

"I'm glad you're still here. I know all the children love you." she said as she patted his back and smiled.

"I's loves dem too. All of em."

It was the summer of 1850 and berry-picking season. April and Cecil promised the children they would go pick berries the next day. They had seen many berry patches the week before in the woods, but they hadn't ripened. With the summer heat, they would be ripe.

The children's metal pail and gloves had been laid out on the hall table in preparation. The next day, after their chores, they were going.

"Jewel, would you spend some time with us tomorrow. We are going to pick wild berries. The children would like it."

"I've no time for such nonsense, got things to do in Charleston. I'll be taking the plantation ferry tomorrow. I'll be home late."

The next morning the children got up early, eager to go.

April remembered the time Cecil and her heard them picking berries and pretending to be slaves. They would softly moan and sing the songs they'd heard the others sing. When the children realized it amused Cecil and April, they sang loudly with more feeling. Cecil and April laughed at their playacting.

The children went running into the hall to get their pails and gloves.

"Let's go before the sun heats up the day. Benjamin, Samuel, where's Carolyn?" she asked looking around the room. "Her pail and gloves are gone. Where is she?"

"I thought she was with both of you. I heard her in your room. When did she get her things?" April asked.

"She must be hiding mama," said Samuel. "You know that's her favorite game. I bet you we can find her fast if we spread out. Benjamin and I will look upstairs; y'all look down here. Beat you upstairs," yelled Samuel as he raced up the stairs with Benjamin in hot pursuit.

Cecil and April looked in every room downstairs, even behind furniture. Carolyn's name seemed to be echoing in the house as they called it, and begged her to come out. The other house workers helped in the search.

"Carolyn, you win, we give up. Come out so we can go!" yelled Benjamin in the now quiet house.

"Carolyn, this is not funny. You come out this very instant!" April called in a loud voice.

"Mama, something is wrong. Carolyn would have come out the moment we said she won," said Samuel. "She's not here."

"Oh my Lord, where is she! Did she go out by herself?" no one in the house had seen her leave. Cecil ran down to the cabins, no one had seen her there either.

"Miss April, no one has seen her since yesterday."

"Well, I put her to bed last night. She was here early this morning." April said biting her nails.

"Mama, she came to wake us up when papa was up. We heard them talking after she left the room. She didn't shut our door. He was in her room." Samuel said.

"That's where she's at mama. She's with papa. You know she goes with him a lot. Let's go and leave her. We don't need her help anyway." Benjamin grabbed his pail and headed for the door.

"You're right. She would have pitched a fit to go with him. He was probably in her room helping her pick out an outfit. Your father will be the death to me yet. I nearly had a heart attack thinking she wandered off. No telling what would have happened to her." April said while leaning exhausted on the hall table.

"We'll go pick berries tomorrow when she's back. You two go out and play before it gets to hot." April said with a weary smile.

"That's not fair! Carolyn always gets her way. I wish I didn't have a dumb sister. She's nothing but trouble!" Samuel pouted as he stomped out of the door to play.

Benjamin copied him word for word, and stomped out right behind him.

"My boys tickle me to death the way they copy each other." April said shaking her head. "You'd think they were twins. Don't you agree?" she said as she turned to look at Cecil.

"Yes em, I's shore do. I glad she be with her pappy. I's feels like tanning her hide for giving us such a scare. You ought not to be letting her do you dat way

Miss April. Master Jackson should done told you he take her too." Cecil said as she folded her arms looking out the door as the boys played. They were swinging on the swing that Grandpa William had made them. It was a wooden board tied to two long ropes attached to a large limb. Grandpa William had field hands climb the tree to hang it.

"When I get a hold of her, she won't have plans of ever doing this again. She's only six years old, and I need to know her whereabouts," finished April as she wiped the sweat that was already forming on her brow. It was going to be an another hot day.

It was late evening when Samuel came running down the stairs yelling that he saw buggy lanterns coming down the lane. All four of them went running outside to greet Jewel and his wayward daughter.

"What brings this great welcoming to a tired and weary man." Jewel said as he pulled the buggy into the drive.

"Where's Carolyn daddy? We're going to beat her up for messing up our day. Is she asleep in the back?" Benjamin asked as he ran to see for himself.

"Mama," screamed Benjamin, "she's not here. Where's my sister daddy?" he yelled up to his father.

"What on earth are you talking about. Carolyn is not with me! I kissed her good-bye this morning in her room. She's been here all day.... hasn't she?" demanded Jewel to April as he jumped off the buggy.

When April realized Carolyn wasn't with her father, she became dizzy. Her precious little girl was gone...and had been gone all day long. April fainted when the truth hit her. Jewel just let her hit the ground.

Cecil bent down to April with tears rolling down her cheeks as she helped April back to her feet.

"Don't worry Miss April, we's gonna finds dat child. She' be all right, you'll see. Everythang gonna be fine. Da Massa here now, he gonna take over. She's be out there somewhere. We's find her. Come on, git yourself together, we got to find her... and soon." Cecil said as she helped April back towards the big house.

The boys followed her.

Jewel jumped on his horse, and rode to the cabins to get some men to help in the search. He told them to bring lanterns and torches and spread out starting from the big house. He wanted every inch of land searched until his daughter was found. Jewel then rode to his father's plantation for more help. It was the night of a full moon.

Before the night ended more than four hundred slaves were out searching for Carolyn. Jewel and his father were leading the search party. At daybreak, more men arrived. M. J. Perry had rode all night telling everyone of the missing child.

That entire day people came to help. Finally there were so many people out searching you couldn't count them. On the third day of searching, some of Carolyn's things were found. Her metal pail, gloves, and bonnet... all covered in blood. The pail still had black berries in it.

The ponds on the plantation were dragged, the swamps were searched, and bloodhounds from Charleston were used. For a solid week the search continued, but Carolyn's body was never found.

April blamed herself for not knowing she wasn't with her father. The boys blamed themselves for wishing they had no sister. Jewel blamed April.

"I wish it were you that was dead!" he screamed. "You have always been unfit as a mother and a wife." Jewel said as he spit on the ground in front of April when walking by her. April lay down on the ground and covered her face and cried.

Cecil was the only one who believed Carolyn was not dead.

"Iffin a body ain't found, den a death ain't happen. Dat child still breathes and lives. I knows it in my heart." thought Cecil as she helped April off the ground and into her room.

Chapter 28

The Hanging

Two weeks after the disappearance of Carolyn, Jewel decided that she had been murdered. He also decided one of his slaves murdered her. Jewel was bound and determined to find the one who did it. For the next week he beat over two-dozen men, trying to get a confession of murder. After three weeks, he decided someone would have to hang for Carolyn's murder.

Jewel decided it was Old Bald William. He told April and the boys of his plans for revenge. They cried and begged him not to, knowing there was no possible way William could have committed such a crime.

"Jewel, you don't know what you're saying. He loves our children as much as they love him. He would have never taken her life. He can barely walk on his on. He loved her."

As soon as the last words came out of her mouth, Jewel was upon her with his fist flying in the air as he pounding her body. All the rage of Carolyn's uncertain fate was released upon April. It was the first time the boys had seen him beat her. They jumped on his back, pleading for him to stop.

"Daddy, stop! Don't kill her! Daddy stop... you're killing mama!" they both cried out as they struggled to help April.

Jewel was like a madman. He threw his sons off and they hit the wall. He continued beating on April until the rug she was lying on was splattered with blood. Jewel jumped off her and spat at her face.

"Don't you ever claim a child of mine would love a slave. The only fool that could is you, Miss Cothran. It is because of you that my daughter is dead. I regret the day I married you. Why don't you just lie there and die." screamed Jewel as he turned and left the room.

The boys had huddled together and watched in terror after their father threw them against the wall. When he left they ran over to their mother.

"Help..." they both screamed. "Somebody help... mother is dying."

They ran for Cecil and the other workers in the house.

"Our mother is bleeding. Daddy tried to kill her. Please come help!" cried Samuel when he found them. They had gathered in the kitchen knowing they couldn't stop the master's madness.

Cecil gasped when she saw April lying on the bloody rug with her head on Benjamin's lap. Her face had begun to swell.

"Oh my Lordy, what dat man done to her. Quick boys, go git more help. Tell dem brings me sheets and towels. Gits da mens to bring me water. Go git em now." yelled Cecil as she turned April over to remove her bloody dress.

"Hang on child, Cecil is wif you now. Everythang gonna be all right. We ain't gonna let you die too. I's send for the doc," finished Cecil as she pulled the top of the dress down and saw the many red bruises. Broken blood vessels were visible in many of them.

April came to long enough to tell her not to send for the doctor. She didn't want Jewel in trouble. As long as her boys were all right, that's all that mattered.

Cecil shook her head in disbelief. With the help of the others, April was cleaned up and placed in her bed. Her lip had been busted open and was swollen so badly it touched her nose. Her nose continued to bleed and was beginning to swell. She was covered in bright red circles where his fist had pounded. Both her eyes were swollen almost totally shut. A man couldn't have taken the beating she just had.

The beating had taken place that morning and it was late afternoon when April started coming around. Cecil had taken a thread and needle to sew up the cuts above April's eyes and once again pleaded to send for the doctor. April refused.

The boys came running in her room around six that evening pleading for her to help Old William.

"Daddy's got a noose in our tree. He's going to hang him. Mama we got to help!' they cried. "He's gone to get him now."

"Run down to Mr. Perry's. Tell him we need help. Tell him your daddy's gone mad, and to get here quick." April said as she struggled to get up.

The boys ran for Mr. Perry as Cecil tried to get April out of bed.

"Cecil, I've got to get out there. Maybe I can still stop him."

"Lord child, da devil be in dat man. You can't stop him."

Mr. Perry came riding up on his horse to the tree where all the slaves had been gathered. William was sitting up on a horse, with a noose around his neck.

"Mr. Jackson, you know good and well this here slave ain't hurt your daughter. I understand your anger sir, but you are wrong by doing this. You need to let him go." Mr. Perry said in a calming voice trying to talk sense into Jewel.

"You don't tell me what I should do. It ain't your child that was killed. It was mine. You don't back off; I'll kill you both. Him with a noose, and I'll blow you head off." Jewel said as he pulled out his pistol aiming it at him. Mr. Perry backed up on his mount.

Samuel and Benjamin clung to their mother's shirt and begged her not to let their papa kill William.

"Jewel please, listen to reason. He loved her."

"Massa Jackson, please don't kills me. I's loves dem babies of yours. I'd neber harm a hair on da head. Not one hair I tells you. I's help all I's could trying find Carolyn. I's loves her Massa. I's loves her." cried William as he spoke with tears streaming down his wrinkled face.

"I bet you loved her. You're not fooling me. You loved her all right. You loved her to death. Now you going to pay with your life, you filthy slave." he said loudly wanting to bring fear to all that watched.

All the others were crying out and begging to take William's place. Jewel didn't listen to anyone's cry for mercy. His focus was on hanging William; he wanted revenge.

There was a horrible sound of a loud and hard slap on the horse's backside. The horse bolted from his place under the noose. A loud snap was heard and then silence. William's body was swinging back and forth in the tree. The swing that William had made for the children was swinging empty back and forth from the force of the hanging on the limb.

After a few moments the air was filled with a loud weeping. Tears were seen falling off the face of the now hanging William.

The last words uttered from William's lips before the horse fled were, "I's truly loves dem young'uns. I's loves Carolyn da mostis."

Chapter 29

The Letter

In September of 1850 May received a long letter. She knew something terrible had happened. May asked Lilly and Philip to watch the children and went outside to read the letter in private. The letter began;

Dearest May,

I need to share with you this nightmare I'm in. My sweet Carolyn is gone. I believe she may be dead. My sorrow is so deep, I find there is no end to it. We had planned to spend a day picking berries with the children, Cecil and I. They knew how that years ago you and I use to pick fresh berries every summer. For the past five years, it's been a chore they look forward to. We always carried a lunch, and made a day of it.

When it was time to go, we couldn't find Carolyn. My son Samuel told me he thought she left with Jewel. We waited until he arrived home that evening, and discovered she wasn't with him. It was horrible. I realized my daughter had been in the woods all day, alone. The burden of this is more than I can take. I will never have more children, for Jewel refuses to share our marriage bed. He stays in a room alone.

I don't know why he turned on me. Now he has reason to. He loved Carolyn more than anyone.

We searched for her with hundreds of others for more than a week. The only thing we found was her bonnet, pail and gloves. They were soaked in her blood. I've never stopped looking for her. I daily walk into the woods and call out her name, searching for any sign of her. Deep in my heart, I know I will never see my baby again in this life. I feel like my soul has been ripped out.

Three weeks after her disappearance, Jewel hung one of the slaves. He beat some of them before deciding whom to hang as a lesson to them all. May… it was Old Bald William. Do you remember him? He loved my children as much as the rest of them. He walked with his cane daily to see them. My children called him Grandpa William just like the others.

I begged Jewel not to harm him. He beat me in front of my boys. The boys thought he was trying to kill me.

He then hung William in the old Oak in the front yard. Mr. Perry even tried to stop him; Jewel threatened to kill him too.

I believe Jewel killed William because our children loved him. He couldn't stand that they loved a slave. He told me I ruined our children by letting them love him. He said I was a fool.

After the hanging, Jewel refused to let anyone cut William down. He sat on the porch with a musket and pistol and was drinking constantly. He was out there for three days, aiming at anyone who dared to walk too close to the tree. Everyone stayed in the cabins as much as possible. My sons refused to come out of their room. They could see William still hanging outside. I could do nothing to stop Jewel.

He wouldn't eat or sleep. He stayed outside and watched over William's body. At night he fired into the darkness. Thank God no one else was killed.

The third day was Sunday. I begged Jewel to let them cut him down. He aimed his pistol and took a shot at me. I'm lucky he was stone drunk, for he has a good aim. Right before dusk, I heard a loud commotion on the porch. I ran out to see what was happening. Mr. Perry had tackled Jewel to the ground. He was about to beat him to death. I ran over to stop him. Jewel jumped up and ran for his horse, screaming he would get revenge. Then he rode away, cussing to us both over his shoulder.

Mr. Perry and the others cut William's body from the tree. I gave them one of Jewel's best suits to bury him in. They placed him in an unmarked grave near the fields. Mr. Perry told me he would be glad to kill Jewel for me. He told me my papa would have killed him long ago. He said he'd no longer work for me. He has been on this plantation all my life; it pains me to see him leave.

He said he devised a plan to kill Jewel and carry his body out into the ocean. He would then throw his body into deep waters for the creatures of the deep. He said he would move back north, where his family lives. No one would ever find him. May, I almost told him yes. I didn't want Jewel's blood on my hands or his. If anything went wrong, we would have both been hung. He told me if I ever change my mind, go to Duffy's store. That's his cousin, and he could get a message to him. He gathered his things and left that night. Jewel was gone for two weeks. I do not know where he went, and I do not care. He came back angry. Nothing has changed. Now the boys are afraid of him. They hide from him and won't let him get near.

One night I heard weeping from Carolyn's room. I ran to the room hoping to find her sitting there. It was Jewel sitting on her bed surrounded by her dolls. He was crying like a baby. I wanted to comfort him thinking that maybe he had changed.

The moment I walked into the room, he began to scream at me and threw a china doll at me. It shattered at my feet. There is no way to reach him. He is beyond my help and love. I can never leave him, for we are bound together by God. This is hell I live in. No one knows the burden I carry. I hate my life.

I'm having a tombstone carved for Carolyn. It will bear her date of birth and that she was a loving daughter and sister. It will have angels carved into the stone looking towards heaven. On the bottom will be these words: "Suppose to be Dead." This is all I know to do.

I would give everything to see you again. Please be happy. Pray for my sons and me.

Please pray for Jewel's sanity.

Forever your sister,
April

May folded the letter and slipped it back into the envelope. She sat there for a while longer thinking of April's life. So much had changed. She wanted to go to her, but knew she couldn't. In the southern states, the moment a free slave entered the plantation of it's previous owner, they can be claimed as property. Jewel would love for her to come back.

Chapter 30

The Scent Of War

May went back to the cabin and wrote April. It took her awhile to find the right words. May's letter read;

My Dearest April,

To read your letter was to have my heart broken. I cannot imagine the pain you must be in. I will pray daily that your Carolyn is found alive. I do not understand the hatred that Jewel must harbor in his heart. April, it's not you. Jewel is a cruel man. I tried to tell you years ago. I will pray for God to touch his heart and change him. There is nothing you can do to change him. Jewel must learn he is creating the hate he feels. It exists because he wishes it so.

Do not give up April. Your boys need their mother. You have to teach them to be men. It is good that you've taught them to love.

April if I could, you know that I would be there for you now. Over the years I have been learning to let go of my pain. I cannot come back to the southern states as long as slavery exists. I do love you my sister. Hold onto your faith.

Freedom feels good,
May

May begin to spend more time with her children after she read of the disappearance of Carolyn. Wesley was the same age, and she couldn't imagine losing him to an unknown fate. To lose even one child would be more than she could take.

Six months after her last letter, she received another from April. She said Jewel had hired a new overseer that seemed to be crueler than him. Some of the slaves were beginning to run away. April said she had even thought of sending for M. J. Perry. Her sons were terrified of their father. They realized he had the power to kill, with no one restraining him from doing so. They were afraid he would turn on them.

May could think of no words to advise her. Maybe Mr. Perry did carry the only answer. May knew Master Cothran would have never allowed his slaves to be treated so cruelly. He would surely have killed him with his bare hands.

In the year of 1860, South Carolina voted to secede from the union. Philip came running into the kitchen to tell May the news.

"May, smell the air around you. Can you smell the changes coming? South Carolina pulled out of the union of the states! Do you know what that means?" asked Philip in an excited voice.

"Philip, what on earth are you talking about? Is something big about to happen? How can a state pull out of the union?"

"South Carolina don't want to give up slaves. More and more people believe it's wrong. If other southern states decide to join South Carolina, then we are going to have ourselves a war. A war that will put a end to slavery!" Philip said, then picked May up and twirled her around.

"What in the world makes you think this means war? Just cause you say it will doesn't make it so. We've heard rumors of war for years now. It's just wishful thinking to believe that whites would declare war to free blacks. There are not enough whites that would be willing to do that. Are they?" she asked confused.

"That's not the only issue, just the main one. I read that South Carolina is saying that states should be able to pull from the union by will of the people. They think the government won't protect their property, which are slaves. South Carolina has asked all southern states to join them. There will be war if that happens." he said walking back in forth in the room, talking with great excitement.

"Philip, do you really think so?"

"There's a man I been hearing about in the city. His name is Abraham Lincoln. I think he may be our next President. May, he's against slavery. He says so in speeches I've heard of. If he comes into office, he could be the Moses you say that slaves been praying for. He would have the power to free them."

"You think?"

"Everyone I talk to thinks the south is looking for a fight. If war starts, I'm going! May I feel it in my bones, changes are going to sweep across this land, and I'm going to be ready."

"Philip, stop talking of this war. You're scaring me. In war, people die. There's already enough blood in the southern soil, why spill more? Why can't our president just tell the south to free the slaves? Don't they have to listen."

"That's why South Carolina pulled out of the union. They don't want to abide by the same laws as everyone else. They want to form their own laws and be separated. That way our laws won't apply to them. You wait and see. They're probably trying to convince other southern states to join them. War's a coming May. War's a coming. I can almost smell it."

"All this talk of war is making me feel sick. I got four children to worry about, now you go talking about a war. If there is a war in the south, then poo:

April will be right in it. That's the last thing she needs. A war." May said as she laid her head down on the kitchen table.

In 1861 other southern states followed: Mississippi, Florida, Alabama, Georgia, and Louisiana. On November 6, 1860 the man named Lincoln had been elected President of the Union. On February 22, 1862 Jefferson Davis was elected as President of the Southern States. That year in the month of April the first shots of the war were fired on Fort Sumter. The War Between the States had begun.

Philip was upset when he wasn't allowed to join in the fight against the south.

"Said they weren't accepted black recruits. Doesn't make any sense. Why won't they let us fight? Guess it will be a long time before things change." Philip said shaking his head in disappointment.

Many of the free blacks had gone into Philadelphia trying to enlist, being turned away due to their race. They wouldn't be allowed to fight with whites, and no black regiments existed.

"Praise the lord, you're needed right here. If you join our boys would try to follow you. We need to have you home." May said when Philip told her.

"May, I will keep trying to enlist. I feel it's my duty to fight in this war. The south needs to be taught a lesson. The states need to stay a union as much as all men need to be free."

Chapter 31

The War Begins

The plantation had been in an uproar over all the events that had begun to take place. Many slaves had tried to run after the hanging of William. A few of them tried to escape but were recaptured. Jewel hired a new overseer that appeared to be as cruel as he was. Beatings were now an everyday event. The share of food given to the slaves was reduced to almost nothing. Jewel had destroyed their gardens when he was drunk. He wanted his slaves to depend completely on him.

April could not control his rages. Once he lined up five men in a row to be beaten. He claimed he caught them trying to steal meat from the shed it hung in.

"Jewel, please don't. They're hungry, that's why they tried to take a ham. You work them too hard and feed them too little. Look at them, you can see their ribs. Jewel, they're hungry I tell you."

"Get away from here woman! You have no say in this matter. I've told you a hundred times before; I'm the master. You are just a filthy slave lover." Jewel said as he backhanded April and she hit the ground. She pulled herself up and headed for the big house.

In March, Confederate soldiers started arriving in large masses on their plantation. They set up their tents in the fields and took any food they wanted. They talked constantly of battle.

"Them Yankee's need to be taught a powerful lesson. They need to mind their own business. If we go after them, they'll learn a lesson fast. We'll tear into them like a bobcat would a rabbit," Jewel said sitting on his porch talking to some officers. April walked out and heard this comment. She was afraid for her sons.

"We need men like you sir. Men that understand our cause. It's for gentlemen like you that we may undertake this confrontation. You deserve the right to own property, be it land, personal, or human chattels."

"Amen to that, young man," Jewel said as he raised his glass in the air. He was drinking straight whiskey.

In April of 1861 shots were fired from Charleston onto Fort Sumter, the entire south was up in arms. Every able-bodied man was called to fill the ranks, to defend the southern states, because their way of life had to be protected. Jewel decided that he and his sons must be true to the south and join the fight. Samuel was 21 years of age and Benjamin was 19.

"Jewel, they're too young, they mustn't join. Who will help me? I need them here. Please let them stay." she begged as they followed their father out to the stables for their mares.

"Mitch Brown, our overseer, will be here to take care of the slaves. You've handled this plantation before; you can do it again. This war won't take long. They have no backbone. One good battle, and it will be over."

"Mama, I'll watch over Benjamin. We'll stick together." Samuel said.

"Now get out of my way woman before I run you down." Jewel said as he jumped on his horse.

Samuel and Benjamin both took time to hug their mother good-bye. There was a regiment leaving from their plantation and Jewel and the boys were joining them.

"Come on, don't act like such mama boys. It's time to become men," Jewel yelled as he turned to the boys who were with April.

"We'll write mama. Don't worry, we'll be all right." Samuel said as he rode towards his father.

"Pray for us all, mama. Pray for us all." Benjamin said as he rode out to them both. They were all afraid of Jewel, not daring to cross him or disobey his demands. April stood near the stables and watched her sons ride away, waving each time they turned around. She felt a sinking feeling inside. She had waved good-bye now to all those she truly loved.

Mitch Brown seen fit that week to tie a woman to the post for a whipping. She had wasted time out in the fields and not done her fair share of work.

"Miss April, please come quick. Da gots Sally tied to da whipping post. She be four months wif child. Miss April, he gonna kills dat child."

"Oh no he ain't," April said as she ran to the library and took down the Kentucky rifle from the wall rack and ran down to the cabin yards. The slaves parted a way when they seen her with the rifle.

"Mr. Brown, you hold it right there." she said as he snapped his whip on the ground in front of Sally preparing to whip her. He loved to snap the ground to frighten the other workers as they stood in a circle around the whipping post. Everyone, including children, were made to watch.

"Put that gun down. You ain't the master of this place. Jewel Jackson is. He told me to stay put, no matter what you say or do. I know of your slave loving ways. Now get on out of here so I can do my job." Mitch said with a crooked smile.

"Is what you're wearing right now suitable to you?" asked April as she placed the rifle on her shoulder and looked down the site.

"Suitable for what?" he asked with sarcasm.

"Why to be buried in, for I'm tired of playing this game. You are leaving right now. This is Cothran land. You don't even have to pack. I don't care if you live or die. It's totally up to you." April said with more firmness in her voice than ever before.

"You're plum crazy. He told me you was. You dumb enough to shoot me, ain't you?"

"Yes, I do believe I am." she said. "Learned to shoot from my papa. You care to check my abilities?"

"I'm outta here. It ain't worth no amount of pay to work here. Master Jackson's gonna be mad. You gonna pay for this." he said as he curled up his whip and went for his horse.

April followed him to the stables with the site staying on him. Some of the slaves followed behind her.

"You nothing but a fool woman. You ain't never gonna run this place on your own. You done lost your mind."

"No, I believe I done found it. Leave now, or stay here six feet under. I tell you this is Cothran land, and it will stay that way from now on. Now get out of here," she yelled.

He kicked his horse and took off down the dirt road. The slaves picked up rocks and were throwing them at him as he rode away. The air was filled with his cussing.

"Praise da lord, Miss April be back. We's now standing firmly on Cothran ground. Y'all heard dat.," said Cecil with her hands on her hips as April walked back to the big house carrying her gun.

Soon after, April heard music coming from the cabins. They were celebrating her return from Jewel's grip.

The Confederate soldiers arrived on the plantation unannounced. They'd demand for the slaves to do their bidding. They'd take food and what ever they needed. Several young girls had been taken to the woods and raped and the soldiers had beaten some of the men. The officers would be speaking kindly to April, while their men were causing turmoil. Although some officers did take charge while they were on the plantation and controlled their troops. Those were the soldiers April gladly fed and let rest on her land. Everyone told her to sacrifice for the cause.

Panic would break out in the cabins when they'd see troops entering the grounds, never knowing if they would be controlled. Their stay was usually short, no longer than two days, but much could happen in just two days.

There was a large reward posted for runaway slaves by the southern states. The chances of reaching the North had gotten worse. The Underground Railroad was still in place, but many of the people from the safe houses had been captured and sent to prison, with their homes being burned. The punishment for helping runaway slaves was death by hanging.

The daily struggle to survive was long and hard. No sooner had they stored a little food, soldiers would come by and claim rights to it. President Lincoln had placed a blockade against the Confederacy in 1861 as one of his first acts. Food shortages were common in all cities. Substitutes were made for many products they could no longer receive.

"I swear, this Confederate coffee has the flavor of dirty water. I can't wait till this war is over so I can drink a decent cup of coffee." declared April as she poured her coffee onto the ground.

"Me too, Miss April. Me too." Cecil replied.

Coffee, salt and sugar had disappeared quickly when the war began. Honey was substituted for sugar, but there was no substitute for salt. Many of the meats now spoiled with no way to cure them. Chicken and fish replaced red meats.

Parched okra and parched wheat were added to coffee to stretch it, adding a strange new taste. It took some time to get use to it.

The dead and captured soldiers were listed on bulletins in town. Once every week, April rode into town to check for her boys and Jewel. In the middle of 1862, Jewel was listed as captured. April was confused by her emotions. He'd been cruel to her, but he was still her husband. She had three children from him; that had to count for something. Yet April couldn't cry for him, she was void of feelings.

On her way home, she looked out over her plantation. There was so much to do, with not enough workers to do it. Some of the men had run off to join the Yankee navy. Late at night, the navy would dock near the banks and run inland to search for recruits. Then they sneak back through the swamps and woods to take them to the ships. April learned of this through Cecil. It was a problem all along the southern coast. The slaves were eager to join the fight for freedom. Only half her fields had been farmed, soldiers used the rest.

April decided that day to try to save what was left in the big house. With so many soldiers beginning to stop by, she'd noticed things had started to disappear. She came up with a plan to save her valuables.

The slaves built large wooden crates to store her silver and gold. The crates were reinforced to be strong. Larger crates were made to hold her finest furniture, her china and the family paintings. Everything was wrapped in cloth and packed tightly.

Deep pits were dug in the woods in open areas. The crates were carried by wagon and then by poles to these areas. Once they were placed in the ground they were quickly covered and the ground stomped down. The excess soil was carried and spread in the fields. April drew a map to the pits and hid it behind the loose brick in the fireplace, along with her promise of sisterhood to May.

"Let them take it now," she declared. The Confederated soldiers were told that the plantation was stripped by troops before them. They never questioned the southern lady who had both her sons and husband fighting for the cause.

April worked side by side with the workers. She was amazed and surprised at how good it made her feel. At night she was exhausted, but the plantation was surviving. Later on she had to sell off some of the land to buy food for everyone.

Not a day passed that April did not watch for her sons. Once a week she rode into town to check the list of dead, captured, and wounded. Next she'd check the post office for mail.

When letters arrived she quickly read them, memorizing each word. She kept all letters in a box under her bed. Jewel never wrote her. Her whole existence seem to surround the letters from her boys and May. April wrote May often but couldn't get letters to her boys, for they were constantly on the move. The last letter she received said they were heading out for a town called Gettysburg.

Chapter 32

The Letter From Gettysburg

April was sitting on the porch when she saw a lone confederate soldier walking down the road towards the plantation. She thought it to be her son. She ran off the porch and down the lane to meet him. April started crying as she ran. From a distance it looked like Samuel leaning on a cane. April began to call out his name.

"Samuel, Samuel!" she cried. April held her arms out to greet him. The soldier stopped dead in his tracks and waited for her to reach him. April could tell from a distance that he was weary. His leg appeared to be causing him great pain because he was leaning heavily on the cane.

As she came closer to him her heart began to sink. It wasn't either of her boys. This was a younger man, looking no older than sixteen. His hair was long and shaggy; his clothes were torn and dirty. His eyes appeared to be that of an old man, sunk in with dark circles under both. When she reached him she saw he was skin and bones.

"Young man, are you all right? Do you need some help?"

"I'm looking for the mother of two men I saw at Gettysburg. I have a letter from the one named Benjamin. Are you their mother?" he asked.

"Yes, they wrote that they were leaving out for Gettysburg. Are they all right? You said you saw them. Did they speak to you?"

"Ma'am, I've been walking for days. I had to shoot my horse. Can I have some water and maybe a bite to eat? I can't believe I've made it. I've come from Gettysburg," then the soldier fell to his knees.

April called out to those who had gathered. "Come help me get him to the house. Let's not waste time, we must help him."

Two strong men came running to carry the wounded soldier to the big house. He cried out in pain as they carried him by holding him under his arms and his thighs. His left leg had wooden sticks tied to it. It was swollen and broken. April had him taken to her son's bed, and began cleaning him up. Cecil helped her clean the dried blood that covered his body. His clothes were stiff with old blood. He'd been shot in the right arm and his leg was swollen twice it's size. They raised his head and gave him some water. April sent for Doctor Alright. You could see maggots moving about in his wounds making the wounds look alive. A stench of rotten meat filled the room.

Cecil and April put a clean nightshirt on his frail body. He whispered, "Thank you," then lost consciousness. April wanted to read her son's letters, but the condition of the young boy turned her thoughts towards him. She knew somewhere a mother was praying for his safe return.

When Doctor Albright arrived that evening, he was amazed the young boy had not died from infection.

"This young man is eat up with the fever. Infection must be running through his blood. I think we need to take this leg," he said looking at the open wound.

The young man had been drifting in and out of consciousness all day. He awoke when the Doctor began to speak.

"Sir, please don't take my leg. My father and brothers are all dead. I'm all that's left. Please try.... Save my leg." he said as he lifted his head up off the pillow pleading with the doctor.

"Son, I can't promise you anything, but I'll try." he said patting him on the shoulder as he shook his head. "I'll try." The soldier then lay back on the pillow.

"April, have some of your workers go and gather leaches from the swamp. I'll need fresh adult ones. Tell them to hurry." he said as he rolled up his sleeves.

April sent some men out to the swamps with lanterns to gather the leeches. She and Cecil went to find clean linen for bandages. The bullet had to be dug out of his arm and the wound sewn shut.

"April, since the blockade, I haven't any medicine. I'll need you to see if any of your slaves can help with their Herb's. I know they have some they use for open wounds. I can't get quinine anymore. Everything is sent to the army."

"Yes, Cecil knows Herb's. She's right here," April said as she pulled Cecil to face the doctor.

"Iffin we gits some dogwood, cherry and willow bark and boils it real good to gather, and add some whiskey, dat oughta work."

"Good, April please find the bark and boil it, then write down how it's made. I need all the help I can find in these times."

April and Cecil hurried to find and boil the mixture. The slaves returned with three jars of fresh leeches within the hour.

The young soldier screamed out in pain as they cleaned the wounds. He was given a belt to bite down on when the bullet was removed. The pain was so great the doctor was afraid he might bite down on his own tongue. The men who gathered the leeches helped hold the solider down.

When the doctor was finished he wrapped the arm and left instructions for April to follow until he returned.

"This is the best I can do for now. He's mighty young, that's in his favor. He may be able to pull out of this, but don't get your hopes up." he said as he wiped the fresh blood off his arms in the water bowl. "This war is hell, pure hell."

"Thank you for coming. I'll stay up with him tonight. He's made it this far surly God is with him."

"I hope you're right. He's mighty young." Doctor Albright said as she walked him to the door. "Keep a cold rag on his head, it will help his fever. Don't load him down with cover, it'll make it worse. I'll be back in two days to see how he's doing. Leave the leeches in the wound and keep it uncovered. They'll be eating the infection. Maybe they're hungry," he said as he walked out the door.

April and Cecil both stayed up with the soldier that night. If one fell asleep, the other would take over. Cecil taught April how to sling the rag in the air in a circle to cool it down when it became hot from being on his head. All night long you could see that rag whipping in the air. When the doctor returned, the leg appeared to be healing. The leeches and the herbal medicine he was given to drink were subduing the infection. April and Cecil watched and cared for the boy as if he were their own.

On the eighth day the soldier was well enough to sit up in bed. He was able to eat and his strength was returning. That evening he began to tell April his story.

"My name is Emory Shockley. I'm from Lauren's County. My family has been farming for as long as I can remember. I joined the ranks with my father, and three brothers. I saw my father and two of my brothers' shot down at Gettysburg. I'm not sure if my youngest brother is alive. I was forced to bury the dead in Gettysburg in mass graves. They were so many dead Confederate soldiers," he said with tears in his eyes. " So many."

The soldier talked with a slur in his voice. Taking time with each thought, as if it were bringing him pain.

"Ma'am, what I have to tell you pains me. There were two confederate soldiers lying at the bottom of Cemetery Ridge. I was told to bring their bodies to the wagon where other dead was thrown. By the way the soldiers were laying; I felt they were kin. The soldier on the bottom had been wounded in the head, with bandage wrapped tight around it. His left hand still held tight to his rifle. The other soldier was lying on his left side holding his hand. I cried like a baby when I saw that. I figured they were brothers or cousins, or someum. Look like the one on the side tried to protect the one with the head wound. He'd been shot in the back," he said looking at April who was turning ashy white.

"Stop, I can't hear anymore. What makes you think they were my sons? How did you get my name? Where is the letter you spoke of? They're all I have left," cried April as she walked from the bed to Samuel's dresser. She picked up his comb and held it to her heart, as if she were once again holding Samuel.

"Ma'am, I'm sorry to cause you so much distress. I felt like after what I did, I had to repay them, and get you this letter. You want me to go on, or just stop."

Cecil had now walked into the room and saw that April was upset.

"Miss April, what be da matter. You all right?"

"I don't think I'll ever be all right again," she said as she turned to look and Cecil and the soldier.

She then crossed back over to the side of the bed and sat down hard into the chair.

"He says my boys are dead. He says he saw them."

"No, Miss April. Da can't be's dead. Da too young."

"Young man, please continue."

"When I started to load them into the wagon, I saw a leather pouch in the pocket of the one shot in the back. I figured it might hold money or something of value. I stole it. I put it in my bootleg. Ain't never stolen nothing before. Don't know what made me do it. I was acting crazy. I felt it would do me more good than him," he said as he turned towards April.

"After we buried the bodies, I was put back in a wooden fence they kept us confederate prisoners in. Late that night I sat by a fire alone and opened the pouch. Inside I found a letter to the mother of those two soldiers. I realized then what a terrible thing I done. I asked God to forgive me. In my heart I knew the only way to be forgiven was to place the letter in the hands of the mother who was loved so dearly. I'm asking you to forgive me, and allow me to give you the letter."

April held her head and began to cry. The soldier was crying and begging to be forgiven for bringing such sad news.

"Ma'am, I would give my soul to read a letter from my paw or one of my brothers. I felt duty bound to bring you the letter, and speak to you of their death," he said as he reached for April's hand.

"Yes, I know you mean well. But they were all I had. I forgive you. I'm sure they would forgive you and be proud of what you've done."

"Thank you ma'am."

"Please show me this letter," she said.

"It's in my jacket, sown into the right panel. I tried to protect it," he said pointing to the Confederate jacket lying with his bloody clothes in the corner.

Cecil went to the jacket and tore the panel and removed the leather pouch She felt a shiver run up her spine. It was covered in dark red blood. The blood of a boy she helped raise to a man. As she carried the pouch to April, she began to softly weep. She gently handed it to her.

April reached out in slow motion and took the pouch. April then stared at it thinking if she didn't open it, none of this would be true. Deep in her heart, she knew they would never be coming home. She knew this the day they left. She slowly got up and walked out of the room with the bloody pouch clutched close to her heart.

"Cecil, take care of Emory. I need to be alone."

"Yes Miss April."

April walked into her room and closed the door behind her. She sat on the bed and laid the pouch down. She stared at it awhile and thought now she had no one. Then she heard the crying of the wounded soldier and knew she still had meaning to her life. If it were only to help bring this young man back to health and return him home.

She picked up the pouch and untied it. She pulled out the letter from its hiding place. As soon as she saw the writing, she knew it was from Benjamin. It was dated July 3, 1863. The letter began;

Dearest Mother,

There is not a day that goes by that I don't think of you and home. I can see our place at night when I close my eyes. I dream of walking down the long road that returns us to home. I pray you're safe and happy. I hope to be coming home soon.

Mama, I believe this war is wrong. I've seen horrible things that you wouldn't believe if I told you. Do you remember Duffy's son, Israel? I saw him on the battlefront yesterday. He was a Union soldier. He'd taken a blow from a cannon ball and was lying in the field. I didn't know it was him. He saw me and begged me to shoot him so he could die. Mama, his limbs were blown off his body. They were scattered around him. I couldn't believe he was alive. Mama, he was my best friend. I had no hate for him, only compassion. Another soldier came and took his life. I stood there crying and telling him I was sorry. Mama, Israel shouldn't have died like that. He should have married and had a family. No one deserves to die on a battlefield. No one.

We are fighting under the charge of George Picketts. Tomorrow we plan to battle for control of a hill. The Union soldiers now are stationed there. We are to overtake them and claim it as Confederate ground. They say this will help us win the war. When I think of why we're fighting, I'm filled with shame. I have loved many of the slaves we've been raised around. There is no difference between us. They breathe the same air, have the same bodies, and bleed as we do, and love as we do. Why are they slaves? Who gave anyone the right to buy or sell them? The only thing I see different is their hair and skin. Is that all it takes to declare them slaves? Mama, I know your slaves love you, but they deserve to be free.

When I talked to my commander of this matter, he told me if I try to leave he would have me hung. He said I have to defend our right to form our own nation, and continue our way of life. He said it was the will of God. Mama, the Bible I read says God freed the slaves, so that means men are to be free. The Bible says all men are created in his image, not just white men, all men. I'm confused by my feelings. I know I don't think the way most southerners do. I don't think I ever have.

I've seen father mistreat the slaves, but I never understood why. Samuel and I have talked of this often. He feels the same way I do. As soon as we leave this place of living Hell, called Gettysburg, we're running. If they catch us, we will be hung or branded with a 'C' for coward. I've seen men in prison camps with this mark. They are court marshaled and branded. I will choose to be hung rather than carry a brand on my face. There are too many soldiers to run now. We wouldn't have a chance.

Samuel was shot in the head last week. It's not a serious wound, so they are making him stay in the ranks. He hasn't spoken since, and he won't release his weapon. He holds onto it even when he sleeps. I think he is afraid this is the last battle. Don't worry, I'll stay by his side, and bring him safely home. He's always watched over me, now I'll watch over him. If he dies, I die.

When everything is quiet, and the cannons can't be heard, I look around at this place called Gettysburg. They have the finest farmland I've ever seen. Cornfields and wheat fields surround us. The gardens have been trampled and lay all around us. It's hard to believe that a battle could take place here. It is strange to think this place is where God chooses for human lives to end. Or is it God who has made this decision? Were we brought here by the foolish thoughts of foolish men?

We are taught to give a rebel call before every wave of battle. I've been told you can hear it for miles. Some Union soldiers, that are our prisoners, told me they call it 'The yell from hell,' they said it made the hair on their backs stand up, and they thought that we were the devils own sons. Mama, some of them are younger than I am. Some are badly wounded, and our doctors give them very little attention. I wish I could help them.

These people around here line the hilltops in buggies to watch us battle. To them it must be a social event. I can sometimes see the outline of hoop dresses and small children. I do not understand people who have the desire to watch men die.

This farmland smells of death. It feels like a thick cloud of anger and pain surrounds us all. Sometimes I feel like no one will ever leave this place the same. If we survive, we'll be changed forever. Mama, we can get no information on father. He is a prisoner of war. I wished he wouldn't have taken us into this war. I wish we were home. I have to close now. I need to rest for battle. We are to be in the first wave of troops sent up the hill. I pray this letter reaches your hands. I miss you and the life we once had. I miss Grandpa William. I wish you well, and send all our love your way. Pray for us.

Your son,
Benjamin

When April finished reading the letter she lay on her bed and cried herself to sleep. She dreamed she saw her sons walking down the road to home, waving and smiling from ear to ear.

Chapter 33

May Remembers

April had not written May in months. The news from the plantation was always filled with such sorrow it made May wonder how much longer April could survive. May sat thinking of the many letters she'd received in the past. The last letter had spoken of the horrors they were enduring from the soldiers. April spoke of the soldiers taking supplies they needed when they passed by. Jewel and her boys had joined the fight and April was left alone. April was still confused by Carolyn's disappearance. The bonnet and berry pail were the only items every found of Carolyn's. April still spoke of wandering the nearby woods and swamp looking for her daughter.

May shook her head when remembering April's tale of hiding her possessions and livestock. The valuables were hidden in wooden crates put into deep pits and covered with soil and trampled down. May smiled at April's plan of hiding the livestock. April had the remaining workers to build large pits and make ramps to herd the cows, horses and pigs in and out. The chickens had all been eaten. When word reached the plantation of coming troops, they would hide the livestock in the pits. Her plan worked for two months until the hungry pigs made such a fuss, the soldiers found their hiding place. The cows and pigs were all slaughtered and the horses were confiscated to replace the sickly Confederate horses. April was allowed to keep the horses left behind.

"You must do your part for the cause. Everyone must sacrifice to support our troops and Confederate states," April was told. April had written of eating whatever they could kill in the woods and surrounding swamps. Alligators, possums, raccoons, squirrel, and snakes were now considered fine eating.

May was able to tell by her letters that April's ideals on life were changing with the war. What had once been consider not acceptable was now common and accepted.

One of the strangest letters that May had received was of the Cherokee Indians moving about on April's plantation. April was frightened of them, thinking they were spies for the north. The slaves claimed to see them wandering in the woods near the plantation hiding as they watched the slaves work. There had been tales of Indians who stole slaves to trade with the soldiers. Although the rumors were proven false, the workers insisted it was fact.

One day when April and Cecil were resting, sitting in a chair on the lower porch, they saw three Indians on horseback approaching the plantation. They stopped 100 feet from where they were sitting and stared at April. She decided the only solution was to confront them.

"Cecil, bring me the rifle. Get it, now," she ordered. Cecil jumped up from her chair and ran into the house, soon returning with the Kentucky rifle.

April then said she marched right out to the three Indians with Jewel's rifle over her shoulder. She felt it would show she had no fear, and they would think her brave.

April said she began to scream at them and shoot the rifle in the air, as if she had great power. The Indian men stood their ground and watched her. She began to stomp the ground and carried on like a mad woman until she was worn slap out. April said she didn't know how long she carried on like that but it didn't scare them at all. Although her slaves who saw her actions fled to their cabins thinking she had gone mad, Cecil stayed on the porch watching.

When she could do no more, she just stood there. April said the Indians were clothed in brightly colored shirts and light brown pants. Their heads were shaved except for a patch of hair on the crown of their head, which was long and braided. Their faces were smooth and their skin had a rich sun toned color. She could see in the distance a larger group of Indians on foot standing in the road leading to her plantation. She saw more men with women and children.

Finally, they began to speak in a language April couldn't understand. They tried to use their hands making motions and made faces of someone in great pain. April said it seemed important to them that she understood their actions. Maybe they had seen a great battle, or had killed soldiers, or soldiers had attacked them. April had no idea what they were trying to relay to her. Finally they too grew tired and shook their heads and rode back to the people who waited for them down the lane. April watched as they all turned and walked back down the road they had traveled.

"I don't know what they're up too, but we better git ready. I think they might attack."

April had warned the slaves before she went back to the big house. She had called them all out to the road and told them to keep watch that night and the next. The Indians were never seen again, although not a day went by for months that they weren't watched for. April decided the Indians were afraid of her, thinking she was fearless and crazy.

May found herself thinking of the incident often, wondering what had actually taken place. Maybe time would bring the answer. May remembered the Indian Chiefs she saw on her journey north, and imagined April acting crazy for them. This always made her laugh.

In the year of 1863, during the winter months, Philip was accepted into a colored regiment in the Union army. May's worst nightmare had come true. She begged Philip not to go. She knew their older son would want to follow him. Philip reminded her of when he first spoke of war.

"May, don't be afraid. Remember I told you long ago, this is a battle that needs to be fought. Many lives will be changed forever. We have God on our side. It is written in his word. It's His will that man should be free. May, I have to go." Philip said as he held May tightly in his arms as they stood in the kitchen.

"I don't want to speak of God's will, Philip. I need you here, more than you are needed in any war. Let the young fight. They have the spirit to fight. I am tired and weary. I refuse to give my only love to the blade of a Confederate soldier. Don't leave our family. We can't make it without you," May said, then sobbed into his shoulder.

"Wait a minute, you already speak as if I'll die. Have faith in our Father who watches over all his beloved. In this war, I will place my care in His hands. Remember he watches over the sparrows and knows their needs, surely he'll be watching over me. And don't speak of not making it without me. You have made it through more than I could ever dream of. You were once a slave. You climbed great mountains and crossed great rivers to be where you are now. Do you realize who guided you through every step? You once told me you felt the presence of God's spirit many times in your life. Do you not believe that same spirit will not be with me? It is truly God who brought you to me. Keep your faith where it needs to be, not with man but with God." finished Philip as he raised May's face to his, and gently wiped away her tears.

He then kissed May with such passion, she felt her legs begin to tremble.

That night would be forever remembered. Their love would never die, even if this would be their last time to melt into each other's arms. They were truly one soul and body.

With the breaking of dawn, Philip gathered his small bag to join his fellow soldiers.

"Children, I will be back before too long. Watch out for each other and help your mama and Grandma. Make sure you do your chores and do everything your mama says."

Philip then held each child in his arms and kissed them good-bye. He held tightly onto Lilly and begged her to take care of May.

"Lilly, take care of May. Assure her I'll come back home. I've got to do this."

"I's know. Iffin I's was a man, I'd be heading out too. You go and help dem wins. May will be fine, just fine," Lilly said as she patted his back.

May did not cry when she hugged Philip. She stood strong for the sake of her children. She and the children watched as he rode off on his horse. He turned to wave to them all.

"Mama, will God be sending angels to help daddy? Will they be big or small?" asked Joshua , the youngest.

"No, I think little angels are sent to guard sweet little babies." replied May. "I'm sure God has a special angel to watch over your daddy. He will be big and strong so he can help daddy if he gets in danger. Don't worry, daddy will come home."

May gathered them back into the house and appointed them chores, to take their minds off Philip leaving. Then May walked outside to chop the wood for the week, and cried.

Chapter 34

The Battle Of Recognition

May and the children survived the winter. The winter of 1863 had been hard and long. Twice the roof almost caved in from the weight of the snow. Hot soup was eaten most of the winter, because of the food shortage. May could only imagine what Philip was going through.

Philip's church was turned into a Union hospital for the many wounded soldiers that were arriving. May rushed to the church when a new wagon full would arrive, looking for Philip. Many of the men from their church had joined the Colored Regiment when Philip did. The ladies of the area were knitting socks and sweaters that were sent to the field for the soldiers. May and Lilly were learning to nurse the wounded.

It was a beautiful spring day when she received her first letter from Philip. She cried when she saw his handwriting.

The letter began:

Dearest May,

I long to hold you. I carry your photograph with me always. I look upon your face every night and yearn to hold you again. I think of our last night together to bring me comfort. I pray for you all daily.

It has been hard living in tents for they are thin and the wind blows right through them. Some of the men have suffered from frostbite. We have been lied to about our pay. They said in the beginning that we would receive thirteen dollars a month, now they say we must pay three dollars a month for our uniforms. The white soldiers do not pay this fee. Our Colonel Steven Morgan was furious when he was told. He went to the paymaster and demanded we receive our full pay. The army refused. He has written the President about this. Our Colonel is a good man. I am in a good regiment. We train for battle as the white soldiers do. Some white soldiers say we are not capable to do battle with the grays. I believe they are wrong. They say the war is for our need to keep the union sound and united. To us it is a war for freedom. The cause of freedom is greater than the cause for a sound union. I have seen no colored men of rank. I have been told many color regiments stay busy doing fatigue duties instead of drilling for battles. Fatigue duty is back breaking work, much like given to slaves. Many colored regiments resent this. They have joined to fight the Rebels, not to dig out houses.

I've found many whites still do not think of colored men as true men. I do not understand this madness. What must we do to prove our worth?

The weapons we have been given have to be rebuilt. They have a brass plate on them which reads: Colored Regiment Issue. I wonder what kind of battle's they want us to fight with broken guns.

Our Colonel has drilled us for battle. He gathered us together and told us that he'd trained white soldiers that didn't learn as quickly as us. He told us we would make fine warriors. He said he would be proud to fight beside us. We all grew a foot taller after his talk.

Give each child a hug and kiss from me. Don't worry, I will be just fine. I will come home as soon as I can. Remember that you forever hold my heart in your hands.

Loving you, Philip

It was the end of June before May received another letter. She had been worried, and was happy to once again see his writing. The letter began:

My Darling May,

What I'm about to tell you took place at Tyler's Point in Virginia. Our regiment was moving to take up battle in Tennessee. This story is hard to believe.

The men in my regiment have begun to call it 'The Battle of Recognition'. Read on my love and believe me when I say it's true.

Our regiment had not yet been involved in any battles. We had heard talk of the many battles, but never had the chance to fight. Colonel Steven Morgan had received orders to carry us to Tennessee to engage in battle. We were all excited to finally be able to prove that we were able to fight. It was near the end of the month of May. The days were warm, yet the night still cold. We'd been marching for three days through the mountains and valleys of Virginia. We stopped to camp along rivers and lakes, catching the best tasting fish I've ever eaten.

On the evening of the third day, our scout came back with the news of a rebel camp not but a few miles ahead of us. To continue the route we were told to take, we would have to confront the rebels. The men were all excited to hear that our first battle lay right in front of us. The Colonel gave the orders to advance forward, and get our ranks in position for battle. He sent word to the fort we left, and told them of our battle plans.

We quietly moved forward through the night. By morning we were set up directly across from the enemy. They were camped out in a group of trees, with a large field separating us from them. We set our camp across the field from them They were surely surprised to awaken and find our cannons facing them. No sooner than we loaded our cannons with grapeshot, the enemy began to fire upon us. They seemed excited to do battle.

The sounds of the big cannons can shake your soul. I felt like every nerve in my body was charged with the desire to do battle. The cannons cause a thick smoke that lingers above the ground. Several rounds were fired across the field in both directions, killing and wounding several men. I was sweating and breathing heavy waiting for the call of 'Charge'. The smoke made the field look like a misty dream. We were lined up for the first wave of battle. My musket was loaded and ready to go. My heart was racing so fast, I thought it would jump from my chest. Then we heard the call to battle. All that were in the first wave began our run towards the enemy. That is the first time I heard the 'Rebel Call'. It is a loud scream rebels yell when on the attack. It almost made me want to turn back towards our camp. I felt fear for the first time. When we could, we disengaged our guns into the enemy. I could see men falling to the ground, now screaming in terror and pain. I couldn't stop to help; I had to press on. When we reached the enemy, we used our bayonet's to kill. May, it was horrible. I just kept telling myself it was for freedom. I pray God will forgive me for the suffering I caused men that day.

Thirty minutes later we heard the bugle blow to signal retreat and regroup. Both sides retreated back to regroup for the second wave of battle. We all took hold of the wounded and dragged them back to our sides to our doctors.

Our Colonel began to speak to us of the plan for the next wave of battle. He praised our bravery, and pointed out all the gray coats lying dead in the field. May, blue coats also lay dead in the field. It seemed we no longer thought of them as men, but as colored coats.

We loaded our muskets and cleaned our bayonets. Cannons sent another round of grapeshot to the other side. It was time for the second wave of battle.

Suddenly, we heard a voice cry out from the middle of the battlefield. Someone living was left among the dead. Both sides became very silent as we listen to the voice cry out to God for help.

The smoke began to clear, and we saw the out stretched arm of a gray coat reaching out to our side. He must had been knocked out by the blows he suffered, because he was confused and begging us for help. He called out to God, as he reached out to our side. I felt like he was reaching out just to me. His voice was carried and it sounded as if a great choir was calling for his help. We all lay there in position frozen, not knowing to kill him or save him.

What happened next, I can only explain as the power of God taking hold of the situation. Before I knew what was happening I stood up, laid down my gun, and unfasten my musket ball pouch. Then my feet started moving towards the voice coming from the gray coat. The Colonel ordered me to come back, but I couldn't if I wanted to. Someone of higher rank was guiding me across the field. I could hear my heart beating rapidly in my ears. I felt every move my body made; every muscle movement and each breath I took. I knew that by the end of the day, I would be dead. I could see the gray coat crawling my way, still crying to God for help. I began praying that God was in control. No man would ever believe this sight. Before I reached the gray coat, he had stopped calling for help and had begun to cry.

I was surprised at the silence. I could hear the birds calling to each other as if a battle had not disturbed this day. As I approached the gray coat, I saw he was lying on his stomach. One hand had been digging into the ground, trying to move his body. I bent down on one knee, and turned him over. May, this was a boy no older than fourteen years.

His face was muddy and covered in blood. He appeared to have only one eye. He looked up at me, and fainted.

I picked him up as if I was picking up one of my own sons. This could have been my son. I began to cry. For a second I hesitated, then turned to take him back to his front. I could hear my regiment scream out for me to stop, but I couldn't. The boy came to, and placed his left arm around my neck. He pulled his bleeding head closer to my body. I knew he could hear my beating heart. His right arm dangled by his side. Both his legs had taken musket balls.

As I started across the field I began to pray for you and the children. I prayed you would understand this foolish act I was part of. I never expected to survive. I could see all the enemies' muskets pointing at me the closer I came.

I prayed for each of our children and that God would take care of you all. Then I began to pray for the young boy in my arms. I prayed that if my life had to be given to save him that his life would be joyous and filled with good works. I looked upon his face once more before I reached the enemy's line. This could not be the face of the enemy. When I reached the enemy's line I was weeping. I stopped and waited for them to make the next move. They all just stared at me in disbelief. Finally two men were ordered to take him from me. They came running from the trees and carefully took the wounded young man from my arms.

As they removed his arm from my neck, he looked up at me and said, Bless you sir."

"God be with you, son." I said.

Then I stood at attention waiting for my life to be swept away with the firing of the enemy's guns. I closed my eyes, so none could see the pain in them. I stood like that for several minutes. When no guns were fired, I opened them to look at the faces of the enemy. They seemed to be as shocked to see me, as I was to see them. I began to look up and down their ranks. Some of them appeared to be not much older than the boy I carried across was. Others looked too old for fighting. They were all dirty, bloody and tired. I could see it in their eyes. The eyes of the enemy appeared to look much like the eyes of any man. Everyone seemed to be puzzled about what to do. Even their Colonel just stood staring at me. I must have looked a sight. The blood of the white soldier covered me, and my face was dirty and tear stained.

I will never know if they thought me to be the bravest man they ever saw, or a fool. No one raised their musket to me. I believe no one wanted to kill me. I was yearning to go back to my regiment. I had to say something, but great words of meaning did not come to my lips. I simply said, "Good day to you all."

Then I turned and started my journey across the field. It was then I heard a commotion with the muskets, and realized they had waited to shoot me in back. The sound seemed to ring in my ears. I said aloud to our Father above that I was ready.

That's when the first one called out. In a very southern voice someone yelled, "God bless you!"

Then another voice echoed the first. Then another, and another. All the way across that field, with each step I took, it could be heard. I could see the men in my regiment begin to stand up and watch what was taking place. I couldn't believe the way it made me feel. I've never felt so proud in all my life.

When I reached our side, I gave God thanks. It was God who made me go, and God who brought me safely back. May, I wish every man could see the enemy as they are. As men. Men who are just following the order to fight, just as we are. Nothing more, nothing less.

It wasn't too long after that, both sides packed up and moved out. Neither wanted to fight after we'd been witnesses to that great event. The hate had been melted away, and we stood purely as men.

You will probably never read of this battle in any history books. No man of war would want to remember. Lives were lost that day, but many more were saved. Never will I be sent on a greater mission. I plan on giving a great sermon on this event when I reach home. I will close for now my love. Kiss each one for me and tell them Daddy loves them. God has delivered me safely from the enemy, surely he will deliver me home. Till we meet again my love, I shall blow kisses to the wind and pray they find your lips.

Your loving husband, Philip

May read the letter aloud to the children and Lilly. Then they all got down on their knees to thank God for keeping their father safe. Never before has the power of God over man seemed so real.

Chapter 35

Emory Returns Home

Since the end of July 1863, Emory Shockley had been living at the plantation. It was now the middle of October, and cooler weather was setting in. Emory's leg had healed enough that he could walk with the use of a cane. He was grateful to be alive. Caring for Emory had helped April overcome the sorrow of losing her sons.

The day of his departure had arrived. April had sent a letter to his family, and they came to carry him back home. Emory's mother was filled with joy when she saw him. He was the only son she had left. Emory's father and brothers were all killed at Gettysburg, buried in mass graves.

"Mrs. Jackson." said his mother Lizzie, "I can't thank you enough for caring for my son. If it weren't for you, he'd be dead too. My family couldn't pay for a doctor. We have no money. All we have now is each other, but that will be enough."

"Your son has done a great service for me," said April softly. "He brought me a letter from my boys, risking his own life to do so. I will always remember his bravery, and I'm grateful for his compassionate heart. It was a letter pinned by my son Benjamin the night before his death. It let me look inside my son's soul, and I was proud of what I saw. I will never forget your son."

April reached out to hug Emory good-bye and kissed his cheek. She then gave him her gold wedding rings and a long gold chain with a heart of small diamonds. She'd received the necklace when she turned thirteen from her parents.

"Take these and get whatever you can for them. May God shower you with his blessings," finished April smiling with tears in her eyes.

"No ma'am, I can't take this. These are your wedding rings." pleaded Emory as he tried to give them back."

"They hold no value for me now. Do as I say and keep them. You will need the money they bring for your family. I wish there were more to give you. You have missed them so much, and this is your day to rejoice."

Emory reached out and gave April a long tearful hug, then climbed aboard the clap buggy board with his mother and sisters. They all waved good-bye and started down the lane.

"Wait...wait!" called out Cecil as she hurried out the door with a basket of food she'd help prepare. "Here's somepun for ya'lls journey. You gonna git hungry down da road apiece. Help fix it myself."

"Thank ye. We shore appreciate your kindness. Take care of your mistress. She's a fine southern lady," said Emory as he reached down to take the basket.

"I's shore will do dat," Cecil said with a big toothy grin. "You take care of dat leg now," she said as they rode away.

Emory turned to face April standing in the yard and waved farewell. She heard him yelling back to her.

"I'll never forget what you done for me. I'll never forget you."

The day after Emory left, April called all the slaves to the front of the plantation. It was early evening and the sun was beginning to set. The sky was alive with bright colors that seem to glow off the clouds. Everyone stood with sweat clinging to their clothes and their bodies still dirty from working the fields. They were all hungry and tired.

April had been working with them in the fields until that afternoon. She had left them and came back to the big house. Now she sat in a wicker chair near the steps leading up to the porch, with a large stack of papers in her lap.

"I need to speak to you concerning a matter that has been on my heart for awhile. All of you have been good, and helped me with the problems that came my way. I trust all of you completely. Ever since the death of my parents, life has been hard for me. But you all have been here for me. When we had no food, you helped me grow it. Some of you have hunted game for us to eat. For quite some time now, we've lived more like a family. I finally realize that's how it should be. We are all but one family, stemming from one tree."

The slaves began to look at each other in puzzlement over April's words. Cecil sat on the steps near her chair and looked up with her brow wrinkled.

"I must tell you about my papa's journal. He wrote of his own confusion about owning slaves. He said it was all he ever knew. Near the end of his life, he questioned its moral value. My son's saw the cruelty of slavery at the hands of their father. The last letter I received from Benjamin, he spoke of missing Grandpa William. They truly loved him, just as I love May. The color of her skin meant nothing to me," April said as tears formed in her eyes.

"We knows you love May. We understand you were just a child. No one hold dat against you. You did right by us. You does da best you cans to protect us from da soldiers. It ain't neber been your fault how Master Jackson done us. He was beating on you too. I's seen it wif my own eyes," Cecil said looking up to April. "Don't cry now. It gonna be all right."

After a few moments, April once again began to speak.

"Master Jackson is still prisoner of the Union. By law I'm now legal master of you all. And as master of you all I shall do what should have been done years ago. To each here, I will give freedom papers. From this day forward, you own yourselves," said April now smiling. A great gasp went out among all the slaves

They couldn't believe what they'd just heard. They stood staring up at April. Cecil stared at her with her mouth dropped open.

"In my lap here are your papers." She turned the papers over and held one up. "This is freedom papers for Jeffrey Cothran, already signed by me. They have been filled out since the letter from Gettysburg. Slavery is wrong, and I pray one day you will find it in your hearts to forgive me."

"Freedom papers, for me?" Jeffrey asked pointing to himself. "You'll let me leab dis place?" Jeffrey asked.

"Yes, you may leave. You will all get your papers today. You can stay on my land as long as you like. Not as my slave, but as my friend. Those of you who do stay, will be rewarded when the war ends. I will give those who stay 30 acres of land and help you build a home. If you leave now, I can only give you my blessing. If you stand by me, and help the plantation survive, I will put it in writing that the land is yours. I have a map here plotted for the ones who will stay. Just show me the land you wish to own," April said as she spread out the map on the porch in front of her.

"After the war, you can start building on your land. But we must do this in secret, for the Confederates would kill me and take all that is mine. Now who will stay?"

Everyone was silent. Then Cecil stood up tall.

"I'll stay Miss April."

Then one by one most of them came up to the porch and looked down at the map pointing to a plot.

"Geb me dis one. Dat be mine."

"Ober here, dis be mine."

April got down on her knees to write in the names on different plots. Then she handed out the papers of freedom. At first everyone was stunned. They just stood there looking at the papers in their hands. Finally one young man let out a joyous 'whoop ba da doo.' Then they all began to let out screams and calls of joy. Everyone began to wave their papers in the air and dance about. Even April danced around with them, never feeling so alive in her life.

That night the plantation was once again filled with music and dance. Everyone had a reason to be happy. April felt like a great load had been lifted from her. She couldn't wait to share this day with May. Now maybe May would completely forgive her.

Chapter 36

Freedom's Song

April was filled with joy that night and when the party was over she went in to write May. The letter began:

Dearest May,

I have to share my joy with you. Yesterday Emory's family came for him. It was a glorious reunion for them. His mother had lost her husband and sons at that dreadful place called Gettysburg. To see her face when she saw Emory was worth it all. It did my poor heart good. I hope they make it through the winter. I'm sure the next year will be better for them. I felt so happy to be able to deliver him alive into the hands of those that love him.

I wish you could have been with me today. May, I gathered all the workers in the front yard. There were no more than seventy-five of them left, counting the children. All the others have run, or joined the Union navy. I gave them all papers of Freedom. I do not own humans any more. I promise those who stay with me that I will give them land and help them build a home. Most of them will stay as my friends and help me run what's left of my plantation.

You would not believe the excitement that has followed. Everybody is so happy, we've been dancing and singing all night. They made up a Freedom Song. It's fun to sing. My heart is so filled with love for them. All of them have been so good to me. I never knew how much they meant to me, until I lost all those I loved.

I started thinking about how I have always felt about the people that live here. I never stopped trying to protect them, even when Jewel would beat me for it. I've always worried when they became sick, and helped nurse them back. To see that all were fed and clothed has always been my goal. But I never understood this to be love. I would have gladly taken Old William's place in the tree, or Joseph's place behind the horse. Not because I felt sorry for them, but because I knew and loved them. I have been living blind, now I see things for the first time. I wish I could share this joy with you. I wish this feeling would stay with me forever. I know Papa would be proud of me. All but five are staying here to help me.

Last week the tombstones arrived for my sons' graves. I had them placed in the family graveyard in remembrance of them. Their names are on them, along with the fact that they are buried in a mass grave at Gettysburg. Each has an angel with wings spread to fly away. I know you think I'm crazy for insisting to have tombstones for empty graves. It is important to me that people know that they once were here. They were my family. Each one of their lives was important. When I'm gone and cannot speak of them anymore, it's important that people know they once lived.

I pray that when all this is over, you will once again come home to see me. I miss you so much. I pray one day you will find it in your heart to forgive me for everything.

Your Sister Forever
April

Chapter 37

May's Life

May was happy when she read April's letter. She ran to find her mama and her children to tell them of April's decision.

"Mama, they all free. April has set them free." May said jumping up and down when she found Lilly.

"Lordy child, don't be fooling me. Da really free? Da moving north?"

"No, most of them are staying with April. She promised them land and to help them build a home. Ain't it wonderful!"

"God bless her." Lilly said.

May's children gathered to hear the news.

May reread the letter word for word. They had all prayed together for the freedom of the Cothran slaves, now all would know how good freedom feels. They all hugged and cried tears of joy, although the children had never known the pain of being a slave. It was hard to comprehend if you had never experienced it.

Anthony had left that previous October to join the Union ranks in a colored regiment. Posters had been posted in the city and on trees for the need of colored men to fill the ranks. When May first saw them, she feared for all her sons. Young men were being accepted as young as fourteen.

May kept the letter that she found on Anthony's bed that cold October morning. His brothers came for her when they saw he was gone. It simply read:

Dearest Mother,

I can wait no longer. I am a man, and my country needs me. I know this is not what you want, but I must go and fight. I will fight for those you still know in bondage. I will fight to keep our great nation whole. Please forgive me and pray for me. I will return.

I love you all, Anthony

Soon another year had gone by. Life for Lilly, May and the children was hard. There was never enough money or food. Everyone was suffering due to the war. May was told in the city of the severe shortages the south was having due to the blockade, she knew April was suffering twice as much.

Lilly and May worked long hours at the make shift hospital at the church. The soldiers told them of unspeakable horrors. They claimed that colored prisoners were being shot instead of taken to prison camps. They told of the "Fort Pillow Massacre", where three hundred men were murdered. The rules of war were that all prisoners were to be treated fairly, yet this wasn't applied to colored prisoners. The rebels deem this law unnecessary. It shook May up to hear such tales, but she needed to know what Philip and Anthony might be going through. There were tales of Union colored troops being marched right back into slavery, sold at cheap prices to replace runaways.

May thanked God for every letter she received from Philip and Anthony. Anthony had joined a regiment that had seen many battles. He wrote of seeing many of his friends dying with dysentery. He claimed it took as many lives as the battles took. There wasn't enough doctors or medicine within their field camps. Anthony believed most of the medicine was being used for the white soldiers.

He told of the games that they played to pass time away and wait for battles. The oddest involved a hot plate and large cockroaches. The metal plate was heated and roaches were placed in the center. Men would bet on which roach would escape the plate first. The roach's wings were colored so they could tell them apart. May was grateful that at least the men found some amusements in their painful surroundings.

On a warm sunny day in June, Lilly came charging up the road on her horse to fetch May. The year was 1864. She'd been at the hospital when new soldiers arrived.

"May, come quick. Da someone you just might bring home. Someone who can't wait to lay his eyes on you. You better hurry child, times a wasting.

May jumped on her horse and took off like the devil himself was chasing her. You could see her horse kicking up a dust storm as it ran. Lilly had beaten her back and was standing at the altar. May jumped off her horse before it came to a full stop, falling down then jumped up to grab the rope to tie him up.

May's skirt was dirty and torn when she ran into the church hospital. Lilly was standing at the altar holding someone's hand and grinning from ear to ear.

"Here she is now. I told you she'd be quick. Don't start crying. Here she be," Lilly said to the man as she released his hand.

May's heart was pounding in her ears. She ran up to the altar were her mother stood. She looked down at a swollen face wrapped in a bandage. At first she stood frozen, not knowing who it was. Then he spoke, "May, my darling May."

"Philip, is it really you? Oh Philip, I thought I'd never see you again," cried May as she fell to her knees and threw her arms around his body. She began crying and couldn't stop.

Philip began to stroke her hair with his good hand.

"Its all right now, honey. We're back together again and the family is whole From this day forward all will be fine. I just need to heal. And I need your love to do it." smiled Philip through his bandages.

Philip didn't know that Anthony had joined the ranks. Before May had time to tell him, Lilly spoke up.

"Don't you know, Anthony done run off to join da Union? Said he wanted to be like his daddy, and fight for freedom. He looked up to you, you oughta be proud of dat young'un. He don't eben know what it feels like to be a slave, but he be willing to fight for em."

"May, is it true?" he asked as he gently lifted May's chin with his good hand.

"I'm afraid so Philip. I wouldn't allow him to join, so he ran away. The last letter I received he was in a state called Louisiana. Said he had already been in two battles. His first Colonel was mean, but was killed in the first battle. His Colonel now is a good man. The letter's are at home. You can read them," May finished.

"This war ain't a place for no human to be. Some things that happened, I can never tell. I am a grown man, and it's been the hardest thing I've ever done. Anthony is yet a child in a man's body. He will be made to kill, and only God knows how it will effect him," Philip said with a shaky voice.

They both held onto to each other tightly and cried.

Philip was well enough to come home after two weeks. He'd been hit with grape shot in the head. It almost cracked his skull. His leg had been broken in battle when a large man fell on him in death. The other wounds were deep inside, which only God could heal.

In July, they received a letter from Anthony. He was still in Louisiana, but leaving out for Georgia. The letter was filled with his desire to come home. There had been too many battles, on and off the battlefields.

Chapter 38

Jewel Returns

April was thrilled to receive May's letter. May told her she was proud of her. April cried when she read that Philip had been wounded but was now home. April felt in her heart that Jewel might one day come home. Maybe the war had changed him, yet she dreaded the day.

On a hot sticky August day in the year of 1864, a small troop of Confederate soldiers came riding up the plantation road in parade uniforms. April was in the front yard hoeing her flowerbed, what was left of it.

"Y'all looking for something? What can I do for you?" she asked as they dismounted their horses.

"Ma'am, are you the mother of Samuel and Benjamin Cothran?" the tallest soldier asked.

"Yes, I am. But they are deceased. Buried at Gettysburg. You'll not find them here," she said leaning on the hoe propping up her chin.

"Ma'am, we come to show honor to our fallen comrades and give you medals in their behalf. We'd like to put the Southern Cross on their graves, if you erected any in memory of them."

"Shore I did. They are in the family plot. Would you like something to drink before we go there, it's mighty hot today," she said.

"Thank ye ma'am. Water would be nice, if it ain't any trouble.'

"No trouble at all. I'll be right back," she said as she laid the hoe down and walked inside the big house.

She came back with three glasses of water, which they quickly drank. April took the empty glasses to the porch, and went back to the men.

"The family plot is this way," she said as she pulled up her skirt a little and began the walk up the small hill that led to the gravesite.

The graveyard stood under a massive Oak that had some branches that hung low to the ground. Moss hung heavy in the tree, making the site beautiful. A large pond was to the right of the site. The soldiers commented on it's beauty and feeling of peace.

"We are here to present to Benjamin and Samuel Medals of Honor for the bravery they showed to the Southern states. They fought with great valor and in a self less act to protect our Southern states," the one with the beard said as he hung the medals on the side of their tombstones.

"We also have letters in honor of each of your sons from President Jefferson Davis. He'd like to applaud you and Mr. Jackson for raising such fine southern men. He wants you to know their lives were not given in vain. The south will be able to carry on its great traditions due in part to your sons valor," the short fat one said as he handed April the letters.

April had tears in her eyes as the letters where handed to her. She remembered well what the last letter from Gettysburg had said. They'd wanted to flee the insanity of it all. Now, here was a President commenting on men he never knew. He surely didn't know they thought him to be foolish.

The soldiers then surrounded the graves of her sons. One began to play a bugle while another beat softly on a small drum hanging around his hip. The instruments were decorated with gold tassels and rope, with the uniforms of the soldiers finely decorated. When the music stopped, one soldier, not much older than 16, placed a bronze cross on Samuel's grave. Then the tall soldier placed one on Benjamin's.

April had never seen crosses like these before. They told her they were called 'The Southern Cross'. Each end had been flattened out with a raised letter on it. A rebel flag was in the center. The letters were 'C', 'S' and 'A'. The crosses stood about one-fourth the size of the tombstones.

The soldiers then saluted the graves and bid April farewell as they headed back to their horses. They had other fallen comrades to honor. April was left standing at the graves, staring down at the crosses and the medals that hung on each tombstone.

She tried to imagine what her sons would now say or do. The she did exactly what she felt they would have done. She tore the letters up and threw them to the wind. Then she took the great medals and slung them high in the tree. Finally she pulled up each cross from the graves and ran down to the pond and threw them in. She then walked back to the plantation with a tear stained face holding her head high. She felt in a small way that her sons' death had just been avenged. To hell with the war.

The months quickly passed by, and soon it was the month of April. Flowers had began to peek from there resting places where they hid from the bitter winter. This was a lovely month to be alive. The sound of riders was heard coming up the Oak lane. They were screaming and shouting. When they came closer, April could hear their words.

"The war is over! The war is over!"

They screamed it as if it were a song. Then April heard bells ringing in the distance, and knew it to be true. April ran to find Cecil and the others. This would be a day of great celebration. The South lost, the slaves were free. Now no secrets had to be kept. April's people could truly walk free.

What a wonderful day. Now they could began working on their homes on the land April had promised. Everyone who played an instrument had begun to make music. The great celebration had begun. After the tears came laughing and dancing by all.

April was true to her word. They all helped her dig up her belongings and she took everything of value to sell in Charleston. The people who bought her gold and silver were amazed at how she had buried her possessions and managed to keep them. They laughed at her attempt to hide her livestock. The paintings were harmed by mold, but they could be repaired. Both armies had searched her home for valuables, but had found nothing.

When April returned, she used the money to help buy supplies to build their homes. She allowed the workers to tear down the old slave cabins and use the timber and bricks to build their own homes. New bricks were now made on the plantation in the large ovens that survived the war. Everyone was busy helping each other. They'd all helped build one house at a time. Then they'd move on to another. April was more than kind. When it was time for harvest, they all worked together to get it in. She gave each family their fair share of the crops. April was the happiest she'd been in a long time. Once again her life held great promise.

The letters from May were becoming longer. April felt that she had finally been forgiven. May shared the great events that happened. Philip had healed, and walked with a cane. One wonderful day, when May was hanging clothes, she saw a man walking down their dirt road. It was Anthony coming home. He'd made it through five battles without physical harm. May said he was weary and thin. He was nervous and anxious, but seemed to be improving.

April and Cecil had tried their best to keep the plantation house livable. It was in grave need of many repairs. Cecil had decided to live in the plantation house with April.

"Cecil, if you will stay with me I'll give you five acres more of land. I'll even help you get started on your own cabin. I can't stand the thought of living here alone. Please stay."

"Miss April, I's be glad too."

Cecil's husband Henry had died from the fever not long after her baby. He'd been sold to another plantation, and it was near the end of the war before Cecil heard of his death. He'd been dead for four years when she finally heard about it.

"Been a widow all dis time and didn't know it. Don't dat beat all," was all she said about it to April. But April knew it hurt her deeply.

It was now winter, and one of the coldest nights of the year. Cecil and April had brought down their quilts and were sleeping in the main parlor near a fireplace that held logs three feet long. The room could become warm enough to heat the soul. They sat by the fire and talked of all the things that needed to be done.

All of a sudden, they heard pounding at the front door. April wrapped a quilt around her and went to answer.

"What poor soul would be out on a night like this?" she said before she opened the door.

As soon as she opened the door she saw him. It was Jewel. He still had on a thin and tor n Confederate jacket, and he was shaking violently from the cold.

For a moment April stood frozen, not knowing what to do. She thought he was surely dead. It had been six months since the war ended, and she'd not heard from him. Now he stood half frozen in front of her. She then did the only thing she knew to do. She reached out for his arm and helped him walk in. She led him into the parlor and laid him on the couch close to the fire. She told Cecil to bring more quilts. Cecil ran upstairs to get them.

Jewel never uttered a word; he just let them cover him with the quilts. His eyes followed April as she walked around the room. She made him hot coffee and lifted his head to help him drink. Cecil heated the soup they'd had that evening, so that Jewel could have some.

April fed him like he was a baby. He ate every bite offered to him never taking his eyes off April. When his body had warmed, he drifted off to slept. April and Cecil were both confused by his arrival and his behavior. They'd never knew Jewel to be passive. Maybe being a prisoner had changed him. They couldn't figure out where he had been.

Jewel slept soundly for the next two days. Waking only to take a little fluid. April couldn't find any of his family to tell them he was back. The Union soldiers had burned them out.

The story on the incident was that his slaves told Union soldiers of the suffering Master Jackson gave out. The Union soldiers decided he needed to be taught a lesson. They tied him to his own whipping post and beat him in front of his slaves. Then they set his plantation on fire. Master Jackson and his wife were made to watch their home burn down to ashes. April didn't know how much of the story was true, but she'd seen the smoke from the burning house. It had filled the air for miles.

Jewel's silence went on for weeks. He was able to move around and take care of himself, but he wouldn't speak. April found him to be pleasant. He would smile at her when she greeted him or brought him food. He would move by and let her pass if he stood before her. He began to chop firewood for the many fireplaces and started doing odd jobs around the plantation. April was beginning to hope that maybe he had changed. She didn't mind him being speechless, for he was kind. Maybe he would once again share their marriage bed.

One day she saw him walking back from the family gravesite. He appeared to be upset, and his steps were quick. April thought he knew about their sons, for he never asked her about them.

He came up to where she was sitting on the porch and uttered his first words to her.

"What happened to my sons?" he demanded. "You'd better tell me now woman!"

This was the Jewel that April knew. She hadn't known the other Jewel, or where he went. This was the angry Jewel she married.

"Please Jewel, come inside. I will give you all the letters I received from them. Then you will know what happened," pleaded April. He followed her inside and slammed the door shut behind him. He went into the parlor and waited for April to return with the letters. You could see the veins standing out on his neck.

April returned to the room with a box full of letters from them. She was surprised to see Jewel looking so strange. It was still cold outside, yet Jewel had begun to sweat. His face had flushed to a bright red. He looked like he might explode. April felt like running, but she sat motionless down into a chair.

She watched as he took each letter and read them in the order they were written. April could see the tears welling up in his blue eyes. His hands had begun to tremble as he read. Finally he came to the last pouch, with the blood soaked letter from Gettysburg. He stopped for a moment and looked up at April. She saw his jaws begin to set.

He pulled the letter out and began to read it. The muscles in his face grew tighter and tighter. Sweat began to pore from his forehead. April recognized it too late. Jewel was going into a rage.

Jewel threw down the letters, and jumped over to where April was sitting. His fist connected to her jaw so quickly that she flew from the chair to the floor. It took her a moment to realize what was happening. She tried to get away, but it was too late. His boot found her back and he kicked her with such fury, she thought she would die.

He began to scream, "Look what you've done. You made my sons love slaves so they couldn't fight as real men. You filthy woman, I should have killed you long ago! Because of you, I now have nothing! I have no one! Do you hear me, no one!" he screamed as loudly as he could.

He reached down and picked April up and slammed her against the brick walled fireplace. She moaned out and begged him to stop.

"Jewel, no. You don't understand."

He kept pounding his fist into her and calling her filthy names.

"This is the day you die woman. I've had all I can take from you and everyone else!"

He then took her by her long hair and pulled her across the floor. Her hair had fallen down from the bun when the beating began. He stopped twice to kick at her body. He dragged her over to a table where a large knife had been left out. He grabbed the knife and sat on April's back. Jewel pulled her head up and placed the knife on her throat.

"Today is the day you die!" he screamed.

Jewel felt the cold metal at the temple of his face. Then he heard Cecil's voice talking back to him.

"No sir, dis is da day you die iffin you lay one more hand on Miss April. I suggest you drop dat knife!" she said with such force that it stunned Jewel for a moment.

"Leave this place Nigger. I am a man, do you hear me? You are nothing more than a slave, my slave," Jewel said with the knife still to April's throat.

The rifle was pressed harder into his temple, so hard his head moved. Then Cecil slowly uttered these words.

"You call me Nigger one more time, you gonna be a dead man. Now git off her and git out of dis house. I has an overpowering desire to blow you straight to hell!"

Jewel realized then that she was more than willing to kill him. He dropped the knife to the floor and removed himself off April. He began to back out towards the front door, with Cecil following him never taking her eye off the gun site. As he reached the hall, he grabbed the pistol he used during the war off the table, then fled out the door.

Cecil locked the door behind him and ran to help April. April could hardly breath.

Cecil ran to call out the back door for one of the men chopping wood near the plantation to fetch Doctor Albright.

Jewel had broken April's nose, four of her ribs, and busted her jawbone. All of her body was covered in dark bruises. This time April told the doctor that Jewel had beaten her. Jewel had been nothing more than a mad man.

The doctor was there later that evening when they heard a gun go off. It sounded like it came from the family gravesite.

Cecil and the doctor took lanterns to the gravesite to find out what happened. In the family graveyard, lying between the tombstones of his sons lay the lifeless body of Jewel Jackson. He had taken his own life with the pistol still in his mouth. On him he had pinned a note, which read:

Bury me between my two sons. Keep me far from were she will be laid to rest.

Jewel Jackson

April cried when they told her the news. She'd begun to understand where his anger had come from. He grew the same hate his father knew. Jewel had been taught to hate slaves. Jewel was never given a choice. It was bred within him. He hated April when he realized she truly loved everyone. To him this was evil and wrong.

April believed Jewel would have killed himself even if her sons still lived. Jewel would never be able to except the fact that all men were to be free. It was not how he wanted it to be. His father had set his fate when he filled his heart with hate.

Chapter 39

The Good Years

May thought that after the war ended, life would settle down. But what was closer to the truth was that life was entering a new stage. When the soldiers came home there was wedding plans to be made. Alicia was engaged to a furniture maker from the city of Philadelphia named Michael. He was Anthony's boyhood friend. He came to their cabin often as a small child to play with them. Alicia and Michael had always fought as children, acting more like siblings.

Once Anthony and Michael had tied the out house door shut with rope while Alicia was in it. Alicia was stuck in the outhouse until Grandma Lilly came back from the fields. On that hot summer day she spent 3 hours waiting to be rescued. It was not an event that she soon forgot.

Before summer was out, she scored her revenge. Alicia wrote love letters to the ugliest girls in the county and signed them with Anthony and Michael's names. She claimed she was the go between for the boys and would pick up and deliver letters for them. She went so far as to propose marriage to one in Anthony's behalf. That night an angry father came to see Philip because his 15-year-old son was trying to court his 12-year-old daughter... behind his back. Anthony was whipped with a hickory switch for the letters. Only after they were delivered to Anthony that he realized who wrote them. Alicia had smiled sweetly at him at the dinner table.

"Almost as bad as the out house, huh."

"Why you devil."

"Learnt my devilment from you, dear sweet brother," she said with a smile. Although Anthony was furious about the plot, Michael had found it amusing. Not long after, it was Alicia he came to see. He said he loved her sense of humor. No hickory switches had persuaded him other wise. That's how their romance began.

"I can't believe my only daughter is about to marry. Life has passed by so quickly. I feel like I haven't been given enough time to be your mother," May said as they sat down at the kitchen table making plans.

"You'll always be my mother. Now maybe you can also be my friend," Alicia said as she leaned over to hug her mother.

Alicia had continued her schooling during the war, and had received her certificate to teach. Michael had begun building their cabin as soon as the war ended. He and his father had filled it with the fine furniture they made. It was to be Alicia's wedding gift.

Michael and his father had established a reputation of being the finest furniture makers in the state of Pennsylvania. People came from across the states to purchase their goods. Michael's father had learned to make furniture from an Englishman from the low country. It was a fine living. And Alicia had found a job teaching in a three-room schoolhouse for colored children.

Anthony had been accepted into law school. He wanted to eventually become a public defender and to further the colored race in their fight to be equal and treated fairly. The war had changed him, showing him many sides of men he didn't know. Philip and May were proud of his decision.

Their youngest sons had not yet decided on what to do with their life. They had discovered the opposite sex, and this took all their efforts. The war didn't have a chance to change them, for they witnessed none of its violence.

May looked forward to the letters from April. Over the years they had shared their lives through the written word. May's feelings of angry had long ago softened. If it were not for April's foolish choice to burn her, she would have never come to this point in her life. She had received her freedom early on, had found the love of her life. Her children and people she loved surrounded her. One event could not have happened if the others were missing. Maybe it had all been in God's plan for her. It all fit together to form a very good life.

May was shocked to read what Jewel had done to April and himself. She knew it was a sin, but she was glad to hear that Jewel was dead. May thought it was a bold thing that April did with the Confederate honors. She felt it would be exactly what April's sons would have wanted. She wished she could have met them. April had raised some fine young men. She felt in her heart that they knew of her, just as she knew of them. The letters had let the sisters manage to share their whole lives. May prayed that April would now be given the chance for a good life. She needed for April to finally be happy.

In September of 1870, May received a letter in an unknown writing. It was from the Cothran plantation, and pinned by Cecil in child like writing. It read:

Dear May,

April knows not of dis letter. She been begging you to come see her again. She been waiting a long time. If you loves her, come. She is dying. Doctor says someun grows in her head. He can does no more. She calls for you. Come see bout her for it's too late.

Cecil

May's hands began to tremble as she read the short note. It had to be wrong. It was April's time to be happy. She had to go back. Somehow, she had to go.

May run outside to find Philip and Lilly clutching the letter to her heart.

"Philip, she dying."

"Who's dying."

"Philip, I got to go back. I got to be with her," she said as she buried her face in his shoulder.

"Sweet Jesus, not April," cried out Lilly as she heard what May said. "Dat child been through hell on earth. How we gonna git you there?" she said as she stroked May's hair.

"Don't worry none Hon, we'll do it some how. I get you to April."

"Oh Philip, what if I've waited too long? What if I never get to see her again?" cried May as she reached out for her mother.

"I promise, you'll see her. Now lets call a family meeting, and see what we can figure out. I'll go to the church if I have too. They'll be some who can help. Don't worry, we'll get you back."

At the family meeting they all decided to sell some of their livestock. Michael's parents sent some money to help with the journey. When the church found out they took up a love offering for May. Two cows, three horses and six pigs were sold for the journey back to South Carolina. It was decided that Philip would go back with May and Lilly. May found it hard to believe she was going home. Lilly was excited at the thought of seeing some of her old friends again. Philip wanted to meet the woman who gave up so much to give May happiness. It had been 31 years since May had been a Cothran slave and had stepped foot on southern soil.

Chapter 40

With My Last Breath

April buried Jewel as he wished, between the tombstones of his sons. Jewel had taken his life on the 30th day of November, 1865. He left April so beaten she couldn't come to the small funeral that was given him. No one from the Jacksons family could be found. It was if they had all disappeared. Someone said they moved to Europe to live with Mrs. Jackson family in England. Only a couple of elder colored men attended, mostly to be sure he was dead. Cecil went for April. No flowers were placed on his grave, and no tears were shed.

It took April three months to overcome the last beating from Jewel.

"Cecil, what on earth made you come home that day. You were to be gone all day helping Willy Joe and his family cut down trees."

"Miss April, it be the strangest thang. We was chopping wood, and I's got dis feeling urgent like.. to git myself back home. Almost felt like being pushed. Heard dat man yelling, and commence to running. Found him fixing to slit your throat," Cecil said as she used her finger to illustrate.

"I's gladly kills him you know."

"I know. I'm sure glad you came. You saved my life. Won't never forget it."

"Ah, it wurn't nutin. You save me too given da chance. Wouldn't ya?"

"Sure I would, given the chance."

"See dare, we eben," Cecil said with a big smile.

In the spring of 1866 life began to look up for April. She and Cecil got along well. They helped tear down the slave cabins, and move wood to various plots for the free blacks to live. They all loved April. On Saturday many came to help them work on the plantation. They got all the farming tools in working order, and helped her keep most of the fields plowed. The rice paddies were abandoned. April loved to work right beside them. She had given up her society life years before. She now understood what was truly wonderful about life. Helping others survive.

The only trouble April ever had was her fainting spells. She had fainted easy all her life, so no one gave it much thought. And many times Cecil would have to go into the woods and find April. She would find her roaming around and calling for Carolyn as if she were in a trance. This had been happening since Carolyn disappeared years before. Cecil hoped that time would help April, but time made it worst. After her sons were killed at Gettysburg, she made weekly trips to the woods. The urge to find Carolyn had grown with each year. Cecil could do nothing but find April in the woods, and guide her back home.

"It be all right, Miss April. Dat child be somewhere happy. I promise you dat. Now let's git home fer you git sick. You ought not come out here barefooted. Snake gonna git you one of des days."

Most of the time April was full of joy. She loved to talk of the many memories she had in her younger years, and of her children. She'd talked for hours about May's life as if she shared it with her. Once a year Cecil and April made it to the beach, just as they did with the children. Once, after the war, they camped out right on the beach. God put on a show for them that night. The stars shone brightly against the pitch-dark sky. A crescent moon was up high. They had caught huge crabs that day, and boiled them over an open fire for their evening meal. Both had said it was the best night of their lives.

Several times a week during the season, they'd ride to Charleston to sell at the market place. It always proved to be exciting for them both. Many of the society people walked by April without recognizing her. She had long ago given up the fancy attire. Now hers was simple but pretty.

"Git a load of dat dress. Looky at dat hat. It be bigger dan her head." Cecil said in a whisper.

She and April both giggled as the lady strolled by leading her fancy dog, which looked Chinese.

"Members when you dressed like dat? You miss it?"

"Heck no, not one bit." April said under her breath. "Now I just like to raise fancy vegetables." They both giggled again.

They were good friends.

April began to have terrible headaches in the year of 1869. Sometimes they were so bad, even light made them worse. Doctor Albright was sent for many times, always telling her it was from too much sun. He urged her to stay out of the fields. The great Doctor had gotten on in years and now walked with a cane. He was the only Doctor outside of Charleston. He told April to hire workers for the field. April was now 47 years old. Cecil was reaching the age of 53.

"Cecil, do you think May will ever really forgive me?" asked April on the porch swing one evening.

"Miss April, I can't be's da one dat knows dat. Only May knows da answer. I do thank you done right by her, giben her freedom long fer da rest of us. By what you says, she done had a pretty good life. Looks like to me, she order be bout ready to forgive."

"My prayer is one day I can see her again, and tell her what happened on that day face to face." April said as she stared at the rocker.

"Cecil, I didn't do it by accident, it was on purpose. I thought it was to save her from Master Jackson. I was young, and didn't realize I was doing it for me.

wanted her to stay with me, and Master Jackson was buying her from papa. I heard them talking."

April began to cry. "I was as bad as Master Jackson. I had no right to hurt her with the soap. I truly had no idea what it would do. She'll never forgive me."

Cecil sat near her and let her cry. There wasn't anything she could say. She finally knew the truth. April had been tormenting herself all her life over the truth she kept inside. April had made many wrong choices, which shaped the life she had to live.

By the beginning of 1870 April's headaches had become so bad that she wouldn't go out into daylight. She kept the heavy drapes closed in the house. She began to lose her balance and hearing. By August of that year, she was bedridden. She never wrote May of her illness for she wanted May to come back out of love, not pity.

Finally the doctor told April the truth. Cecil was by her side when he gave the grave news.

"April, I've been dreading this day with all my heart. I'm the doctor who brought you into this world. I have taken care of you all of your life. It is with great sadness I tell you that what you have cannot be cured. I can only give you something for pain. You have a brain disease. We don't know much about the brain yet, but I've seen this many times before. I thought you had it three years ago, but I prayed I was wrong. I saw spots on your eyes that showed pressure on the brain. There has never been anything I could do to stop it. Your hearing and sight are growing worse. These are the final stages. It won't be long till you pass over. April, do you understand what I'm saying?" he said with a shaky voice and tears in his eyes.

"Don't cry. I'm ready. I understand that I'm dying. I'm tired and ready to go." she said as she reached out and patted his hand.

"It's I who should be dying," he cried. "You are still young, and should have a chance to be happy. My life has been full, and I just keep growing older. It should be me."

"What would the people do without you. Think of all the babies you've delivered, and the lives you've saved. You are a person of great value. Always remember that," said April as she closed her eyes to rest.

"You are too my child. You are too," he said.

The doctor sat there a while longer and watched her breathing, wishing he could save her from the pain he knew would come. Once again he found himself asking God to show mercy to this young girl. Just as he had asked for May.

Cecil watched daily for May's arrival. It had been weeks since she mailed her letter. She knew May would come. If there was any way possible, May would come to April.

It was September 24 when Cecil saw a large carriage coming down the Oak lined road. She didn't wonder who it was, she knew. She ran to wait by the walkway as the carriage made it's way to the house.

As soon as it stopped, the door opened. Lilly was the first to step out, gazing up at the plantation. She then saw Cecil, and softly called her name.

"Cecil, is dat you gal."

"It shore be, Lilly. Me in da flesh. My, you look fine." Cecil said with her arms opened wide. Lilly walked into her arms, embracing her tightly.

"Welcome back home!" she said as she looked at Lilly. " I still members da day you left. We's all wanted to be riding to freedom wif y'all. Dat was a good day."

"Shore was."

Philip was the next to leave the carriage. He stepped down from it and tipped his hat to Cecil and bid her good day.

Finally, May herself, came from the carriage door. She slowly looked up at the plantation and began to weep.

Cecil came to her, and gave her a long embrace.

"I's knows you'd come. I's knows it," she said as she kissed May's cheek.

"Welcome back home. Dis is where we all began." she said with a sweep of her arm.

May was shocked at the difference of things. The slave cabins were all torn down, and just a few buildings remained. The plantation house still stood tall, with ivy growing on all sides. The war had left no scares on it. Only time had changed its appearance.

She turned to Cecil and asked in a soft voice, "Where's April? Please take me too her. I must see her. Don't tell me she's gone."

"Miss April's still here, but she ain't da April you left long ago. She's changed. She might not wake when you speak. She's under drugs. It's almost time. She's been waiting fer you," Cecil said with a quivering voice.

Cecil led May and them up the plantation steps. Once again May was in the home of her childhood. The memories came rushing back. She could hear their laughter as children. She could see them sliding down the long rails of the staircase. She could almost see her mother as young and Miss Betty standing with her hands on her hips and her finger wagging at them. She reached out and touched the dry wooden walls. She remembered how they used to shine with oil. They used to fill the house with their wonderful woodsy smells. Tears began flowing as she remembered the past glory of the house. In her mind, it had never changed. Now she stood in its half-empty hull. She saw what war and time could do.

The door to April's room was open as they came down the candle lit hall. Outside was a glorious day, but inside seemed more like a dark coffin. She could hear the rattled breathing coming from April's room. She knew the sound all too well. When she worked at the Union hospital, they called it the death rattle.

Cecil took May's hand and led her to the bed. May couldn't believe what she saw. April looked like an old lady laying in wait for death. Her dark and now graying hair was tucked under a bed bonnet. Her face was thin and frail. April's arms lay on her chest as if she were already asleep in her coffin. Her skin had an ash color to it, her lips dried and cracked.

May sat slowly on the bedside and began to stroke April's forehead. Her skin felt cold and life less. It seemed to just hang on her body. She leaned down and whispered in her ear.

"April, can you hear me?" she asked softly as a tear rolled off her cheek onto April's.

April's eyes slowly began to open. As if she were in a brightly lit room. Yet the only light was from a candle by her bedside.

"May," she whispered. "Is it truly my sister? Are you really here, or am I dreaming again?" she said as tears rolled down to her pillow.

May softly kissed her forehead, and took hold of one of her frail small hands. "Yes April, it's really me."

"May forgive me, please forgive me. I cannot leave this place unless I know you forgive me. May, you are my only sister. I've always loved you," April said in a fading voice.

"It is I who should asked to be forgiven. I've stayed away too long, now there is no time for us. I've missed you so much, and I do love you."

"I'm sorry for what I did to you long ago. You must understand; I didn't want to lose you. If I could go back, it would be me that was burned," she said as she slowly reached up to touch the burn on May's face, caressing it softly.

"April, do not cry for me. My life has been good. The scars never made me stop loving you. I'm sorry I punished you with my absence. We were but children and neither of us understood life," she said as she leaned into April's hand, touching her hand to it.

April then grew weak and let her hand fall back to the bed.

"May, they've all been here. They say I should follow them. Papa and mother came first. They said it wouldn't be long. Yesterday Samuel and Benjamin came. They said everything is ready for me to come. I'm waiting for Carolyn. I don't know why she won't come. I've called out to her, but she still won't come. May, now that you're here, I'm ready." she said as she closed her eyes.

"The pain is with me always. If I leave, it can't follow. I want to go home May. I want to go home."

Cecil heard April's words and went to the other side of the bed and took her other hand and gently rubbed it.

"You can leave us now April, we's all here. Even Miss Lilly came back." Cecil said as she began to cry. Her eyes already swollen from the days of crying.

"Lilly? You here too?"

"Yes Miss April, here I am." Lilly said as she walked closer to the bed and saw April for the first time since she left. Suddenly all the anger she had felt towards April slipped away. This was the sweet baby girl she nursed and helped raise. This woman laying here was April.

Philip stood at the bottom of the bed, thinking much, but saying nothing.

May stood up and walked over to the fireplace. It was the one she knew as a child. It took her a moment to find the loose brick. The paper was still in its hiding place. The oath of their sisterhood. May remembered the childhood day they made it and hid it from all eyes. It now seemed like a lifetime ago. She carried the paper to April's bedside.

"April, only miles separated our bodies, but never our spirits. I have always been with you, just as you've always been with me. I give you this to prove you are forgiven. I've never forgotten one moment of our life together."

The spirit of love touched everyone's heart in the room, they all began to cry softly.

May leaned down close to April's face and started to sing the old song they loved as children. They had heard it in the fields being sung by the slaves.

"Ain't worrying no mo.. Ain't crying no mo.. My eyes done seen da lord....He's coming for me.. just wait and see... for my eyes done seen da lord....Don't look for me.. around here none.. for my eyes done seen da lord."

When the song was finished April opened her eyes, and once more looked at May. She mouthed these words, with no sound being heard, "I love you, I always have."

Then her eyes closed for the final time. Her body grew still on the bed. Gone were the tears and the pain she knew for so long.

Cecil and May looked at each other knowing she was gone. Cecil had lost her friend, May had lost her true sister.

They both fell to their knees and sobbed. Lilly tried to comfort Cecil and Philip went to May.

When the room finally grew silent, May asked everyone to give her some time alone with April. They quietly slipped from the room, and May closed the door. She went to the windows and pulled back the heavy drapes. Sunlight filled the room with a great brightness and warmth. She then walked over to the bed and crawled up beside April, just as she had as a child. She sat up against the backboard, and began to talk. May told April all the things she'd been wanting to say about her life. She told her how much she thought about her, and of the many memories she still carried of their past. She spoke of her life, and that of her children. She thanked April for the letters over the years, and thanked her for her freedom and the wonderful life she had because of it all. Then she stoked her hair and lay by her side and hugged her one more time. April body was still soft. It was hard to believe she was gone.

Two hours later she left the room to join the others in the parlor. Cecil came up to her with a letter that April was going to send her. It was the last letter April wrote.

My Dearest Sister May,

It has been years since I've last seen you. I dream of seeing you again. I so want to speak to you, face to face. There is much that I've never been able to tell you, now I feel I must.

The day you were burned I heard Papa and Master Jackson talking. It had been a bad harvest and Papa was in great need of money. Master Jackson offered him a large sum for you. Papa agreed to take it. When I came running to find you, I wanted us to run for the free states. I wanted to go with you so we could always be together. Those were my plans. I thought the soap was an easy answer to our problems. May, I didn't know how bad it would hurt you. I never would have thrown it if I knew.

Many times I relived that day, and changed the events in my mind. But it could never change the reality of what I did to you. You really should never forgive me, but I pray one day you will.

Sometimes I wondered why I was born. When I die, there will be no part of me left living. All my children are dead. Then I'd remembered the good I've done. After my sons died, my eyes where opened to the many wrongs I've committed. I tried to correct them and do right by everyone.

The only thing I'm not sure of is if you will ever truly forgive me. One day May, you'll know that you are and always will be my sister. I will say this till my last breath is gone.

Your Sister Forever, April

May held the letter close to her heart when she finished. April's handwriting had become small and frail, almost fading away. When May read what really transpire that day, she felt true release. It had been the act of a child. A frighten child who didn't want to lose her sister. Nothing more, nothing less.

On September 26,1870, Mrs. April Marie Cothran Jackson was laid to rest. A wake was held for two days. The ones who April freed and given land to came with their families. They'd been given a great deal from her. Her love and respect for them was treasured most. Although they were now free, they were not treated as equals to whites. Only by a few, and April being one.

All the windows of the house where opened and sunlight streamed into every room. The house was once again filled with laughter as they all reminisced the many events that had transpired on the plantation. No one talked of the pain; it hurt too much to remember. The rotten wood of a swing still hung on the Oak on the front lawn where Old Bald William hung for days. He was remembered and spoken of in life, but not in his death.

The towns people and people from Charleston that knew April came. At first they were shocked to see all the blacks that were there. They all roamed freely around the plantation. Freedom had come, but accepting the fact all men were free was still hard for many.

April hadn't been to church in years, and had no minister to preach her funeral. She and Cecil read from their Bible's daily, but did not believe in the way it was taught. Philip went to May and Cecil and asked if he could have the honor. He had heard of April for years, and felt he knew her. So Philip led the funeral rights.

It was a beautiful day when April was laid to rest. The sky was bright blue and the birds all sang as if in a huge choir. Around the Massive Oak, they all gathered. April was to be buried next to Carolyn.

Philip preached a lovely sermon on April's life. He told how she'd grown to love the many people around her, and understood their need to be free. He spoke of how her faith in God had brought her through many of lifes sorrows. Her life had many troubles that most would never realize. He thanked God for April and the freedom that now all men knew. He asked God to change the hearts of the people who still choose to hate.

When it was over, everyone came by and placed flowers on her grave. Once again flowers were piled high as your knees. April had truly been loved.

Everyone left the graveyard except May. She sat by April's grave for a very long time. Sometimes you could hear her singing the old Negro spirituals they both knew and loved. So much of their lives had been so entwined. When May arrived at the plantation house, she felt like she was coming home. She'd never thought of the plantation as home, but when she returned she knew it to be true.

The next day they were all getting ready to go back to Pennsylvania. Cecil was going to stay at the cabin of a former slave until her cabin was finished. A loud knocking was soon heard at the front door. Cecil went to answer it. In the doorway stood a tall man in a fancy black suit.

"Good morning," he said, "I'm looking for a Mrs. May Cothran Redbone Would you tell her I'm here please."

"Yes sir," said Cecil as she went to the kitchen to find May.

May came to the door and the man looked shocked. May could think of no reason that anyone would be seeking her.

"Can I help you sir?" she asked. "I'm Mrs. May Cothran Redbone."

Philip walked up behind her and stood by her side. The man looked again at the papers he was holding, then back at May.

"I don't understand how this could be possible, but it's legal and binding," he said in a rough voice.

He pushed the papers towards May and hurried off the porch. He jumped into his small carriage and drove quickly away.

They all stood at the doorway and watched him ride away.

"What in the name of heaven was wrong with him. You would have thought we did something to make him mad," said May as she closed the door.

May opened the papers and began to read.

"Philip! Philip! I can't believe it, I just can't believe it." May trembled as she handed the papers to Philip, then sat down in a chair.

Philip began to read out loud. The papers were April's last will and testament. They were written and posted in the year 1868. April had willed to her sister May, all that remained of her estate at her death. She asked for Cecil Cothran to be allowed to live for the rest of her natural life at the plantation, if it were her desire. If Cecil ever decided to build on her land, she wanted her to have an additional twenty acres. The total amount of acres remaining was seven hundred and eighty eight. The plantation and all remaining were to be her sister's.

May sat in the chair shocked. Never had she thought April would consider her to be true blood kin. She thought the estate would go to the family of the now deceased Uncle Andy.

May cried when she realized the total extent of April's love. They were truly sisters, legal and binding.

Within the next few years the plantation was brought up to it's former glory. May and Philip's children had all moved to South Carolina. All except Alicia, who stayed in Pennsylvania with Michael. She was given the old homestead and the land surrounding it.

Cecil had decided to spend the rest of her life at the plantation. She had her own room as Lilly did. Soon she and Lilly became fast friends. Life for them had taken some pretty big changes.

The town people didn't like the plantation falling into the hands of previous slaves. It even made the Charleston paper, making quiet a stir in the city.

May placed a beautiful tombstone on April's grave. It stood higher than the rest, and had the face of an angel carved on it. "She Truly Loved Everyone" was carved below April's birth date and death.

One day three years later, they were all sitting on the front porch drinking cold tea. It was summer, and the air was hot. They saw a buggy come charging up the lane. Cecil had gone into town to buy supplies. She pulled up with great excitement. Her eyes were wide, and she could barely calm down to speak.

"You ain't gonna believe dis. I ain't beliven it. My heart almost stopped. I's was walking down da street minding my own business. It was in front of Duffy's store. I's saw an Indian dressed woman wif two small chillens. She held one in each hand. I's swear to y'all, she looked just like April. I's think I's seeing a ghostis, so I's call April's name. Dat Indian looked right at me, like she knows who I called. Den she turned and walked away. I swear to you all, I thinks it was April's ghost." finished Cecil.

"Glory be to God," said May with her hands clasping in front of her, "It's gotta be Carolyn."

The End